AN IMPROPER PROPOSAL

She was not too breathless to be temporarily overwhelmed by the gentleman's perfect features. His hair was dark and thick, his coat faultlessly tailored over wide shoulders and as blue as his eyes. There was something about him . . .

He swept off his top hat and bowed. "I am Julian Donberry."

The pleasant timbre of his voice . . . those blue, blue eyes. Suddenly, her body became quite stiff with shock.

"No, you are not," she said, her voice trembling.

His smile faltered. "I'm not?"

"You are Lord Merlyn, the magician," she pronounced.

The smile disappeared entirely, then returned. "Oh well. It was worth a try. There was always the chance you would not recognize me, since I was wearing a mask the last time we met. But I suspected you were too sharp for that, Miss Lyons."

If she were not so curious, she would run away. "Why—why are you here? What do you want?"

His eyes twinkled while he considered her questions. Then, as if throwing caution to the winds, his grin widened recklessly. "I'm here to renew my offer, Miss Lyons. I have come to ask you to be my wife."

Abby's knees went weak. She was alone with a madman!

* * *

The shining talent of Marcy Stewart is showcased in *Charity's Gambit* . . . an appealing heroine and clever plot."

—*Romantic Times*

"A fun-filled Regency romance . . . readers will delight."

—*Affaire de Coeur*

"Excellent."

—*Rendezvous*

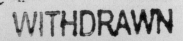

ZEBRA'S REGENCY ROMANCES
DAZZLE AND DELIGHT

A BEGUILING INTRIGUE
(4441, $3.99)
by Olivia Sumner

Pretty as a picture Justine Riggs cared nothing for propriety. She dressed as a boy, sat on her horse like a jockey, and pondered the stars like a scientist. But when she tried to best the handsome Quenton Fletcher, Marquess of Devon, by proving that she was the better equestrian, he would try to prove Justine's antics were pure folly. The game he had in mind was seduction—never imagining that he might lose his heart in the process!

AN INCONVENIENT ENGAGEMENT
(4442, $3.99)
by Joy Reed

Rebecca Wentworth was furious when she saw her betrothed waltzing with another. So she decides to make him jealous by flirting with the handsomest man at the ball, John Collinwood, Earl of Stanford. The "wicked" nobleman knew exactly what the enticing miss was up to—and he was only too happy to play along. But as Rebecca gazed into his magnificent eyes, her errant fiancé was soon utterly forgotten!

SCANDAL'S LADY
(4472, $3.99)
by Mary Kingsley

Cassandra was shocked to learn that the new Earl of Lynton was her childhood friend, Nicholas St. John. After years at sea and mixed feelings Nicholas had come home to take the family title. And although Cassandra knew her place as a governess, she could not help the thrill that went through her each time he was near. Nicholas was pleased to find that his old friend Cassandra was his new next door neighbor, but after being near her, he wondered if mere friendship would be enough . . .

HIS LORDSHIP'S REWARD
(4473, $3.99)
by Carola Dunn

As the daughter of a seasoned soldier, Fanny Ingram was accustomed to the vagaries of military life and cared not a whit about matters of rank and social standing. So she certainly never foresaw her *tendre* for handsome Viscount Roworth of Kent with whom she was forced to share lodgings, while he carried out his clandestine activities on behalf of the British Army. And though good sense told Roworth to keep his distance, he couldn't stop from taking Fanny in his arms for a kiss that made all hearts equal!

Available wherever paperbacks are sold, or order direct from the Publisher. Send cover price plus 50¢ per copy for mailing and handling to Penguin USA, P.O. Box 999, c/o Dept. 17109, Bergenfield, NJ 07621. Residents of New York and Tennessee must include sales tax. DO NOT SEND CASH.

ZEBRA REGENCY ROMANCE

Marcy Stewart

Lord Merlyn's Magic

ZEBRA BOOKS
KENSINGTON PUBLISHING CORP.

ZEBRA BOOKS are published by

Kensington Publishing Corp.
850 Third Avenue
New York, NY 10022

First Printing: October, 1995

Printed in the United States of America

For
Ken Froemke
with love

1816

One

Sparkling in the light of a thousand candles, the lobby of the Pendragon was more magnificent than anything Miss Abigail Lyons had ever seen. Gilded walls and ornate mirrors decorated High Chipping's new theatre, and red carpeting stretched up a staircase railed in vines of wrought-iron ivy. Surrounding her, richly gowned, jeweled ladies murmured and laughed and tapped their fans on the arms of their escorts, who rivaled them in the elegance of their dress and manner.

Scarcely knowing where to direct her gaze, Abby tried to look at everything at once, her wide brown eyes lit by a hungry fire.

"Stop gawking, Abigail," commanded her companion, Philip Demere. "You are behaving like a peasant who has come to the city for the first time."

"I cannot help myself; there is too much of interest," Abby said. "Do you not find these people amusing, Philip? Look at that lady by the stair. Her tiara is as tall as a fan, and it keeps slipping from her head." She gave a little gurgle of laughter. "There, do you not see? She has narrowly missed stabbing her escort in the eye!"

Philip turned in the direction indicated, then stiffened. "That is Lady Anna Wentworth. If she notices you laughing at her, we shall both be ruined."

Abby lowered her lashes resentfully and mumbled an apology. But even Philip could not dampen her spirits for long;

not here, not where bright lithographs dotted the walls promising an incomparable evening's entertainment provided by Lord Merlyn the Wizard, Prestidigitateur and Mentalist of World Renown.

Keeping her head downcast, she studied one of the broadsides now. The darkly handsome man depicted there, his face half-hidden behind a black domino, cut a figure more romantic than anything she had ever seen. He was certainly more colorful than Philip, who aside from a white shirt with a high, starched collar and silk cravat, was dressed entirely in shades of grey.

She looked from the magician's image to Philip and back again and again, until she realized it must appear as if her eyes were rolling in her head. She settled her vision on the magician and sighed faintly.

Philip missed very little, and he responded to her distracted air by tightening his grip on her arm. "I hope you're not expecting him to look like that. They always have the artist paint an idealized version of themselves, or a younger one. I'll wager the fellow's past sixty if he's a day."

Abby's mouth quirked in annoyance, but she gave the lithograph another glance—a dubious one this time. "You cannot know that for certain," she protested weakly, then blinked as her escort's eyes flashed in disapproval.

But he said nothing more, and after a moment she shifted her shoulder a little to tell him he was hurting her. However, the hand on her arm did not relax, and she did not wish to ignite him further by speaking of it. He had, after all, been generous enough to give her this outing—one of only a few such entertainments she'd had in the years since she'd come to live with her grandmother—and what was a little discomfort in comparison with that?

They were moving toward a set of wide double-doors that led into the auditorium. Philip bestowed practiced smiles on distant faces he recognized in the crowd. Although she saw no one she knew, Abby smiled and nodded, too, causing several people to look doubtful and glance behind them.

She had little opportunity to make friends, isolated as she was with an ailing relative in the furthest reaches of the Hampshire countryside, but if she were friendly enough, perhaps she could make a few this evening.

Tonight she was prepared to enjoy everything put before her as a starving man would embrace a full table. And tomorrow? Tomorrow, she would have new memories to lace into her dreams.

And who knew? Perhaps more would come of this evening than memories. Perhaps this outing was all she needed to clear her mind, to find a solution to her dilemma. If her grandmother thought she was going to marry the high-tempered man at her side, she was in for a grave disappointment.

But these were bold thoughts indeed for timid Abigail Lyons, and she knew it. Her spirits fell just a little.

Her reverie was interrupted by a gentleman edging through the crowd crying her escort's name. When he reached them, he clapped Philip's back while darting interested looks in her direction. The man was dressed in a knee-length brown *frac,* a yellow-and-black-striped waistcoat and ivory trousers. His side whiskers appeared even more wiry and abundant than her companion's, and his long, sharp nose put Abby in mind of a drawing of an anteater she had once seen in a book.

"Harold, well met!" Philip declared, pumping his hand. Then, noticing irritated looks from other patrons trying to pass by, he pulled them both through the doorway to stand against the back wall. "Haven't seen you since we sold out. Where have you been?"

Harold laughed uncomfortably. "On a fool's errand, trying my hand at making a fortune in Australia. Didn't work, dash it all." His gaze slid pointedly toward Abby.

Philip turned to her. "Abigail, allow me to present my friend, Harold Crumb, who fought Boney's Frogs by my side. Harold, my betrothed, Abigail Lyons."

Abby's brows lowered during the final portion of Philip's speech, but Harold did not notice, only seized her gloved hand and pressed it to his lips. "Enchanted," he said. As he continued to stare at Abby, his eyes lost focus, seeming to look beyond her. "Lyons, Lyons . . . Isn't that the name of your neighbor, Philip? The one whose estate joins yours?"

"Yes, Abigail is Matilda Lyons's granddaughter."

Harold's gaze sharpened as he looked back and forth between them. "I see," he said, his plain features brightening. "Your luck has taken a change for the better, hasn't it, old boy?"

Philip smiled thinly. "We are all responsible for our own destinies. I don't believe in the whims of fortune."

"Hah! 'Tis just as well." Harold fixed his protuberant blue eyes on Abby and grinned. "Miss Lyons, I was in the army four years. The only time I came close to being planted was when Philip's gun discharged while he was cleaning it. The shot blew a row of hair off the side of my head, nicked my ear, and dented the captain's favorite saber. And Philip says he don't believe in luck. Hah!"

Abby gazed with wonder at her escort, whose face was clouding dangerously. Could this stranger possibly be speaking of the man she knew? Dignified, proud, intimidating Philip, who tolerated nothing less than perfection in himself and everyone else?

Struggling to keep her features composed, she ventured, "Perhaps that was an example of your own misfortune rather than his. Or, since you were not grievously injured, your *good* fortune."

"Oh, well, I might think so were it not for all the other things. There was the night he set the tent on fire with his pipe, and the time he escorted a badly needed shipment of boots that fell in the river—"

"The boy is snuffing the candles, so we had better find our seats," Philip interrupted hastily, then frowned into Abby's amused eyes. "Will you join us, Harold?"

"Can't. Mother's so glad I'm home she sprung for box seats and is waiting upstairs. Don't guess you did the same, though, even for your lovely lady, or you'd be up there. Still as tight-fisted as always, eh?"

"We have perfectly good seats up front," Philip replied coolly.

"Right in the pit with the ruffians, I'll wager," Harold said. Then, seeing Philip's face, he added hurriedly, "Well, I'm off. Hope to see you in town sometime."

As Harold fought his way upstream, Abby thought she heard him murmur, "Stiff stick," but could not be certain. The mere possibility that he had brought a smile to her lips.

Philip did not appear to see it as he nudged her into the aisle and toward the stage. "Harold wants for good sense, as you could judge for yourself by his leather-headed reminisces," he murmured in her ear. "You shouldn't have encouraged him."

"Had I said nothing, you would have accused me of being dim-witted as you did at your mother's dinner party last month." She gathered courage and added, "I wish you had not told him we are betrothed."

Philip's eyes were inscrutable as he guided her to a seat in the second row behind the orchestra and sat beside her on the aisle. She sighed in relief when he removed his hand from her arm.

"Well, aren't we?" he asked innocently.

"You know we are not."

"But your grandmother believes we are. You wouldn't want to disappoint her, would you? Not when she's in such poor health."

Abby made no answer. She didn't know what she wanted, except she was certain it wasn't Philip. But somehow in the past four years since her parents died, her wishes had slipped beyond her control. She floated adrift in the desires and demands of others, led this way and that as stronger wills dictated her decisions.

Her only solace was her dreams. She often retreated to an imaginary world of balls and teas and dinners, a world where cheerful friends sought her company and handsome gentlemen loved her just as she was.

But her fantasies had not served her well. She could not put her finger on the very moment, but sometime during the past year while Abby dreamed, Matilda's hopes for a wedding between Philip and her granddaughter had changed into certainty. Now, without even a formal declaration, it seemed that one more decision had been stolen from Abby's hands. And this the greatest one of all; one that would affect her entire future.

In the dimming light, she tossed her head a little, shaking off the weight of her thoughts, determined to enjoy this moment. The musicians in the small orchestra had tuned their instruments, and now a quartet of violins began an eerie melody, the lower strings joining them in a tense tremolo. When the harpsichordist struck a tinny arpeggio, the crimson curtains parted, and an excited hush fell over the audience.

The set was painted to resemble the stone-walled interior of a castle. Leaded windows revealed a lonely moor and craggy peaks in the distance, and a real door intersected the center. The only furniture, two chairs and a wooden table covered with a velvet cloth, were placed centerstage.

In the shadowy, flickering footlights, the scene was surprisingly real. When a crack of thunder sounded offstage, several ladies cried out in surprise and fear.

Abby grinned delightedly and would have clapped her hands had Philip not cast her a quick look of disapproval. But even he shifted a little in his seat when a loud knock sounded and the door creaked open. Behind it stood a very frightened young woman whose milkmaid's dress skirted the top of her ankles and barely contained a brimming cleavage.

"Is—is anyone at home?" she asked in a quavering voice. Several masculine whistles and catcalls greeted this query, but she paid no attention, merely swept back her tumbled red locks and crept inside, calling hopefully, "I've lost my way, and I seek shelter from the storm."

"Come here and I'll shelter you!" cried a young man in the first row, who was immediately shushed by his neighbors.

The maiden's glance fell upon the table, upon which sat a man's top hat. She walked toward it cautiously and lifted it, peered within, then tilted the interior toward the audience so they saw nothing was inside. After placing it back on the table, brim side up, she sighed heavily and began to walk about the stage in a desultory manner. Suddenly, little puffs of smoke came from the hat, then huge billows that clouded the table. She stood back, her arms raised in alarm.

When the fog dissipated, a tall, wide-shouldered man stood there, clothed all in black satin except for his cloak, which was lined in red. The jeweled domino he wore could not disguise the clean line of his jaw, the straight, fine nose, nor the startling brilliance of his blue eyes, which Abby believed must be visible from the furthest row of the balcony.

More than a few ladies sighed in appreciation.

Abby could not help murmuring, "Sixty years old?"

When Philip glared at her in the darkness, she pretended not to notice.

The action on the stage continued. "And what fair maid is this who visits Merlyn's castle on such a dark and gloomy night?" asked Lord Merlyn in a mellow voice, his inflection lending humor to the melodramatic words.

"It is I, Hilda of Silverwaithe Farms, my lord, seeking refuge from the storm."

He bowed to her. Then, staring into the audience, he said meaningfully, "Who am I to deny such a simple request?" While the audience tittered, he continued, "Are you hungry, fair Hilda of Silverwaithe Farms?"

"I am, my lord."

"Then you shall eat." He swept his cloak backward and passed his hands over the hat several times. Plunging his fingers inside, he brought forth two white doves and handed them to her. "I hope you know how to cook." While she struggled to hold onto the flapping creatures, he pulled a bouquet of flowers from the hat. "For the table. And of course, no meal is complete without wine." A champagne bottle followed.

As Hilda hurried offstage with the items, the audience applauded politely. Abby was disturbed to note that Philip was growing restless. But she refused to allow his grumpiness to destroy her enjoyment and returned her attention to the stage.

"I perceive you are no longer hungry," Lord Merlyn said as the maiden came back empty-handed. "Perhaps I can now amuse you with a little entertainment."

He then proceeded to perform a number of illusions. He collected coins from Hilda's ears, pleased the gentlemen by pulling a long, long scarf from her bodice, and frightened the ladies by tossing a glass of wine toward the audience, a glass that changed into a ball of paper, all done with Lord Merlyn's thumbs tied and covered with the hat.

There were fewer snide comments as the performance progressed in difficulty and the audience's loyalty was won by the magician's charm. He did not seem arrogant as Abby had feared he might be from the imposing look of his posters.

But as the applause became louder and increasingly appreciative with each successive trick, Philip seemed to grow more and more disgruntled.

And then, near the end of a routine with cups and balls, Lord Merlyn asked Hilda under which cup was the ball hidden, and Philip's impatience could be restrained no longer. "The ball is in your pocket!" he shouted. "I've seen it done a hundred times!"

To Abby's mortification, the audience grew silent as though eager to see how Lord Merlyn would deal with this, for such a loud heckler could surely not be ignored. But the magician made no answer, only lifted his brows and stared directly at Philip, his piercing eyes seemingly unfazed by the darkness that shrouded the spectators.

Abby felt her cheeks burn as the conjurer's eyes shifted

slightly and appeared to look at her. The moment stretched an instant too long for comfort, and she thought she saw something flicker in his expression, some little look of doubt or hesitancy, but it could have been her imagination. And then the moment was gone, and he was switching the cups with deft fingers again, around and around and around; and when Hilda tapped one of the cups, he lifted it to reveal a peeping baby chick that he gave her, to the delight of the audience.

A roughly dressed man sitting several seats down leaned toward Philip, grinning. "Sure had that'n figgered, din't ye, mate!" he said loudly.

Philip did not lower himself to answer.

When the crowd grew quiet again, the wizard said, "And now, fair Hilda, perhaps you are growing tired. I regret I do not have a bed to offer you, but perhaps the chairs will suffice." When Hilda sat in the chair, he said, "No, that cannot be comfortable enough. Here, lie down between them."

When the maiden protested that the chairs were not of sufficient length to support her, he passed a hand before her eyes. "Sleep," he commanded, and she stiffened and closed her eyes. Carefully he aligned the chairs and assisted her to recline across their backs. When he removed the one beneath her feet, gasps were heard as she remained suspended by only the chair beneath her head.

The curtains closed to foot-stampings and yells and wild applause. While several boys rushed to light the wall sconces, the stage manager walked onstage and announced that lemon ices and other refreshments would be available in the lobby during intermission, after which Lord Merlyn would return to amaze them with card tricks and mental illusions in a quarter-hour.

As the orchestra began to play and people stirred to their feet, Philip said, "Let's go, Abigail; I've seen enough of this nonsense."

"You mean to leave *now?*"

"I see no reason to remain. The performance is as foolish

as I feared it would be, but you wanted to come so badly. Surely the first half has satisfied your craving for a diversion."

Abby stared up at him as he touched her shoulder. Her heart was pounding so hard she could feel it beating in her temples. The old weakness, the tired old thoughts that said it was easier to give in than object, almost made her yield to the hand fingering her sleeve. But once, just this once, she was determined to have her way.

"No," she said firmly. "I'm not leaving."

He could not have looked more surprised had the chair risen up and slapped him. "But Abigail, I insist."

"If you intend to force me to go," she said, staring hard at the cello player, "you will have to sling me over your shoulder in front of all these people."

A light flared in his eyes, and for a moment she feared he might meet her challenge. But though he tapped his fingers against his trousers, he held his temper in check. "Very well. I had no idea you were enjoying yourself so much. I wouldn't wish to cause you distress. Would you care for an ice?"

Thinking that the lobby was that much nearer the front doors and Philip's carriage, Abby thanked him and shook her head.

"I shall return directly, then," he said, and turned away from her.

When he came back some ten minutes later, his mood had not been improved by the roasting he'd taken in the lobby about his outburst. Harold and a few other acquaintances had thought it highly amusing to see him "put in his place by a *theatre person,* for Gawd's sake," as one had so elegantly put it. When Philip sat down, he neither looked at nor spoke to Abby.

She was relieved. Her singular act of rebellion had almost robbed her of speech.

When the curtains parted once more, Abby was glad to see no sign of Hilda, to whom she had taken an instant and unaccountable dislike. Lord Merlyn, having exchanged his red-lined cape for a blue one during the interval, now addressed the audience directly and performed several card tricks that involved the participation of volunteers, tricks that dumbfounded her comprehension

"How could he know which card that lady held?" she asked after the magician selected a designated card from a deck spread facedown on the table. Philip did not answer, only snorted his disgust.

And then, all too soon for Abby's taste, it was time for the final portion of the program. After guessing correctly a number of personal objects held by audience participants while blindfolded, Lord Merlyn removed the hood and said, "For my last exhibition, I shall need two volunteers whom I have never before met and who will tell me their darkest secrets through their thoughts alone."

"Rubbish," Philip said under his breath.

As though hearing him, Lord Merlyn turned in Philip's direction, his gaze searching the area behind the pit, his cloak swirling and shimmering in the candlelight.

"You," he said, pointing to Philip. "And you."

Abby's breath caught in her throat. He was staring at her.

A lantern-boy hurried down the aisle and shined his light on their faces. As he did, Philip shook his head angrily, and for once Abby was in agreement with him. She did not want to go onstage. Her green velvet dress was three years old and there were shiny places in it. Moreover, the ribbons in her hair did not match it precisely, and though Grandmother had insisted the hues were close enough, she knew they clashed.

Most of all, she was afraid to stand so near Lord Merlyn. It was not impossible she would faint if placed in such a position.

"Ho, Philip!" called a voice from one of the boxes. "Onward and upward and into the breach!"

"You're not afraid, are you Philip, old boy?" cried another from the balcony.

Setting his jaw grimly, Philip clasped Abby's hand and

pulled her to her feet. "This is on your head. You wanted to stay, remember?"

There was a smattering of applause as the pair ascended the steps to the stage. Abby thought her legs had turned to stone; she could not feel her feet when her slippers met the floor.

Lord Merlyn seemed aware of her discomfiture and gestured toward the chairs, which he had aligned side by side. She sat in one while Philip settled into the other, crossing his arms over his chest and glowering into the darkness that cloaked the crowd.

But the spectators were not entirely hidden, Abby saw as her eyes adjusted to the glare of the candles at her feet. The orchestra and the first few rows were visible; beyond that, the presence of the multitude could be sensed, if not seen. It was more than the little sounds of shuffling feet, throat clearings, and whispers that reached her ears. She could almost hear their hearts beating.

But perhaps it was only her own heart she heard; it was hammering so hard, she half-expected it to pound its way through her bodice and fall onto her lap.

Lord Merlyn smiled at her reassuringly, and she was distracted for a moment from the worst of her stagefright. Abby wondered if the rest of his face matched the beauty of his smile. She wished he would remove his mask.

The conjurer walked a few paces away and turned so that both they and the spectators could see him. Addressing Abby, he asked, "Have we ever met before this moment, miss?"

"No, we have not," she said, surprised that her voice sounded clear and steady.

He faced Philip. "And you, sir?"

"No," Philip answered. He moistened his lips "To be truthful, I have no desire to meet you now."

Surprised laughter greeted this sally. Abby was relieved to see the magician also laughed as he walked closer to her companion. "An unwilling volunteer, I see. Well then, we shall shorten your agony and begin with you instead of the lady."

Lord Merlyn began to pace as he spoke to the audience. "You have perhaps noted that there is nothing so personal as the human touch. One can learn much from a man's handshake. His strength, for example, or lack of it. The state of his nerves, and perhaps . . . his character." He returned to Philip. "And now, if the gentleman will be so kind as to shake hands with me, I will reveal the secrets I learn."

The magician extended his hand, his eyes totally blank as he gazed down at Philip. Abby glanced back and forth between them, fearing that Philip would refuse. But after a moment's hesitation, he thrust forth his arm and clasped Lord Merlyn's hand.

After the first instant of contact, a surprised look crossed Philip's face. As the seconds ticked past, long seconds that went far beyond the length of a normal handshake, he pulled against the magician's grip, tugging softly at first, then wresting his hand back with an angry jerk.

Abby hardly noticed his reaction, so absorbed was she in observing Lord Merlyn. As soon as he touched Philip, his eyes had darkened to black, the pupils expanding so rapidly that only the smallest edge of blue remained. She had never seen a human's eyes do that; only a cat's, and she shivered as she watched. And then those strange, feral eyes turned to gaze into hers, though their expression was so remote she doubted whether he actually saw her.

For almost a full minute after Philip withdrew his hand, Lord Merlyn's fingers remained outstretched, seemingly paralyzed, while the color receded from his cheeks and perspiration beaded his brow. The silence was growing uncomfortable and the audience communicated it by the scraping movement of boots and many nervous coughs.

A colorful movement backstage caught her eye, and Abby glanced toward the wings and saw Hilda. The milkmaid was now outfitted in an emerald silk gown and looking elegant as well as beautiful, but her face was worried as she gazed at the magician. And then, as Abby watched, the stage manager and another man dressed in servant's livery came to stand beside Hilda; the three of them spoke softly while casting concerned looks toward the stage.

This was not, Abby realized with a sudden throbbing behind her eyes, part of the act.

Philip was growing angrier by the second, his chest rising and falling in shallow breaths. "Well?" he said at last, a challenge in his voice.

The spell was broken, and Lord Merlyn slowly came back to life. Straightening his shoulders, he forced a smile and said, "Your name is Philip."

"You heard them calling me that in the audience," Philip snapped.

Lord Merlyn continued as if he had not spoken. "Philip . . . Philip . . . something about the sea . . . Philip of the Sea?"

"Philip the horse's arse, more like!" cried a man sitting in the front box seat.

While a querulous feminine voice screeched, "Harold!", several hisses and guffaws were heard.

As the noise died down, Lord Merlyn smiled tolerantly and asked, "Is your name Philip Demere?" When Philip admitted it, scowling, the conjuror continued, "And you are a gentleman farmer, is that not correct?" Again Philip assented.

The magician walked toward the audience as though contemplating weighty thoughts. Suddenly he whirled back, sending his cape into dramatic ripples. Pointing his finger accusingly at Philip, he approached him as a lawyer would confront a hostile witness.

"And did you, or did you not, Philip Demere, forget a vital charge that was entrusted to you by a loved one today?"

Philip frowned. "What are you speaking about?"

"Did not your mother ask you to collect a certain pair of new slippers that arrived for her at Henderson's? And didn't you conveniently omit to fulfill this simple, reasonable request?"

"There wasn't enough time!" Philip exploded, his face reddening. And then, "How did you know that?"

Several members of the audience gasped, while others laughed. A storm of applause followed, which the magician acknowledged with a bow. "Thank you, Mr. Demere, for your assistance and good humor," he said, gesturing toward the stairs.

The irony was not lost on Philip, but there was nothing he could do but leave the stage. He did not return to his seat, however, but stood watching Abby from the darkness at the foot of the steps.

With reluctance, she removed her gaze from Philip to the magician, who was now standing beside her. He seemed completely recovered from whatever had bothered him before, and his expression was gentle.

"And now, fair lady," he said, his voice soft but somehow projecting anyway, "if you would be kind enough to remove your glove."

Abby obeyed. When she put the glove in her lap, she lifted her hand and placed it in his. Instead of shaking it as he had Philip's, he closed his other hand over it, enveloping her fingers. When he did, she drew in her breath sharply. A tingling sensation ran up her arm and through her body, like hundreds of tiny needles pricking her skin. It was more surprising than painful.

Once more she saw his eyes grow black and distant and wild, as if he had flown to some faraway place that she couldn't reach. His lips parted, and she felt his hands tighten around hers. Though she was tempted to pull back from him as Philip had, she did not.

The moment of contact lengthened until the audience again moved restlessly. Aware of it, aware also of Philip's impatience as he drew nearer the stairs, Abby nevertheless remained motionless as a bird caught in a cobra's spell.

And then Lord Merlyn's eyes were blue again, and he released her hand and backed away. Only Abby was aware of how his fingers shook, and she watched them with an irrational fear swelling in her breast.

When he spoke, his voice trembled momentarily, and that frightened her as well. "The young lady looks deceptively gentle," he said at last. "But I see great strength . . . a royal strength that is raw and powerful." Though Abby found his words thrilling, he uttered them without feeling, as though reading from a card. "I see the king of all power . . . a lion. Is your name . . . Lion? No, Lyons?"

"Yes," she said eagerly, hoping the swiftness of her response would help him. She could not fathom what troubled him, but something was wrong; the watchful figures in the wings confirmed it.

He lifted one hand and rubbed his forehead. "And your given name . . . I'm sorry, it's not clear to me. Something happy . . . Is your name Joy?"

"My name is Abigail." When the sound of disappointed whispers met her ears, she added more loudly, "My mother named me Abigail because it means *source of joy.*"

He smiled a little as the discontented sounds subsided. "And, Abigail Lyons, have you recently lost something precious to you? An item of jewelry, perhaps?"

Instantly, her fingers flew to her throat. "My locket has been missing this week or more." The necklace contained miniatures of her deceased parents, and she had been devastated to lose it.

"You will find it behind your dresser," he said. "The chain has caught on a nail protruding from the back."

Abby stood up, her eyes shining. "Thank you, Lord Merlyn." There was not a doubt in her mind that she would find it precisely where he said she would.

This had been the best evening of her life. Tonight she had discovered that magic was real.

And if magic was real, anything was possible. Anything at all. She could find a way to free herself.

As the audience applauded and stood to their feet, the magician took her hand and presented her to the crowd as though she had done something worthwhile. She tried to smile, but her lips trembled so much she had to stop.

Lord Merlyn then bowed and escorted her toward the stairs.

As the two of them neared Philip, the magician walked slower and slower until he halted. Since he still held her hand, Abby had to pause too; she was startled when he leaned toward her as if to whisper a secret. Feeling a renewed surge of fear, she watched his pupils widen a third time.

"You must marry me," he said in a voice so low only she could hear.

Before she could respond, he rushed back to centerstage, bowed once more to the appreciative audience, swirled his hands in a graceful pattern, and disappeared in rolling billows of smoke.

Two

Backstage in the largest dressing room of the Pendragon, the magician lay motionless on the couch behind the screen. One leg was folded under him, the other hanging over the end. Both arms were gathered tightly to his chest, and his eyes were closed. A frown creased the forehead above his mask.

Persistent knocking on the dressing room door drummed him to awareness. The door opened. He heard several young men—foxed, from the sound of them—beseeching "Hilda" to join them for a late dinner. Roast duck and brandied cherries were offered. Harriet rejected their invitation, and the gentlemen protested.

The magician listened attentively but did not open his eyes. Francis would take care of them. A heartbeat later, he heard a deep, authoritative voice and imagined the menace the young whips saw in his valet's tall, muscular frame. If the lads only knew it, they had more to fear from Harriet (who had never milked a cow in her life) than gentle Francis, except when his protective instincts were engaged.

The door closed and the room grew quiet. The magician feigned sleep as Harriet approached the couch. If only he could return to oblivion; if only the images could be forced from his mind. Yet even in the sleep of exhaustion, there had not been complete unawareness.

He heard the rustle of silk as Harriet knelt beside him and began caressing his hair. He did not move, hoping the tenderness of her touch would throw him into dreams again, though not the ones he had seen on the stage, please God.

Why had he done it? Why had he allowed his brain to be receptive after all this time? He knew better. Yet on a moment's impulse he'd opened himself to the beast again. And all because of a pair of innocent brown eyes in a beautiful, vulnerable face. He was a fool.

He almost gave himself away when Harriet untied the domino and lifted it from him, then began stroking his cheek. The softness of her hand made him aware of the stubble already sprouting on his face.

He could not pretend any longer. Allowing his eyes to open slowly, he encircled her wrist with his hand. "Hullo, Harry," he whispered.

Her lips curved upward. "Hello, Julian. It's time you awakened."

He released her wrist and sat up, rubbing his fingers through his hair. "How long did I sleep?"

"No more than a half-hour. You were out the minute your head touched the cushion."

Her eyes were lively with unasked questions. Not wanting to answer any of them, he looked away. At that moment, a loud knock sounded at the door, then a booming voice cried, "Lord Merlyn!"

Immediately, the magician seized the domino from the dressing table and secured it to his face. Brushing past Harriet, he circled the screen and nodded to Francis, who opened the door.

Cyril Tankersley, stage manager and owner of the theatre, swept into the room and clasped first the magician's hands, then Harriet's. "Wonderful, wonderful!" he shouted, as though still addressing the balcony. His stout form was clad in an exquisitely tailored black frock coat, trousers, and a red waistcoat embroidered in gold. On his lapel he sported a red rose that shook with the force of his words. "Never have I seen an audience so happy! Would that I'd booked you for a week. I don't suppose . . ."

"I'm sorry," Harriet said quickly. "Tomorrow night we are to be in Portsmouth, then Brighton. Afterwards, we have several other performances before making our way to London, where we are to perform at the Egyptian Hall on Piccadilly."

"And you are justly proud of such illustrious bookings, I see," said Tankersley. Returning his attention to Julian, he added, "How I envy you. A comely assistant with a head on her shoulders—would that I had the same in my employ. Can't get suitable help even from the young men I've hired. Have to do everything meself."

"Sometimes I think it is I who assists Harriet," the magician said.

Tankersley chuckled and lifted his chin, exposing an arc of quivering flesh. He drew in a noisy breath, his large nose wrinkling and making his curious eyes look even smaller.

"Don't you ever take off that mask?"

Julian smiled. "Not often."

Tankersley lifted his shoulders in an exaggerated shrug. "Well, it's nothing to me, though I can't help wondering what's behind it. If you're marked or burned or whatever, my sympathies to you. But if you're hiding from the law—," he paused suddenly, as though the thought had only struck him as he put voice to it. But the stiffening postures of the three figures watching him led him to laugh uncomfortably and finish, "But of course, that cannot be."

"No, sir," Francis said sternly.

"No, I know 'tis not possible. Why would anyone of Lord Merlyn's talents need to indulge in criminal acts?" Tankersley glanced from one to the other of them in growing distress. "Thought I'd tell you the customers have all gone, and you're free to move without hindrance whenever you wish."

"Thank you," said the magician, continuing to smile politely.

Tankersley looked queasy. "How—how is it you do that

thing at the end?" he asked abruptly, then closed his lips with a snap.

"You ought to know a conjuror can't tell his secrets," Francis admonished.

"No, I suppose not. But for a moment I thought something was going awry, Lord Merlyn. Even your friends seemed worried. You worked your way out of it very well, but I just wondered . . ."

"A performer grows stale if he doesn't vary his routine a little, Mr. Tankersley," the magician said. "I may have caught Harriet and Francis by surprise tonight, but I assure you it's all part of the exhibition."

"Is that so?" Tankersley's expression was dubious. He squared his shoulders and returned to the doorway. "Well, it was a show worthy of the Prince. Good luck to all of you."

As they voiced their thanks, the owner closed the door, and the threesome stood quietly until the sounds of his ponderous footsteps faded away. Then, trying to ignore the eloquent glances Harriet and Francis were exchanging beside him, Julian removed his mask and began unfastening his cloak.

After another moment of silence, Francis said, "I'll go gather the equipment."

When he left, Harriet asked, "What *did* happen tonight?"

The magician winced and continued unbuttoning his shirt. Harry could be subtle, but never with him.

"Don't pretend you don't know what I'm talking about." She watched him toss his shirt into the corner. When he still didn't answer, she said in exasperation, "That man and girl. They weren't the ones we'd agreed upon. Francis found out about the couple in the fourth row during intermission, just as he always does, but you didn't call on them."

He reached for a white linen shirt hanging in the wardrobe. "You know I don't have to use trickery for everything I do."

"But I thought you didn't like to do it the other way." She paused a moment, watching with fascination the movement of the muscles beneath his skin as he put his arms into the sleeves. "You've always said it's too chancy."

He had no answers for her. He had none for himself. And where was Francis? He was never around when needed. Leaving his master to deal with a curious Harriet alone, indeed; of what use was he?

Suddenly too tired to button his shirt, the magician sat on the stool, propped his elbows on the dressing table and rested his head in his hands.

Her expression softened. "I know that sometimes you are . . . compelled to do things. Was this one of those times, milord?"

He hesitated. "You are making too much of a little lapse. You heard what I told Tankersley. It was merely a variation in the program."

A flare of anger sparked in her eyes. "Do not talk to me as though I'm an infant. Why won't you tell me? Is it because you're ashamed? You were drawn to that young woman because she was so pretty, weren't you?"

"And if I were?" His eyes were cool as they met hers in the mirror.

The pulse at her throat gave a wild leap and began to race. She took a step toward him and wrapped her arms around his neck, caressing his chest with her palms while leaning her cheek against his. "I'm sorry. I know you better than that. In the past you've most often learned something important, something needful. What was it tonight?"

He clutched her fingers, stilling them. Ignoring her question, he asked, "How many weeks have we left on our tour?"

Harriet straightened suddenly, her arms falling to her sides. "Three, counting London."

"Cancel the week in London."

"Cancel . . . *London?*"

"Yes. That will give them time to schedule another act. The others dates are too near to change." His lips twisted into a wry smile. "We don't want to ruin our reputation for reliability."

"But *why,* milord? We've waited so long for this opportunity."

"The opportunity will come again."

In the mirror, her face reflected shock. *"Why?"* she repeated.

His eyes darkened, cleared, then became apologetic. "I can't explain myself in any way that would make sense. Not yet. I haven't even sorted it out myself. Besides, I'm tired, and I know Francis will be glad of the rest." He lowered his lashes. "You'll appreciate the time at home, too, won't you?"

Her face whitened with anger "Just before you left the stage, you said something to that girl. What was it?"

He reached for a silver-plated brush lying on the table and began thumbing its bristles, hoping the gesture would hide the slight tremor in his hands. "You must have imagined it," he said finally, wishing he spoke truth.

Until this moment, it had been his desire that *he* had imagined the words he'd whispered to Miss Lyons. But Harriet's question and the memory of the young lady's shocked face proved he had indeed spoken as rashly as he remembered. It now appeared that not only his thoughts were beyond his control, but his speech as well. What was next? Would he start walking into walls?

Harriet stared at him wordlessly for a moment, then whirled and strode to the door. "I hope you know what you're doing," she said.

You are not alone, he thought with great feeling.

Steeling himself for the sound of a slamming door, he looked into the mirror and saw that Harriet continued to watch him wrathfully from the threshold. He closed his eyes and began massaging his temples vigorously. The visions were returning, and he could not make them stop.

Behind him, Harriet closed the door without making a sound.

* * *

On the morning following Lord Merlyn's performance, Abby entered her grandmother's bedchamber while fingering the locket at her throat and smiling. Even the sight of Matilda Lyons's probing and critical face, swathed between a lacy mobcap and a frilled cambric gown and robe, could not diminish her feeling of pleasure.

As she often did, Matilda was lying on the velvet settee beside the window, her head framed by lacy pillows, her thin body warmed by numerous crocheted and knitted throws. Abby could not blame her for swaddling herself like a button in a cushion; it was always drafty at Sharonfield House, and especially so now that autumn had arrived. Like the regal old lady who ruled it, the ancient house was cold, overlofty, and without ornamentation that might have softened its stark lines.

"You're looking very pleased with yourself," Matilda said, her low voice carrying well across the distance between them. "Sit down, girl, don't stand there like a broom. Is that your mother's locket you're fiddling with?"

"Yes, ma'am." There was only one comfortable chair in the chamber, but it was across the room near the fireplace; and Jane, Matilda's maid, was sitting in it and snoring softly. Abby pulled a tufted bench beside her grandmother and, without thinking, closed her hand around the tiny golden heart of her necklace.

"Well, don't look at me like I'm going to take it away from you. I'm not the one who lost it, am I?" Matilda raised herself on one elbow, reached for a glass of barley water on the small table by her head, and took several sips. Suddenly she seized her hairbrush and hurled it across the room toward the maid. "Do stop that infernal racket, Jane!" she demanded. "You sound like a wild boar snorting in the woods!" While the maid came to astonished wakefulness from the impact of the hairbrush and rubbed the side of her head, Matilda turned back to her granddaughter. "Was the locket where the magician said it would be?"

"It was," Abby said, startled. Her grandmother had been sleeping when they returned last evening, and Matilda's sudden knowledge of the prophecy was surprising. "How—how did you know?"

"Philip told me." She gave a bark of laughter. "Yes, he was here this morning. Don't looked so shocked, girl! Not everyone lies abed as late as you."

That was unfair; Matilda knew she usually rose early. In injured tones, Abby said, "I had trouble sleeping last night."

"So I would imagine, from what Philip told me. He 'twas mightily upset with you. Said you made eyes at Lord What's-his-name, who is of course lord of nothing but his own feeble dreams, and complained you wouldn't tell him what that feller whispered to you. Didn't ask to meet you somewhere, did he?"

Abby drew herself up. "He most certainly did not."

"I thought not, especially since the whole lot of 'em are gone." Seeing the question in Abby's eyes, she said, "I sent Redmond to the Pendragon to find out. The owner said they cleared out right after the performance."

Although she tried to tell herself it could not have been otherwise, Abby's spirits plunged like a stone in a well.

Matilda narrowed one eye. "What *did* he say to you, Abigail?"

"I don't know," she answered, not entirely untruthfully.

Again and again, for at least half the night through, she had heard his words echoing in her brain: *You must marry me.* But she'd surely misunderstood him. A man, even if he were a mysterious magician, simply did not ask a stranger to marry him.

What he *must* have said was something like, *Thank you for your help,* or perhaps, *It was nice meeting such a pleasant young lady.* That the words had translated into a proposal of marriage was no doubt a trick of her ears born of wishing for romance in her life. It couldn't possibly be otherwise; for if he *had* actually asked her to wed him, he would hardly have left town within minutes, would he?

Not that she would have seriously considered such a proposal, of course. However, seeing her grandmother's other eye narrowing in shrewd assessment, Abby couldn't help thinking it would have been a nice memory to stroke on a cold winter's night.

"I believe you know what he said, but you're not telling." Matilda's lips stretched, creasing her cheeks and revealing a mouthful of yellow teeth. " 'Tis all right with me. A woman needs secrets to intrigue a man."

She straightened the bow at her neck, her gaze never leaving her granddaughter's face. "Ha! You're surprised I said that. Like all the young, you think your elders don't know anything about the ways of love or youth. Well, I'll tell you, there was a time . . . there was a time indeed . . ."

The old woman's eyes grew distant, peering past a curtain of memories that Abby could only imagine. Then Matilda pressed a frail hand to her heart and sighed. "But that was long ago, long before my strength failed me."

Abby moved her slippers restlessly, hoping Matilda wouldn't go down the old trails again. It was difficult to believe she was ill, even now, aged as she was. Years ago, Abby's sire had wryly informed her that Matilda had claimed to be dying since his birth.

But Matilda's abdication to her sickbed had never relaxed her dictatorship over the household or Abby's grandfather, who died of apoplexy following a row over whether to plant the fallow field with wheat or carrots.

" 'Twas good of Philip to take you to the performance, wasn't it?" Matilda asked slyly. "You'll be a fortunate woman indeed when you become his wife."

Abby's jaw set. "I'm not going to be his wife."

Matilda clenched her fists on the coverlet. "You have no more sense than a cabbage! Heed my words, Abigail. Life is disappointing. People never meet your expectations, and only the attainment of worthy goals satisfies. You'll find the truth in that as you grow older. And you know that my goal is for future generations, not myself. You must not be so selfish."

It was an old argument, and Abby felt herself drifting away. A small part of her feared she might come to believe her grandmother's philosophy, simply from the weight of many repetitions.

Besides, Matilda's loftily spoken goal was for Philip's estate to be joined with Sharonfield's, and for that to be accomplished, Abby would have to marry Philip. It hardly seemed fair that she should be sacrificed to satisfy Matilda's dream.

She decided to appeal to her relative's sense of reason. "But Grandmother, if I wed Philip, the land will pass into his control, not yours."

"A moot point, surely, when my remaining days are as few as hairs on a fish," Matilda said, her voice becoming suddenly weak. "I told you my vision is for future generations. We shall be the start of a great dynasty, I know it.

"Now, get you off and make certain that pretty jonquil gown is cleaned and pressed. Philip is returning after luncheon tomorrow, and you'll want to be prepared. I suspect he means to make a formal declaration just to please you, since you've whined more than once that he's taken your assent for granted. If he does, you'd better say *yes,* for I shall cut you off without a groat if you don't."

Abby moved to her feet and took her leave, her spirits sagging. The time had come to make a decision. She would run away, just as her father had so long ago.

But it was not easy to prepare for escape.

By the following morning, reality had dampened Abby's decision considerably. She had no money and no friends to whom she could flee. Acquaintances would think her foolish for refusing such an eligible bachelor. And there were countless stories, all of them bad, about young women who sought their fortunes alone.

Still, she would think of a way. Until then, she must accept her grandmother's orders.

Though luncheon had been served only an hour before, there was a hollow feeling in the pit of Abby's stomach as she descended the stairs that afternoon and entered the parlour. When she caught sight of Philip's tall figure at the bay window, the gnawing sensation increased. He did not appear to have heard her arrival, but continued to stand gazing at the workers who were picking apples for the third day in a row.

He's probably estimating the harvest's worth and deciding how he would improve production, Abby thought. *Would that I could disappear in a cloud of smoke as Lord Merlyn did.*

She blinked away her imaginings and cleared her throat. "Good day to you, Philip."

"Good afternoon, Abigail," he replied, turning and walking forward to press her hands. "How lovely you look in that yellow gown; the shade complements your coloring."

Abby thanked him and gestured toward one of two armchairs set into the bay. He stood until she sat opposite him, then settled into the worn depths of the chair with a pleasant look on his face.

She noted his appearance was especially immaculate today, even for Philip, who never ventured in public less than well-dressed and with every shining hair in place. He wore a brown waistcoat, buff vest, tan pantaloons and a brown-striped cravat. If her grandmother had been correct about his intentions, he'd probably attired himself for the occasion. The thought sent her stomach into fresh paroxysms.

She had to admit he was a handsome man, though. If only he didn't *frighten* her so. And leave her in a constant state of anger, because he made her feel so small.

"Abigail," he said, leaning forward, "I want to apologize for my behaviour the other night."

Before she could express her surprise, Walters, the butler, entered the room and asked, "Did you ring for tea, miss?"

She gave a little start and said, "Er—no, Walters, but I meant to do so."

The butler nodded and backed from the room. In the past, her grandmother had instructed Abby to call the servants frequently to serve as chaperones of a sort, since Matilda considered herself too ill to come downstairs. But in the dread of the moment, Abby had forgotten.

"Impeccable timing," Philip muttered, bringing her attention back to him. "What I started to say is that I behaved rudely at the theatre and afterwards. The only excuse I have to offer is that I've no patience for trickery and only went to please you. Unfortunately, once I was there, I expressed my displeasure childishly."

Abby hardly knew what to say to this. She couldn't help thinking he was trying to soften her resistance.

"I don't expect you to forgive me right away," he said, watching her carefully. "But do you think you might?"

"Of course. I—I forgive you, Philip." She glanced toward the hall and wished Walters would hurry. Hoping to distract her suitor from further declarations, she added, "Were you not amazed that Lord Merlyn knew so much about us?"

Philip looked scornful. "There's an explanation for everything he did."

"Then I wish you would tell me how he knew about my necklace and your mother's slippers."

Philip moved impatiently and crossed his legs. "You are such a baby; you'd believe anything."

"Do explain it to me, then," she challenged.

"They plant someone in the audience to discover our secrets or some such. If I knew exactly, I could be on the stage myself, if I were that sort of inferior person."

She had not considered the possibility of deception, and the thought brought a feeling of heat to her cheeks. *Was* she being childish to believe so readily? But who could have told Lord Merlyn about her locket?

"Do you truly think stage people are inferior?" she asked in a small voice.

"Everyone knows they are. Actors, dancers, musicians, magicians—they have no morals at all to speak of. They don't work at a proper job, you see, and earn an honest wage like normal folk. Instead, they play at what they do, then expect decent people to pay them for their exhibitions. Pah! Thieves and tricksters, all of them!"

He rose to his feet, paced across the room to the fireplace, then strode back to tower over her. "You were attracted to that magician, weren't you? That's why you're asking all these questions. Like a silly schoolgirl instead of the woman you'll soon be, you were dazzled by jeweled masks and ridiculous capes. I expected better of you."

"You are wrong," she said, but wondered in her heart if he was. It was true she couldn't remove Lord Merlyn from her thoughts but had hoped it was because she was overstimulated from the entertainment. Was she foolish enough to be infatuated?

It would certainly explain her delusion that he'd asked her to marry him.

"I'm seldom wrong," Philip said. "And the fact that you won't tell me what he whispered proves it."

"I told you before, I couldn't understand what he said."

Philip glowered down at her, then blinked suddenly and relaxed. "I'm sorry," he said, and reseated himself. "I have the devil of a temper. It's been so since I was a child. You aren't aware of that because you've only known me this past year, since I've mustered out. You would be accustomed to it by now if you'd always lived here."

His eyes were bleak as he looked at her, and she almost felt pity for him.

He moved his hands expressively. "Controlling my temper has become even harder of late, and it's your fault. No, I don't mean to quarrel again. The fact is, I am driven mad by your refusal to regard me favorably." He laughed bitterly. "If you don't change your mind, I shall begin to think Harold Crumb was right when he deemed me unlucky. I—I love you, Abigail, though it's hard for me to say the words. I've never said them before, not to any woman, but now that I've broken my long silence, I'll say it again: I love you."

She was dumbfounded. He had never spoken so tenderly to her before. It was a declaration worthy of a hero in a play. Though the fences within her heart remained, she felt them crumbling a little.

"You look surprised," he continued. "I'm sure you know the reason I came this afternoon. You've known for a long time what your grandmother's wishes are, and mine as well. But for many months now, I've wanted to wed you not merely to unite our estates, but to have you as my own. Once that happens, my ill temper will go away, I promise you. What say you, Abigail? Will you have me?"

As he spoke, Abby's thoughts raced. How easy it would be to believe his rages, his possessiveness, were the acts of a man consumed by frustrated love. How easy to say *yes* to him, *yes* to her grandmother, and sweep her own feelings aside.

But could she as easily forget the wariness she felt in Philip's presence? The sense that within his ordered, perfect exterior, there seethed uncontrollable emotions?

If the arms beneath her sleeves were not bruised from his rough escort the night before last, perhaps she could.

"You're quiet again, Abigail. What does it require to convince you of my regard? Shall I—shall I kneel before you?" To her dismay, he slid from the chair to one knee and took her hand, his expression appealing. When she regarded him speechlessly for a long moment, his cheeks began to flush. "Well, say something, do not leave me here creaking on my knees like a penitent."

"Your words are kind, but—"

"But what?" he asked irritably. "Don't you believe that marrying you will make me a peaceable man?"

Instead of answering, she said, "Sometimes I think you feel . . . contemptuous of me. You are always telling me what to think and—and how to speak and what I should do."

His face was a study in bewilderment. After a moment he said, "Oh, perhaps you mistake my feelings when I instruct you about proper behaviour and such. But you see, there are so many things you don't understand because you're not well-acquainted with the world and how things are done. I want to teach you, to help you grow."

At that moment, Walters and Charlotte Ann, the maid-of-all-work, entered carrying trays of tea and cakes.

Walters's attention was centered on balancing the tea set he carried. Therefore he intoned, "Tea is served," without looking at the scene before him. When he noted the man on his knees, he stopped abruptly, causing Charlotte Ann to walk into him. Several slices of petit-fours flew across the carpet like projectiles. The maid squealed as if she had been struck.

"Get out of here, you interfering jackanapes!" Philip shouted. "Both of you! Can't you see that I am . . . searching for my lost snuffbox?"

"Begging your pardon, sir," the butler said dourly, and turned around without missing a step. After casting a stricken look at the cakes on the floor, the maid hurried after him.

Philip closed his eyes for an instant and heaved a deep breath. "I apologize again, Abigail, but a man has his pride. Now. What say you to my proposal?"

Feeling a kind of horrified fascination, Abby studied the face only inches away from hers. Despite his scornful treatment of the servants, his declaration had been sweet and difficult for him. And did any man feel differently about a woman's lot than he?

Without her bidding, the magician's image came to mind. What was it he said about her—that beneath a gentle exterior, she possessed a raw power? It made her want to laugh, or cry.

What would Lord Merlyn think now, if he could see her considering Philip's proposal?

She would like to believe she was powerful and strong, but it was only a fantasy suggested by a stranger. An inferior stranger with loose morals, according to Philip, who seemed to know a little about every subject. Already she could feel his opinion overshadowing hers by its greater logic. Did that alone not prove how wrong Lord Merlyn had been about her?

Feeling something within her die, she said at last, "I shall think upon it."

Philip's face brightened. "At least you haven't refused me." He rose and pulled her to her feet. "And since you haven't rejected me outright, I'll give you something else to consider."

He put an arm around her waist and drew her close. While she pulled back, stunned, he scanned her face and buried his other hand in the curls at the back of her neck, holding her. Then he kissed her, lightly at first, then longer, his lips pressing harder and harder as he crushed her to him.

She struggled until he freed her with a shaky laugh. "That's only one of many things you will learn, but no more lessons for a while; it is too hard to restrain myself." He stroked a lock of hair from her forehead. "I've mussed your hair. Don't let your grandmother know; she will have my ears. Farewell for now, my sweet."

He turned and walked cheerfully from the room, taking care to overstep the confections oozing on the carpet, shouting in the hall for his hat and cane.

Abby sank into the chair and put her hands to her mouth. Her lips felt bruised. Her heart raced. She could not forget the expression in his eyes as he pulled away from her.

It was a look of proud ownership.

"What have I done?" she whispered.

Three

The sounds of shattering crockery brought the magician to wakefulness. Panting, shaking his head to banish the persistent phantoms from his mind, he sat up in bed and swung his legs to the floor. Someone had shouted. A certain rawness in the back of his throat flooded him with an unwelcome suspicion. When the bedroom door crashed opened and revealed Francis silhouetted against the faint light of the hall, his suspicions were confirmed, and he flushed in shame.

"Are you all right, milord?" Francis queried in a worried voice.

"Yes, yes. Go back to bed." The magician stood, intending to force the valet's departure, but something sharp ripped into his foot, and he swore and sat down again.

Francis strode into the room and lit the lamp, his mouth straightening obstinately when Julian protested. Brushing his master's hands aside, he examined the injury. The cut was only bleeding slightly, and he dampened a towel in the basin and ordered the magician to press it tightly against the wound.

Julian, still riding the effects of the dream, obeyed with sour grace. His thoughts were more disjointed than a cloudscape. For a moment he could not recollect where he was. Just before he unmanned himself further to ask Francis, he recalled they were staying at a small inn, The Garden on the Lea, outside Worthing. Almost a week had passed then, and only one more to go before he compounded his madness.

The valet left and returned quickly carrying a broom and

an oilskin. While he swept the shards of broken crockery onto the cloth, Julian watched him gratefully. At least he'd asked no questions.

When Harriet entered the room without knocking, the magician's stomach knotted. He noticed Francis pause in his sweeping to eye her, and no wonder. She looked like an avenging goddess. Her mane of red hair flowed across her shoulders in appealing waves. The golden robe she wore outlined every sensuous curve.

She crossed her arms beneath her bosom and stared hard at Julian, her expression a mixture of irritation and alarm. "The dreams again," she said flatly. "Every night since we left High Chipping. They're getting worse, aren't they?"

Instead of answering, he displayed sudden interest in the bottom of his foot. Francis gave him a mild glance and replied, "Knocked over the pitcher this time. Cut himself a little. I'm making a pallet over there on the floor." He cast a firm look at his employer, as though daring him to refuse.

"No, you won't, Francis, I'll not listen to your snoring." Julian sighed and permitted Harriet to see his foot. "And you go back to bed too, Harry. As you can see, I'm in no danger of bleeding to death. I'm not a child who needs looking after."

Francis grumbled incoherently, swept the remaining dust into the oilskin and twisted it closed, then walked from the room. Harriet lingered, her eyes glittering softly in the lamplight.

"Would you like me to stay?"

Julian caught her hand and pressed it to his lips, but the look he gave her was filled with regret. "We have spoken of this before. I thought we had come to an understanding. I'm sorry—"

She snatched her hand away. "I don't need your pity," she said, and hurried from the room.

Just the same, he spared her a little. But then his thoughts were overtaken by images of one Miss Abigail Lyons, who was beginning to consume his mind. Tonight he had muffed the simplest tricks in his performance, had even let loose one of his doves over the audience, a thing he hadn't done since he was a lad.

But things would be better soon, if he had made the right decision. If not, his brain would be good for nothing but fodder. And he had no one to blame for it but himself.

As the days following Philip's proposal stretched into a week, then two, it became increasingly difficult for Abby to delay giving her answer; and she wasn't sure why she did. *I can still run away,* she promised herself. But where would she go? What could she do? Her education had too many holes in it to support her as a governess or a teacher in a seminary.

She was grateful he'd never repeated his passionate behaviour, though the simmering glances he sent her way suggested he'd like to do so. If he acted as he did when she promised to think about his proposal, she couldn't imagine what he'd do when she finally said *yes*.

The most confusing thing was that his advances had not totally repulsed her. If he were a villain like a character in one of Mrs. Roche's or Mrs. Radcliffe's novels, she should have found his embrace disgusting. But though she had not sought, wanted, nor enjoyed his kiss, there was an element of excitement to it. Like flotsam in a raging river, she'd been swept into the tide of his passion.

Perhaps marriage to him would not be so terrible. Maybe he could persuade her to love him as he'd changed her mind about so many other things. Maybe he could make her trust him.

But I don't want to be persuaded into loving my husband, she told her tear-soaked pillow each night. *I want the love to be my idea alone.*

Strange, fragmented dreams tortured her sleep. Philip would reach for her again, his expression hungry and demanding. At some point while she pushed and fought, his eyes would change from grey to blue. Just as she realized it was the ma-

gician she struggled against, he would transform into a dove
and fly away.

After one such night she paid her morning visit to her
grandmother's room with red-rimmed eyes and the imprint of
her coverlet branded into her cheek. Matilda observed her with
an unfamiliar stab of guilt tempered by annoyance.

"You're a tiresome child, Abigail," she said. "Mooning and
pining and wasting away when you should be rejoicing. No
man's going to want you, not even Philip, if you don't stop."

Matilda placed her skeletal hands on the side of the settee
and pushed herself to a higher sitting position. With a brighter
edge in her voice, she said, "Now I've had a thought. Let's
have the wedding here, at Sharonfield. Prosings would be more
elegant, but I can't be expected to travel in my condition. And
why not have it three weeks from now, well before your birthday. You don't want your anniversary too close to your birthday, you know, or you'll only get half the presents ever after."

"I haven't said I'd marry him," said Abby listlessly.

"No, and the entire world waits at your feet for one little
word!" Matilda cried. "In my day you would have been forced,
but I am too kind for that!"

She snapped her fingers at Jane, who was feather-dusting
a lamp on the bedside table. "Fetch my purse," she ordered.
Turning back to Abby, she said, "I'm giving you a few coins
to spend. When I was a girl, nothing made me feel better than
an outing. Redmond has told me there is a small circus come
to town this week. Get you into High Chipping and come home
with your head back on your shoulders, do you hear? And take
Charlotte Ann with you. I can't spare Jane."

Jane looked woeful at this news, but she handed the purse
to her mistress, who removed several shillings, one at a time,
and gave them to Abby. With her gaze fixed regretfully on the
coins in her granddaughter's hand, Matilda waved her from the
room.

* * *

Abby did not think anything could stir her from the darkness of her thoughts, but as her grandmother's fusty old coach rattled the two miles into town, her spirits grew higher with every bump.

"There is more traffic on the road today than I've ever seen before," she shouted over the clatter of the wheels.

Charlotte Ann turned worried eyes toward the dusty window. "I reckon everybody is going to see the sideshows."

"You don't sound happy about it. Are you not glad to be released from your duties for a while?"

The maid stared at her glumly. Several wisps of lackluster hair had fallen away from her topknot, and she pushed them upward into her bonnet. Abby suddenly realized she had never seen a larger pair of ears on anyone, then stifled the unkind thought.

"Everything will be waiting for me when I get back," Charlotte Ann said in fatalistic tones.

"Oh, I see. Maybe I can help you."

The servant shrugged, then turned her eyes to the glass again. "Most often they advertise these traveling companies weeks ahead of time. But this one seems like it came from nowhere. I hope they don't have the kind of performers that goes about in their smallclothes. I'd hate for the vicar to see me here if they do."

Swallowing her amusement, Abby forebore mentioning that if the vicar saw her, he would have to be present, too. She left the maid to her worries and kept silent for the remaining minutes of the trip.

When Redmond halted the carriage in a large field south of town, she joined the crowd eagerly, leaving Charlotte Ann to follow. A gate had been erected at the edge of the meadow. Abby opened her reticule and paid the entrance fees for both of them, then entered the makeshift arena.

Some twenty or so wagons had been pulled into an enormous half-circle, and performers were displaying their particular abilities before each. There were jugglers, acrobats, contortionists, cages with lions and panthers, a shooting gallery, and Red Indians from America demonstrating war dances. Abby became dizzy wandering from one exhibit to the other. She wished her grandmother had given her more money so she could buy something to eat. The smells of lamb-on-a-stick and dipped apples were making her stomach as hollow as an empty log.

While she stood watching a man eating fire, she felt a tug at the end of her arm. She turned in time to see a lad running through the crowd with her reticule.

"Stop! Stop the thief!" she cried, and began chasing him. One rough-looking man made a half-hearted attempt to trip the culprit, but the boy slithered away like a snake. She could hear Charlotte Ann's yells growing fainter behind her. No one else seemed to care, the spectators appearing to view her distress as part of the entertainment. A couple of rowdies even had the audacity to cheer her on.

The boy kept glancing over his shoulder, slowing himself considerably to do so. He must be a very inept thief, or a beginner. If there were not so many people between them, she could have caught him easily. Finally, the child led her behind the wagons, where he ran headlong into an impeccably dressed young gentleman.

She was not too breathless to be temporarily overwhelmed by the gentleman's perfect features. His hair was dark and thick, his coat faultlessly tailored over wide shoulders and as blue as his eyes. There was something about him . . .

"Whoa there, lad!" said the stranger with a chuckle. "What are you up to?"

"He has stolen my reticule!" Abby cried.

"Well, that will never do. Hand it over, young man."

The boy passed it to him without protest, then ran off. Abby thought she saw a grin on the child's face, but surely she had imagined it. Still, she could not help feeling a whisper of distrust as she looked at the gentleman. Had not his act of rescue been too *easy*?

"Here you are, miss," he said, and gave her the purse.

"Thank you," she said weakly. Her gaze roamed across his face. She was being rude to stare, and the amusement in his eyes made her cheeks sting. What was it about him? Something . . .

He swept off his top hat and bowed. "Since we have met in this rather dramatic way, perhaps I should introduce myself. I am Julian Donberry."

The pleasant timbre of his voice . . . those blue, blue eyes. Suddenly, her body became quite stiff with shock.

"No, you are not," she said, her voice trembling.

His smile faltered. "I'm not?"

"You are Lord Merlyn, the magician," she pronounced.

The smile disappeared entirely, then returned. "Oh, well. It was worth a try. There was always the chance you would not recognize me, since I was wearing a mask the last time we met. But I suspected you were too sharp for that, Miss Lyons."

She felt quite cold. Her awareness of the crowd on the other side of the wagon brought a small measure of comfort. But for the moment, they were alone. If she were not so curious, she would run away.

"Why—why are you here? What do you want?"

His eyes twinkled while he considered her questions. Then, as if throwing caution to the winds, his grin widened recklessly. "I'm here to renew my offer, Miss Lyons. I have come to ask you to be my wife."

Abby's knees went weak. She was alone with a madman. She sank against the hub of the carriage wheel and felt her heart turn over.

He rushed to assist her. "Forgive me. I am being too abrupt. I should have—"

"Abrupt?" she squeaked, anger and alarm making her strong enough to push him away. "Abrupt is hardly the word I'd use. Insane is more like."

He stepped back a pace. "You need not be insulting."

She gave him an incredulous look, then laughed wildly.

"No, of course I need not." She careened away from the wheel and stormed away from him. He caught her before she reached the back of the wagon and guided her around to face him.

"Please, Miss Lyons. Wait."

She stopped. The teasing look had fallen from his face. He looked suddenly vulnerable, and something within her responded in spite of herself. Still, he must be playing some kind of game with her. She tensed and moved her eyes back and forth, searching for a means of escape.

He released her. "I won't force you to stay, but I beg you to remain a few moments. Allow me to begin again. I thought bringing the sideshow was a romantic way to be introduced, that rescuing your reticule might make you regard me in a kindly light. I hoped you would become interested in Julian Donberry, for I feared our initial contact might prejudice you against me. Will you let me explain?"

"You brought the circus to town in order to meet me?" asked Abby, who had absorbed little beyond that statement.

He looked sheepish. "Well, some of the performers are my relatives, and they were touring nearby anyway. Knowing what I do about your interest in such matters, I was certain you would attend."

She stared at him in disbelief. "I have never heard such nonsense. And what does any of it have to do with your proposing marriage?"

"I am trying to explain, Miss Lyons." He paused, calming himself. When he noted her furious eyes, he continued hurriedly, "I should begin by telling you my real name *is* Julian Donberry. I'm the fifth son of the Marquess of Donberry. Lord Merlyn is the stage name I have assumed to avoid embarrassing my family. That is also the reason I wear the domino when I am associated with my role."

"Your father is a marquess, and yet you have relatives in the circus?" she asked scornfully. His story was as full of holes as a beehive.

"My mother was a Gypsy." His eyes bored into hers as if daring her to say something about *that*.

Knowing how tender one could feel toward one's mother, she chose not to dispute him. What she doubted was the story about his father, whom she suspected had probably been a clown.

"Why would a marquess's son need to work as a magician?" she challenged.

"I had to earn my living somehow. My family and I are . . . estranged."

She could almost hear Philip saying, *How convenient.* Evidently he had been right about Lord Merlyn all along. Disappointment flooded her. "I daresay your taking to the stage has not improved your estrangement any," she snapped.

He eyed her warily. "To speak the truth, I'm not sure that they know. I left home over ten years ago and have never been back. Very few people know that Lord Merlyn is really Julian Donberry."

"And yet you have told *me,* a stranger." Was there no end to his lies?

"Yes, I have told you." He sighed. "There is a reason." A hopelessness came into his voice, as if he knew she would not believe him but had to go on anyway. "This is difficult. I'm a little afraid you will think I'm mad."

"Oh, I do not think it," she said with a humorless little laugh.

He gave her the briefest of glances through his lashes, then dropped his gaze to the brim of his hat. He turned it restlessly in his hands and took a quick breath.

"For as long as I can remember, I've had a certain . . . ability."

For the first time, Abby noted the shadows beneath his eyes. There was a haunted quality in his expression, too, that plowed through her skepticism and made her feel more sympathetic. She would have to guard against it.

"An ability that allows you to find lost necklaces?" she asked, her fingers clutching at her locket.

"Among other things." He saw the necklace and smiled.

His claim excited her, but she was not to be won over so easily. Philip had told her she was childish enough to believe anything. "I have heard it said that such accomplishments can be . . . staged."

A slight edge came into his voice. "How do you think I knew about your locket? Do you imagine I sent my servant to your house and had him hide it before I even knew you or suspected you would attend the performance?"

"There is no reason to be sarcastic. I have not said I don't believe you." After an instant, she added, "I have not said I *do,* either."

He gave the wagon wheel a bitter look. "Well, you wouldn't be the first who did not."

Her chin rose, and she regarded him thoughtfully through her lashes. "If you are who and what you say, there is an easy way to resolve this. Tell me what I am thinking."

His eyes hardened to stone. "It doesn't work that way."

She snorted. "I thought not."

"Allow me to explain how it *does* work."

"Oh, pray do; I shall not stop you."

He inhaled quickly. "I cannot guess your thoughts. Occasionally I have dreams that warn me of future events, and sometimes vague feelings. But ordinarily, I must touch a person or something he or she owns before I can sense anything. Even then I often only receive jumbled images—bits and pieces of the day's activities that are meaningless. Sometimes I get absolutely nothing." His gaze fastened on hers. "And, now and then, I catch a glimpse of that person's future."

Pressure began to build inside Abby's head. She could not mistake his meaning. "Is that why you've come? You saw something in my future when you held my hand on the stage?"

He nodded slowly.

She swallowed. Even though she knew he was probably lying, a superstitious chill swept across the back of her neck. "Something . . . terrible?"

A burst of laughter and applause came from the other side of the wagon. A mime ran around the corner, saw them, and brushed past Abby to enter the caravan without comment. The magician put on his hat, tilted his head, and offered an arm. "Walk with me awhile?"

Abby displayed a token hesitation, but nothing would have prevented her from hearing the rest of his story now. Even if it was untrue, she had to know how it came out. She accepted his escort, and they began to pace along the outside edge of the wagons.

As he spoke, he kept his gaze centered on the path ahead. "I saw two different futures. One was when I touched you. The other was from Demere."

Abby waited, her eyes never wavering from his face. She found it frightening that he remembered her name and Philip's after so brief an acquaintance weeks ago.

"When I shook Demere's hand, I saw a series of images. I watched the two of you on your wedding day, then on later occasions." The magician's unencumbered hand rolled into a fist. "I must be brutally frank. I saw him hurting you. Many times. Even after you were in a delicate condition. During childbirth, you . . . died."

If he was making this up, he was a monster. "What—what happened to the baby?"

"Also dead. I observed your funeral, then watched Demere return to his house. Things began to decay after that; the estate deteriorated, as did Demere, until he put a pistol to his head."

She closed her eyes for a moment. Her own misgivings about Philip had never gone this far. It was an impossibly bad future. She would humor the magician, play along until his awful prophecies were finished and she could banish him from her life forever.

"You said you saw two futures. Hopefully the other is better, for I do not like this one."

"Nor do I," he said, dropping his gaze. "In the second future, the one I read when I touched you, *we* were wed."

There was a brief silence while a rush of anger swept from Abby's head to her toes. What was he about? Did he think she was an heiress? If so, he had been faulty in his research, for she had nothing. Or was this simply an unusual approach to seduce foolish young ladies?

"That is very interesting." Her voice sounded falsely enthusiastic, even to her ears. "Now, when you saw this second future . . . was it more satisfactory?"

Hearing the skepticism behind her words, he gave her a searching look. "You have to understand something. I can never see my own future except when it is in relationship to someone else's, if I am involved in some way. I saw you being married through the perspective of my own eyes. This ring was on your finger." He raised his little finger to display a ring of gold filigree. "After that, the images became vague."

"But you believe my marrying you would provide a brighter future for me."

He began to speak rapidly. "It could hardly be worse. I assure you I will never harm you. I know it's unusual for strangers to wed, but not unheard of. What I am proposing is a marriage in name only, one that we may annul later, once the danger to you is past."

She was so incensed she could hardly breathe. Releasing his arm, she stepped away from him. "Do you think I am a complete imbecile?"

His face was a study in shock, as if he had not considered the possibility she would not swallow every word he said. "I beg your pardon?"

"How can you imagine I would accept such a story?"

"But, your locket is surely some proof—"

"I'll thank you not to speak of my jewelry again. No, I don't know how you did it, but I am certain you could find a way. You *are* an excellent magician; that much I will admit."

"Thank you for your kind words." Jerking the hat off his

head, he came to stand only inches away from her. Using the hat to punctuate his speech, he said curtly, "If I've failed to convince you of the truth, perhaps you will be so kind as to explain why *you* think I have made this unusual offer?"

In his wrath, the blue of his eyes had intensified. Abby felt as if he were shining a light into her soul. "I—I don't know. The only thing I am certain of is that gentlemen do not propose marriage to strange ladies!"

She heard her words and blushed. To dispel the sudden spark of humor in his eyes, she blurted, "Not that I am . . . oh, you understand my meaning. If you truly had these visions as you said, why should marriage be necessary? I was already considering rejecting Philip's proposal. Now that you have told me of your premonitions, even though I'm not sure of their accuracy, I shall take them as confirmation. I won't marry him. There. Now you may go; you have done your duty."

"So he has already made an offer." Shadows came into his eyes. "It's not so simple. I believe the futures I saw were the only two possibilities. If you don't wed me, somehow you will, either by your own decision or by force, marry him."

"You are trying to frighten me. It would be simpler for me to go to a city where I can find a position and start a new life. I *am* penniless, you should know. Not an heiress. If you had thought to receive a fortune by marrying, you have made a grave mistake in asking *me*."

Ribbons of color rushed into his cheeks. "I am not interested in marrying an heiress. If I were, I could have done so a dozen times by now—"

"And it is remarkably gentlemanly of you to mention it," someone cried, and Abby looked astonished when she discovered it was herself.

For an instant he appeared as if he might ignite, but he called upon something calm within himself and continued in a softer voice, "The evidence of my life argues against your leaving on your own. If such were a possibility, I should have seen it when I touched your hand. No, I cannot help thinking therein would lie disaster. Demere would find you, and the other future I foresaw would come to pass."

His tone softened her anger a little, but she shook her head stubbornly. "Even if what you say is true, I cannot understand your willingness to do this. Surely mine isn't the first bad future you've foreseen. Do you make a practice of rescuing people?"

"I am not so generous," he said quietly. A starling landed near their feet, and he watched it solemnly as it pecked at the ground and flew away. "I no longer allow myself to know more than anyone else." He gave her a sideways glance. "You and Demere were the first exceptions to that in years.

"Even then, even after I read your companion's future, I might have done nothing, though I was in horror for you. But when I touched you, everything changed because I was involved. The visions are just as strong as they were that first night, and they won't go away. I see them every time I close my eyes."

He passed a hand across his face. "If you won't allow me to help, I shall go mad."

"That is a line worthy of your melodrama with Hilda on the stage," she said spitefully.

He appeared stung beyond the limits of his endurance. "God save me, I had not dreamed I was proposing to a shrew!"

"Do not trouble yourself, my lord," she hurled between her teeth. "This shrew will not hold you to it!"

The heat of their words throbbed in the air between them. Whirling around, she strode away and plunged into the crowd. She thought he might follow, but he did not.

Four

During the next days, Abby sank lower and lower into a morass of gloom. She relived the scene behind the wagons with Lord Merlyn—Lord Julian—repeatedly in her mind. There were a dozen ways she could have acted differently, and every scenario had a better outcome.

She had been foolish to throw away a chance to leave Sharonfield. Had she spoken with more civility, perhaps she could have persuaded the magician to take her to another city without marrying her. She would like to go to London. There were many opportunities there. Perhaps she could become a zookeeper. She had always wanted to see the bears.

But she had reacted with more wrath than she knew she possessed. She had never spoken so freely and angrily to anyone in her life. It had been . . . exhilarating.

Of course, her initial suspicions had probably been correct. He must be either insane or a trickster of some kind. Perhaps he sold young Englishwomen to Arabian sheikhs. Why he would go to such lengths to deceive her, however, she could not imagine.

She should not have been so hasty. Surely he was not so bad as Philip. But now her opportunity was gone. Her spirits fell a little lower every day.

On the third afternoon following her encounter with the magician, Abby returned from a long, dismal walk to find Walters in a disturbed mood. She was eager for any diversion and felt an immediate stirring of interest.

"There is a visitor for you in the parlour, miss," he said in formal tones, then lowered his voice to a whisper. "He's already been up to see your grandmother, and she's all in a dither. Wouldn't take himself off 'til he visited you, too. According to him, he's a friend of your mother's family. Says he's the son of the Marquess of Donberry."

Her depression lifted at once. She was surprised to feel an almost affectionate burst of humour at Lord Julian's fiction about knowing her mother. Was he incapable of telling the truth? Of course if he did, he would not be received here.

After Walters helped her remove her cloak and bonnet, he ushered her into the parlour. The magician rose to his feet immediately, a beseeching expression on his face. She smiled more warmly than she had intended and pretended to be meeting him for the first time.

As soon as Walters introduced them and moved out of sight, Julian suggested they stroll about the grounds for a while.

"Of course," she heard herself say. In her relief to see him again—well, not to see *him* precisely, it was merely the opportunity of escape he represented—her mind had gone shockingly blank. Had he asked her to leap across the garden on her hands, she wouldn't have had the presence of mind to refuse.

She turned and led the way past a disapproving Walters, who had stationed himself against the wall outside the parlour. Moving stiffly, he distributed hats and coats and held the door for them while they exited.

The outside air was sharp with the smell of burning leaves; the shadows were growing long and the temperature falling. Abby did not feel the cold, would not have felt it even if she'd left her cloak inside.

Now that they were alone, she drew breath to speak, but the magician said quickly, "A moment, please," then offered his arm and escorted her down the stairs and along the narrow, flagstoned pathway that led past the orchards. When they were some distance from the house, he started to speak, then paused as a lad carrying a bucket and a rake crossed their path.

"Is there a place where we can talk privately?"

Swallowing her impatience, Abby nodded and led him to the back garden, where stone benches were placed among a profusion of goatsbeard, cornflowers, kiss-me-quicks, and Welsh poppies. They sat on a bench allowing a prospect of both the house and the apple trees.

He removed his hat and placed it on the bench between them. "Thank you for seeing me. I was afraid you might have me thrown out head-first."

Intent upon remaining inoffensive this time, she folded her hands in her lap and appeared to contemplate them. "Upon reflection, I believe I spoke too harshly to you the other day."

He cleared his throat. "Yes. I rather thought so too, if you'll forgive my saying so. I hoped you would see reason after a few days."

Turning her head slowly to look at him, she said, "You were rather rude yourself. No one has ever called me a shrew before."

He chuckled. "I have not come to fight with you again, Miss Lyons. I do apologize for that unfortunate remark."

Her wrath, so easily called forth of late, eased. She glanced back at her hands. "Why *have* you come?"

"I'm here to renew my offer one final time. If you refuse me again, I shall go away, I promise. But please—allow me to speak first."

In her most world-weary voice, she granted him permission to speak; but she could not restrain the spark of hope that flew into her eyes.

He must have seen it, for his smile was dazzling. She had to look away from it in order to catch her breath. "I can understand your distrust concerning my ability. Most people who learn of it either regard me as a charlatan or a lunatic. I have even been accused of practicing the devil's arts."

"The devil's—surely you jest?"

"I wish I could say so." His expression turned grim. "The first time it happened, I was three or four years old. I had a vision of the roof collapsing on my nursemaid's home. When she said she planned to join her family at the cottage on her off-day, I made a terrible row. To satisfy me, she stayed. Not because she believed me, mind."

He leaned down, picked up a stick from the ground, and began twirling it between his hands. "There was a rainstorm that Saturday night. The hut was old, the roof in poor repair and weakened by the weight of water. Her father and brother were killed by a falling beam."

"But your nursemaid was saved?" She could not disguise the disbelief in her voice.

He shrugged. "I lost her anyway. She said she couldn't work with a child who was possessed of the devil. And this from the woman who heard me say my prayers each night."

Abby visualized a sad little boy struggling to understand why his friend left him, and sympathy pierced her heart. But was the story true?

Hoping to trip him if he were lying, she asked, "What did your family think about your ability?"

He pressed the end of the stick into the dirt and twisted a little hole in the ground. "My father ignored it. My brothers . . . well. Let us just say they weren't receptive and were glad to see me gone."

Though he spoke lightly, Abby sensed the pain behind his words. She paused, then asked, "And your mother?"

The movement of the stick stilled. "She died shortly after I was born."

"Oh." Abby was aware of much left unsaid, of old wounds still raw. Of course, he could be fabricating everything in order to secure her sympathy. She wished she were a prophetess so she could know for sure. She wished she could make up her mind about *something*.

"If they believed in your ability, I am surprised they did not view it as a special gift, like the biblical Joseph's talent for visions and interpreting dreams."

He faced her, his eyes glimmering strangely, reminding her

of sunlight on water. "You call it a gift? If such it is, I'd gladly return it. More often than not, it brings trouble. It's a beastly curse."

"How can you feel that way? If such a talent exists, it should be helpful."

"It has not helped me with you," he said softly. "Not so far, at least."

She stared at him for a moment. "I know you would like me to say I believe in your visions, but I cannot. However, I am beginning to be certain that *you* believe them. But can you not admit the possibility that you are wrong about the ones concerning Philip and myself?"

"I have no reason to think so. Occasionally I've misinterpreted what I've seen, but in every instance, later developments confirm the truth of the visions themselves."

She stood and brushed the sides of her skirt, smoothing the gathers and fidgeting. Julian grabbed his hat and rose, watching her hopefully.

"I would like you to dismiss marriage from your mind," she said in deliberate tones. "If you truly want to help, take me to a city far from here. Escort me to London if you can."

Her heart hammered as she waited. She stole brief glances at his face, but he was no longer looking at her; his attention seemed to be caught by a flock of geese flying overhead.

"I can't do that, Miss Lyons," he said finally. "I'm sorry. If you won't allow me to help you in a manner that will truly be of use to you, I will not contribute to something that may cause you further harm."

She told herself she had expected as much, but disappointment clanged through her body. Should she accept his offer, then? Could she trust him enough?

Feeling as if she were stepping off a cliff, she said, "If I did believe you—and I'm not saying I do—my grandmother will never approve such a union. She wants me to marry Philip to join the two estates."

When his face brightened, she closed her heart. He must

think she meant to give in. His words gushed into her ears, persuasive words spoken as attractively as the Pied Piper must have piped.

"I believe you are in the right of it; Mrs. Lyons will never accept me. Which means, unfortunately, that should you decide in favor of my offer, we shall have to elope. For your sake, I'm sorry for it."

Abby planted her feet, piercing him with her eyes. "Elope?"

He sighed. "Whatever you are thinking now, don't. I have no terrible designs on your virtue. Bring your maid if you wish."

Her anxiety eased somewhat, but her mind still swam with questions. "If I do this, what will become of me after the marriage is annulled?"

"I travel through many cities on my tours. Once Philip is no longer a threat, you can make your choice of them. I won't hold you captive, if that's what you're thinking."

His spirits were definitely lifting, she saw. She wished she could say the same, but hers were twirling in a confused mass. She cast him a resentful look and began walking again. They passed the orchard and approached the flagstoned walkway. The unanswered question trembled in the air between them like half-forgotten music.

"I cannot make a decision now. How shall I get word to you?"

"I'll call again tomorrow."

The afternoon was a deceptively peaceful backdrop for the turbulence of her emotions until a persistent tapping intruded. Following the sound, Abby lifted her gaze to the upper story of the house. Matilda's angry face was pressed against the bedroom window, her cane beating a summons on the glass.

"That may not be possible," Abby said miserably.

Julian's glance followed hers. A bright smile broke across his face, and he nodded and lifted his hand in a jaunty wave. "Do as I do," he commanded between his teeth.

"She will be incensed," Abby said, but she obeyed, raising

her hand and smiling. When the tapping became even more imperious, she again followed his lead, grinning and waving with added enthusiasm. "If we don't stop, she will slay me," Abby declared, but her giggles were genuine.

His eyes danced as he led her onward. "I hope not. I like hearing you laugh." A few seconds later they climbed the front steps. "Don't worry about reaching me," he said quickly. "I'll contact you somehow."

He opened the door to find Walters hovering near it, his eyes worried. "Your gloves, my lord," the butler said immediately. "Redmond has gone round to the stable for your horse."

"Er, thank you." Julian gave Abby a look of heavy irony. "I believe I must take my leave of you, Miss Lyons," he said.

While he hurriedly pulled on his gloves, she stood nearby, her head beginning to fill with the significance of the last half-hour. Her life was never going to be the same, no matter what she decided. The dreadful tedium of the past few years was finally drawing to a close.

Her grandmother could never force her to marry Philip now, even if she decided this stranger's offer was too risky to take. He could not know that he had given her a breath of hope, enough to restore some remnants of her confidence. She could do anything. Become a governess. Marry a nobleman. Sing opera on the stage. The entire world was open to her.

The wonder and the joy of it bubbled inside her like a geyser. Julian sensed it, his eyes reflecting her delight as he bowed over her hand and she sank into a curtsey.

"Until next time," he whispered.

When Walters closed the door behind him, Abby continued to stare at the carved panels as if she could conjure Julian's image from them. The butler cleared his throat and glanced toward the stairs.

As if on cue, an indignant voice shouted, "Abigail!"

* * *

Julian wearily entered his room at the Wooden Flagon and tossed his gloves and hat on the bed. Francis had a roaring fire going in the hearth, and the magician was glad for it. He sat in the wooden rocker and held his hands toward the blaze.

There was a knock at the door and Francis entered. With the ease of a man who knows he is more friend than servant, he dropped several pieces of correspondence into his master's lap and settled into the companion chair, then fixed his green gaze on Julian and waited.

The magician snorted. Francis was a man who kept his own counsel, except when he wanted to offer unneeded advice. Beyond a doubt, he was burning with curiosity but would go up in flames before asking. Well, perhaps a little torture was in order. After the frustration of the past weeks, Julian felt like roasting something over the coals.

"Has Uncle Georgio's troupe moved on?"

"All gone, milord. He said the take was better than what they would have received in Steeping."

"Good. Perhaps I've not made enemies then."

"Too bad all that effort was wasted."

Julian's lips quirked. He darted a look at Francis, then glanced at the mail and leaned back leisurely. "What's all this?"

"Cards and letters, milord," Francis answered stiffly.

"I can see that. Who are they from? Who knows we are here? Harry couldn't have written already, could she?"

" 'Tis not my place to read your mail."

Julian lifted a brow irritably and began to thumb through the calling cards and invitations. "Lady Anna Wentworth. The Reverend Whitley Moore. Mister George Strongfellow. Who *are* these people?"

"Locals, milord. The word's out. Everyone of them has daughters eager to meet the marquess's son. Been a procession of them all afternoon in the public rooms downstairs. Some are staying for dinner."

Julian groaned. "If they knew this marquess's son had performed as a magician here weeks ago, they would hang me by my toenails. We'll dine in the room tonight." He threw the cards in the fire, then glanced sideways at the valet. With a little smile he leaned back again and closed his eyes.

The silence stretched. Francis made a humming noise in the back of his throat, as if scratching an itch. Julian's smile widened.

"One of the young ladies is broader than two cows tied together," the valet commented.

The magician coughed. "Unfortunate girl."

"Another one of 'em is quite comely, if you don't mind she has no front teeth."

"In some societies, that is considered an advantage," Julian said without expression.

"Yes, milord. But you should see her mother."

"Lovely, is she?"

"Like the wrong end of a monkey."

Without moving his head, Julian slid his gaze toward his servant. "Francis, I do not believe you are very respectful toward the fairer sex."

The servant appeared to consider this. "No, milord, I suppose I am not."

Julian leaned forward and threw an errant piece of bark onto the flames. "You're not going to ask me how it went this afternoon, are you?"

"Ask how what went?"

"Hah. Mister Unconcerned. Well, to answer your unasked question, I have not been accepted. Not yet, anyway."

Francis sniffed. "I'm sure that will change."

The magician darted a sharp look his way. He thought he detected a cynical note, but the valet was a picture of innocence. A moment later Francis slipped out the door, murmuring something about seeing to their dinner.

Julian rose, stretched, removed his waistcoat, and loosened his cravat. The bed looked inviting. There was time for a nap before dinner. Surely this afternoon had changed things. Perhaps now he could close his eyes for five minutes without seeing confused images of brutality and death. He pulled off his boots and stretched across the counterpane.

As he settled into the contours of the mattress, the disturbing encounters with Abigail Lyons began to file through his mind. She had proved to be as strong as his initial impression of her. She looked soft but was no one's fool. Unfortunately, she now suspected him of half-a-dozen things. Maybe he had handled matters badly, but he had approached her the only way he knew how. He had told her the truth, or at least as much of it as she needed to know. Once she thought it over, she would come around. She must.

She continued to compel his thoughts as she had from the moment he first saw her in the audience. Her dark eyes flamed with life; they expressed every emotion that drifted through her mind. With the amusement of distance, he recalled her excitement this afternoon, her skepticism, and even her wrath. One would always know where he stood with her.

He caught himself wondering if her hair felt as thick and soft as it looked. He could probably encircle her waist with his hands. Before his thoughts wandered farther afield, he commanded himself to sleep.

When Francis returned a half-hour later, he found Julian sitting up in bed with his back pressed against the headboard. The valet paused, then set the dinner tray on the bedside table. He filled one of the goblets with wine and passed it to his master. The magician downed several sips, spilling only a little on the bedspread.

"The bad dream again?" Francis asked gruffly.

"No." Julian turned shattered eyes to his. "Something new, Francis."

By the following afternoon, Matilda's wrath had not diminished, and she was moved to pour some of it upon her visitor. Raking Philip's neat figure from head to toe with scornful eyes, she pounded her cane on the floor with one hand and squeezed her coverlet with the other.

"You'll lose her, you impudent young whelp, if you don't stop scaring her to death. I said she's like a withering vine, didn't I? Don't respond to being told what to do and when to do it."

Philip's fists opened and closed reflexively. "I'm expecting a favorable answer any day now. You know I've taken your advice, Matilda; I've been very careful with her."

The old lady turned her head to look out the window. The afternoon light fell full on her face, highlighting a wattled neck and lined cheeks.

"Well, that's as may be," she said in a softer voice. "But I watched her walking with that feller yesterday, and she didn't stand off from him like a reed as she does with you. Hung on his every word."

Philip's eyes blazed, and Matilda shrunk into herself for a moment, then cackled. "You're a sight, boy! Would that I were Abigail's age. Full of starch, I was. You're the kind of man I always wanted, a man of strength and strong emotion. Not like that velvet-eyed Winston I married. Yes, you and I would've suited very well."

Ignoring the revolting images her words produced, he demanded, "Who is this man?"

"I've told you, he's Lord Julian Donberry, the son of the Marquess of Donberry and a friend on her mother's side of the family."

"And you believed that story?"

"No, I didn't *believe* his story, not right away," she said harshly, then lifted a frilly handkerchief to her lips and dabbed at the corners of her mouth. "I had Jane take a note to Lady Anna this morning. The old crone-face has been in Society and knows a lot of people, as you know. And sure enough, she recognized the name. Said she already knew he was in town. Guess she still has hopes for those three homely daughters of hers. All of 'em had their Seasons so long ago nobody remembers. Ha!"

"Lady Anna knew the name, but I daresay she doesn't know what he looks like. He could be an impostor."

Giving him a mockingly flirtatious glance, she said, "You're a suspicious feller, Philip. I like that in a man."

He sprang to his feet and walked rapidly to the serving table, bringing Jane to wakefulness in her fireside chair. Pouring a glass of Matilda's sherry, he downed it, frowning at the cloying taste. "He'll leave her alone, if he knows what is good for him. Where is Abigail now?"

"I told her to take a walk. Thought it would give me a chance to tell you how the land lies."

Matilda watched him carefully, the humor dying from her face. Despite her enjoyment of Philip's fiery personality, she sometimes suspected his surface anger went far deeper, that he controlled it with the most tenuous of reins. At such times her conscience would nag at her and bring to mind the naive face of her granddaughter. Would Abigail be able to handle this man?

"You know, Philip," she said carefully, "I should like to think you're going to be good to the girl not just now, but later, after you are wed. She don't have town polish. Don't know anything, really."

"I know she doesn't." He clinked the glass back on the table and paced to the window. "Of course I'll be good to her. What do you think? I love her."

Satisfied, Matilda breathed in deeply. "Well, if that's the way you feel, you had best get her agreement. Her birthday is next month. I can't keep the solicitor from her then. Once she finds out this place is hers, she won't have to wed you, and then nothing we do or say will make her, silly chit that she is. If I were her, though . . ."

She winked at him, the wrinkles fanning from her eye like folds in a curtain. Philip made a feeble attempt to smile, then, declaring his intention of finding Abigail, took his leave.

When she was alone except for the nodding Jane, Matilda stared at the brown-splotched hands folded over her blanket. The knuckles were swollen and twisted, the purple veins raised like snakes over crumpled tissue. These weren't her hands. Her hands were white and soft with enough flesh to hide the bones. They had smoothed away her son Andrew's hurts, but not often enough. She had left him to the governess, never knowing she would live far beyond the burying of him.

But they would have had more time together if Andrew had not distanced himself. It was not her fault he could not sense the grandeur of her vision.

If only he hadn't married that woman, Abigail's mother. By so doing, he had lost the chance to unite Prosings and Sharonfield in his generation. He could just as easily have married Audrey Prosings, but no, he would not; so Audrey became Vincent Demere's wife.

Now Matilda had one final chance with Audrey's son and her granddaughter. She would not accept defeat, not this time. Her existence depended on it.

If only Winston hadn't paid that last cruel trick on her. Willing the estate to his granddaughter, a thing he could do because there were no male relatives to inherit. Dear God! He must be laughing in his grave.

But if she could double the size of Sharonfield before Abigail found out about her inheritance, all would be well. Philip had promised to christen the new holding Lyon-Demere, and that was something of worth to live through the centuries. She'd make her mark yet, as would Abigail. When the girl had her own children, she would forget her nonsense about Philip. She would learn about family pride and tradition then, once she held that first infant in her strong, young hands.

Disregarding Matilda's rules, Abby had left the grounds and was walking along the road toward High Chipping, hoping by some lucky stroke of fortune to intercept Julian. But though she had been marching at a soldier's pace for some time and was growing hot and dusty, she had seen no sign of him.

It made her a little angry, which she realized was irrational. But he had promised to make contact, and now that she'd made up her mind, she wanted to see him before she changed it again.

That morning she had decided to accept his offer.

The decision followed a night of inner debate. She could not think of another option providing escape so easily and quickly. And now that the possibility of flight had entered her head, she was itching to be gone. Her grandmother had harangued her for hours after his visit yesterday, bombarding her with questions and demands, making Abby want to leave more than ever.

She was taking a huge risk, she knew that; entrusting herself to a stranger's care. But if she could persuade Charlotte Ann to accompany her, propriety would be served. And if Julian proved to be a criminal of some sort, she would steal away during the night and find a place in one of the towns they would pass through on their way to the border. It would be an adventure.

She could not help feeling a twinge of regret that she'd not had a long courtship full of soft words, meaningful glances, and stolen kisses. Perhaps after she and the magician had their mock-marriage annulled, she would meet someone and have such a relationship.

For some reason the thought did not cheer her.

When she heard hoofbeats approaching behind, she turned gladly, knowing it must be him; but it was Philip, riding toward her like a thunderstorm on hooves. She struggled to keep her face neutral and not betray the ache of disappointment she felt.

He dismounted when he reached her. "What are you doing here, Abigail? Where's your maid?"

"You know I don't have a servant," she answered. "And I'm merely taking a walk. It's perfectly safe."

"A female is never safe alone. Matilda shouldn't tighten the

purse strings as she does; she's not penniless, but she's allowing Sharonfield to fall to pieces. I'm not a spendthrift myself,
but I don't regard a maid as an extravagance. My mother has
one, and so shall you when we're wed."

She wanted to say, *I shall never marry you,* but, although
this was a well-travelled road with open fields all around, they
were alone, and she was not so reckless. But something of her
feelings must have reflected in her eyes, for Philip's countenance clouded with doubt.

He moved closer and touched her hair, pushing a wayward
lock beneath her bonnet. His hand lingered, then trailed down
to her shoulders. Alarm coursed through Abby's body, and she
shrugged him away, reversed direction, and began walking rapidly toward Sharonfield.

"Abigail," he whispered, abandoning his horse to pursue its
interest in the roadside grasses. In a few paces, he caught up
with her and brushed her flailing hands aside. "Stop. Don't
fight me. Have you forgotten the taste of my kisses? You liked
them well enough before, I know you did."

There was desperation in his voice, and rage as well. His
hands were like iron claws on her arms. Realizing the futility
of resistance, she grew still but kept her head downcast. He
forced her chin upward. The anger and desire she saw in his
eyes stole her breath away.

And then, with a surge of hope, she detected movement
over Philip's left shoulder. A rider. Surely it would be Julian
come to her rescue. But as the horseman drew nearer, she saw
it was not. This man was taller and more strongly built than
the magician, and he wore servant's livery. In one hand he
carried a large bouquet of flowers. He looked vaguely familiar.

The rider was coming so fast she thought at first he meant
to pass them by, but at the last moment he drew on the reins,
causing his steed to kick a spray of gravel across her skirt. He
looked down at her without emotion.

"May I help you, miss?" he asked.

"Yes," Abby immediately replied.

"No," answered Philip at the same time.

Cool green eyes studied them. "Would you happen to be Miss Abigail Lyons?" When a surprised Abby confirmed her identity, he leaped off his horse as easily as she would overstep a puddle. "I am Francis Morgan, come to express the regards of my master, Lord Julian Donberry, to you and Mrs. Lyons."

While Philip drew an indignant breath, Francis gave her the flowers, which were late-blooming China roses. Remembering now that he was the man she had seen backstage during Julian's performance, she accepted the bouquet with a keen sense of disappointment. Was she not to see the magician today, then?

But the servant was still speaking. "You look tired, Miss Lyons. Why don't you ride Cracker here, and I'll walk you home."

"She can ride my horse," Philip said, but Francis was already boosting Abby into the saddle, which was difficult for her to arrange herself upon without falling, since it was not a sidesaddle. Philip moved as if to pull her off, but the servant inserted himself between them.

"I shall be all right, Philip," Abby said quickly. "Do you go home."

Bristling, he eyed the width of Francis's shoulders, then the stubborn set of Abby's mouth, and seemed to deflate. "Very well. I'll go because you have asked me, but I shall call on you tomorrow."

Francis slapped the horse into motion, and Abby lurched forward, the saddle horn gripped in one hand, the roses held in the other. Looking over her shoulder, she watched Philip stalk down the road toward his mount. When the roan caught sight of his master, he tossed his head and edged away. Philip's pace increased. The horse moved accordingly. Before long, it was an all-out chase.

Abby's lips trembled until she could no longer contain her laughter. Francis followed the line of her gaze, then looked up at her, his eyes flaring with amusement that quickly faded.

She observed him with some puzzlement. If not a handsome man, he was certainly well-favored. He had narrow green eyes that looked used to laughter, if the crinkles at the corners were a true indication. At some point in his life, his nose had been broken. He possessed a thatch of thick brown hair that fell across his forehead appealingly.

But for some reason, he didn't appear to like her, and while she was used to being bullied and treated like a rattle-head without a will of her own, she had little experience with not being liked. She set herself to win him over.

"The roses are lovely," she said.

"I'll tell milord you said so," he answered.

"Is there a card?"

"Yes, miss. 'Tis in my pocket. Should you like to see it now?"

"I wish I could, but if I release my hold on the saddle, I shall fall." He made no answer to this. She tried again. "Have you been in Lord Julian's employ for a long time?"

He sighed, as though opening his mouth were a burden. "Since we lived at Donberry Castle, miss."

He continued to trudge on in silence, tugging now and then on the reins when Cracker slowed. Abby gave up. "Do you know, I believe I would like to see that card after all. I shall be careful not to fall."

He halted the horse and fished in his pocket, then handed a gilt-edged rectangle to her. It was only Julian's personal card. His name and title were inscribed on one side, and a short message was scribbled on the other; something about enjoying meeting them yesterday.

"Oh," she said sadly, handing the card back. "Perhaps you had better give that to my grandmother."

He nodded, and they continued on without meeting anyone until they reached the circular drive of the manor house. Feeling bereft and not a little bewildered, Abby accepted Francis's assistance from the horse.

She had almost reached the front door when he cleared his

throat. "Oh, miss," he said, speaking quietly. "Milord said to tell you he will be taking a drive at one this morning. Means to halt awhile at the turning of your road. Just in the off-chance you're interested."

"Oh, yes," Abby said immediately, blushing and feeling as if her feet might leave the ground, too elated to wonder why Francis hadn't told her before. "Tell him—tell him I'm *very* interested to know that."

"Thought you would be," he said grimly. When Abby looked at him in surprise, he turned away and busied himself in tying Cracker's reins to the post.

Five

That evening, Charlotte Ann nervously scanned the sky from Miss Abby's bedroom window. "It's dark outside, but there's no fog," she whispered to her mistress. "There's always a fog! Why can't there be one tonight to hide us from the busybodies in this house? I'm going to pray for one."

"An excellent idea," Abby said, her mouth curving into a smile despite her nervousness.

The maid closed her eyes. Her lips moved briefly. When she looked again, the night was as clear as before.

"I just have too many doubts," Charlotte Ann explained. "If my faith was stronger, that fog would have been there, just as it would have for Elijah. That's what the vicar would say."

"I can almost hear him saying it," Abby agreed.

Charlotte Ann scratched her nose vigorously. "I've got to tell you I'm having my doubts about what we're doing, too. At first I thought a runaway marriage sounded romantic, and I have to say I was pleased at your offer for higher wages and lesser duties as a lady's maid. But . . . how do we know he's who he says? What if he's one of them what sells young maidens to brothels?"

"If that were the case, why would he bother to work as a magician? And why come all the way to High Chipping just for me?" Abby whispered crossly. She, too, was feeling doubts, and the maid's suspicions weren't helping. "Besides, he'd hardly tell me to bring my maid, would he?"

"He would if he knew he could fetch two foolish young virgins at one stroke."

"Oh, Charlotte Ann, please do not make me laugh; I'll awaken Grandmother."

"All right, so I'm not so young anymore. But still . . ."

Abby shook her head helplessly, then looked at her pocketwatch. "It's time."

With a moan, the maid jumped to her feet and picked up one portmanteau. Abby lifted the other and pulled the hood of her cloak over her hair. Ever so quietly, they crept from the room, down the hall, down the stairs, both of them skipping the noisy third step; and, having predetermined the back entrance would be safest, pushed through the kitchen door and saw a single candle glowing on the kitchen table.

Walters, a chicken leg at his mouth, looked up in surprise.

Abby and Charlotte Ann froze.

The butler jerked the meat from his lips, set it on the table, and wiped his chin on the sleeve of his nightshirt. Scraping back his chair and standing, he slowly moved his gaze over them, taking in their cloaks, baggage, and frightened, guilty expressions with dawning comprehension.

"Miss Lyons," he said warningly.

Knowing she could never fabricate a believable excuse, Abby cut to the heart of the matter and said in a quavering voice, "If you do not permit me to leave, I shall have to marry Philip."

Walters's eyes softened a moment, then became distant. "You can never hope to escape on foot. They'll find you."

Abby hesitated, then blurted, "I am meeting Lord Julian. We're going to the border to be married."

"A man you have just met, miss?" Walters drew himself up, his chest swelling with authority. "I can never permit that."

Trembling like a leaf in a gale, Charlotte Ann positioned herself in front of Abby. "They hadn't just met. He's that magician Mrs. Lyons took on about so." Instantly deciding not to tell him the part about Julian's warning, for it was the por-

tion of Miss Abby's tale that had been hardest for her to believe, she went on, "He fell in love with Miss Abby soon as
he set eyes on her at the magic show. And don't forget he's a
marquess's son, neither. He takes on a false name when he
does his act so as not to bring shame on his family."

It was hard to determine which of them was more surprised
by this heated defense. Perhaps it was Charlotte Ann herself,
who staggered in a brief wave of dizziness.

Walters pondered for what seemed an eternity. "Mr. Demere
is no favorite of mine," he murmured as though speaking to
himself. "Always full of insults and demands. But if I let them
go, Mrs. Lyons will have my heart on a platter."

He looked at Abby, who was watching him with a desperate,
tearful appeal in her eyes. He squared his shoulders boldly.

"I never eat at night; I must be dreaming," he said, and
walked from the room.

Abby exchanged a relieved smile with her maid. The smile
faded when Walters reentered the kitchen, but he only crossed
to the table without looking at them, picked up the chicken
leg, and withdrew once more. Heaving a sigh of relief, Abby
lifted the lock on the back door, and they slipped out, circled
the house, and scurried down the drive.

Since there was no moon, they occasionally stumbled and
tripped across unlevel places in the gravel. It seemed a lonely
night to Abby, even with Charlotte Ann along. As they walked,
the young lady glanced over her shoulder at the house. Beneath
a backdrop of twinkling stars, nestled among trees that rustled
in the wind, it appeared warm and inviting for the first time.
It is only an illusion of the darkness, she told herself, and
hurried on. But by the time Abby spied the silhouette of Julian's coach and two figures on horseback, her thoughts were
scattered and worried, and her arm was on fire from the weight
of the portmanteau.

It was Julian and Francis who were on horseback, and they
dismounted and relieved the women of their bags. While Francis tossed the luggage to the coachman, Julian greeted Abby

warmly, then Charlotte Ann. Amidst the overwhelming confusion of her feelings, Abby could not help noticing that Francis would not meet her eyes.

"Francis and I will ride awhile so you can sleep," Julian said, then assisted both women into the carriage, closed the door, and climbed on his horse.

Abby saw blankets and pillows awaiting them on the seats. Grateful she didn't have to make conversation with the stranger she was running away with, she divided the linen with Charlotte Ann and stretched out as best she could, as did the maid on the opposite bench.

With a cry of the coachman, they were off.

Abby stared sightlessly into the gloom as the miles began to pass. Although the conveyance appeared new and expensive, the ride was as jerky and bumpy as could be expected on roads repaired only at the whim of every parish they entered; evidently they were avoiding the better-maintained turnpikes. And the coachman, urging the horses as fast as he dared in the dark, was not making it easier. Abby thought she would never sleep, but the softness of her pillow was comforting, as were the mumbled prayers of the maid, and she did not open her eyes again until daylight filtered through the windows.

Feeling lethargic and half-asleep, Abby sat up and made a feeble attempt to straighten her hair. Charlotte Ann, pale and wide-eyed, was sitting erect across from her, the blanket and pillow in a tidy bundle at her feet.

"Could you not sleep?" Abby asked.

"Not a wink," the maid replied, turning her head to look out the window. "I hadn't never been out of High Chipping in my life."

"It will be all right," the young lady said, as much to herself as the servant. The reality of what she had done was beginning to strike her in full weight. She could hardly refrain from shivering.

Within the hour they stopped at a small inn sporting a thatched roof and tiny balconies. Julian escorted her inside with Charlotte Ann and Francis following. After spending a few restorative moments in an upstairs room, the women joined the men in a small dining chamber warmed by a smoking fire and crowded with battered tables and rickety chairs. While Julian seated Abby opposite him, Charlotte Ann hovered uncertainly. There appeared to be no separate quarters for servants.

"Sit with me," Francis offered from a table across the room. Charlotte Ann colored, bumped into a chair, and moved to join him, slowly and painfully.

The inn host, a stout, unshaven man with a dirty apron, brought them tankards of ale, pickled eggs, rolls and butter. " 'Tsall we got this hour o' the mornin'," he said, when Julian lifted his brows. "Wife's abed with our newest boy."

"Congratulations," Julian said. When the man left, the magician added apologetically, "We shall have to take what comes, I'm afraid. No doubt there will be better inns near the turnpikes, which I've avoided until now in case anyone is following us; but I think it's safe enough at this point. Hopefully we can average eight to ten miles an hour today. I should like to spend no more than two nights on the road before we are wed."

Abby felt a moment's terror at the thought of an irate Philip tracking them. "Where are we now?"

"In Gloucestershire. We're not far from the Severn, actually, and I wish we had time to view Kingsweston. The prospect of the estuary from the grounds is remarkably beautiful."

"I have heard of the house." She took a sip of ale and made a face at its bitterness.

Keeping his eyes locked on hers, he offered the basket of rolls. When Abby took one and began buttering it, he said, "I'm glad you decided to accept my proposal."

She set the knife aside and stared at her roll. "Please do not misunderstand. Had I not been desperate to leave Philip, I could never have acted so rashly as to come with you."

Without looking at him, she could sense his withdrawal.

After a moment he said, "How very thoughtful of you to say so."

"I do not mean to be unkind. If everything you have told me is true—I mean, true as you believe it to be—then you are being remarkably generous. If you are lying . . ."

His eyebrows lifted. "Yes? Pray do not stop now. If I am lying . . ."

Her chin began to tremble. "Then I shall do everything I can to ensure that you deceive no more young ladies."

"You amaze me, Miss Lyons. Do you imagine I make it my sport to race about the countryside making up stories like the one I've told you? What possible enjoyment is there in having one's character condemned?"

"I cannot pretend to know what amuses people I don't know well." She took a bite of her roll and chewed it with nervous haste. Why was she here? What had possessed her to run away with this man? She wanted to go home.

A cool look came into his eyes. "Be careful. You will choke."

The bread in her mouth seemed to be expanding rather than growing smaller. Pushing the wad into her cheek with her tongue, she asked carefully, "Is that a prediction, or only your opinion?"

When she heard his sharp intake of breath, she glanced upward, then looked away hurriedly.

"Perhaps we have made a mistake," he said.

Abby thought so, too, but did not want to hear him say it. Her heart began to spiral downward. "Oh?" She made her voice sound very disinterested. "What makes you say so?"

"Can you ask? We don't get on well together, that's apparent. I tell you, Miss Lyons, if I could relieve myself of these visions . . ." He drained his tankard and smacked it on the table. "Perhaps I should have called out Demere and dispensed with all this."

Although she didn't care about the magician at all, his words were crushing her like heavy blows. She washed down the roll with a sip of ale and grimaced. "Well, why didn't you?"

"I suppose the only reason is that I'm not a violent man."

Perhaps that meant he was a coward as well. "Are you not? I am glad to hear it. I wish the same could be said for Philip."

His lashes dropped, and she saw a rush of color flow back into his cheeks. "It is Philip's violence that is at the heart of all our actions, is it not? We should not be quarreling." He popped an egg into his mouth, chewed once or twice, and swallowed. "Tell me about yourself. What were your parents like?"

She felt a little off-balance by his change of mood. "Don't you already know?"

"Pardon me? Oh, I see. I'm not omnipotent, Miss Lyons."

"Well, then . . . I suppose there is not much to say. My parents were gentle, good people. We lived comfortably, though my father was not wealthy. Grandmother insisted his portion be cut off when he refused to marry the woman she wanted him to marry, who later married someone else and became Philip's mother. But Grandpapa sent us funds secretly, and my father also earned a small income from writing biographies of famous architects. We rented a succession of houses as I grew up, all of them in Kent. There were books and friends and outings . . ." She trailed away, remembering.

"It sounds very different from life with your grandmother."

"Yes." Her face darkened. "My parents died of influenza within weeks of one another when I was sixteen. I had nowhere to turn but to my grandparents. As you say, life was *very* different then. Oh, at first it was all right because Grandpapa was still alive and, while he seldom resisted Grandmother's will, at least he was kind to me. But after he died, things became worse. She has always tried to direct every decision in my life."

"Including your choice of marriage partners," he said.

"Yes." His unspoken sympathy soothed her ruffled feelings a little. She ate in silence awhile and glanced at Charlotte Ann and Francis, who were talking sporadically and quietly as they ate. The maid was darting shy looks at the valet between bites, looks he either didn't notice or ignored. Suddenly, feeling Abby's gaze, he lifted his eyes and gave her a cool, measuring stare.

Abby turned away quickly. "What of *your* parents?" she chattered, bewildered and cut to the bone by Francis's dislike. "Was your mother gifted with second sight? I have heard such things run in Gypsy families."

Julian waited as the innkeeper entered with a pitcher of ale and refilled the men's tankards, then asked their host to bring Abby water or milk as she did not like the brew. After swallowing several times, the magician set down the mug. His face was as carefully composed as a mask.

"She was a fortune-teller but without any particular talent, according to the stories I've heard. Like many who earn their living in that manner, she was astute—sensitive, I suppose you'd say—at reading reactions from her clients. You understand my meaning, don't you?"

He affected hauteur, lifting his chin, raising his eyebrows, and speaking loftily, "Lady Claudia enters the Gypsy tent, looking around with regal condescension at the rough furniture, pressing a perfumed handkerchief to her nose. She whisks the handkerchief across the proffered chair, seats herself, then crosses the fortune-teller's palm with silver. The prophetess begins: "I see a long journey ahead," and Lady Claudia's eyes become surprised, even forbidding; then Lady Fortune quickly amends, "But that is someone near to you. A tall, handsome stranger shall enter *your* life." And when Lady Claudia's eyes sparkle, Lady Fortune is off and running."

Abby giggled, then caught herself. If she were not careful, he would disarm her with his charming manner. Trying to dampen the humor in her voice, she said, "It sounds a talent in itself."

"I was told she was one of the best," he said, smiling. "My father was certainly impressed by her. One day in late summer, my mother and the others in her group—mostly family members—made so bold as to encamp on the marquess's property. Father charged to the camp in a lather, determined to run them off for their trespass. And then my mother swayed from her wagon to meet him. She said they were doing him a favor by making use of the land. Told him he had more than any one man needed and that God would punish him if he didn't share. If not charmed by her words, he was by her, and before many moments passed, he was ensconced in her parlour on wheels, having his palm read. The rest, as they say, is history."

Abby thought she heard an undercurrent of bittersweetness in his tone. "Was it very difficult for them to be married?" she ventured, then colored brightly. "I mean—they *were,* uh—," she floundered hopelessly.

"Married?" he interjected quickly. "Yes, they were. I see you hold the general opinion of Gypsies—that they are immoral creatures."

"Pray forgive me. It was not my intention to imply—that is, I mean . . ."

She could think of nothing more to say. There seemed no way to redeem the graceless meanderings of her tongue. She may not trust him, but that was no reason to disparage his family.

Fortunately, the innkeeper entered the room carrying a glass of milk which he placed before Abby. "Fresh from the cow," he announced, and departed.

"Drink your milk," Julian said briskly. "We should leave soon."

Abby choked down a few sips and set the glass on the table. The lump in her throat made further drinking impossible. Julian was proving to be a thoughtful, if prickly, companion. He had made certain she and Charlotte Ann were comfortable in the coach while he rode outside for hours. He noticed she didn't like the ale and had ordered another drink without her asking. And, unless he were a monstrous liar, he was willing to marry and provide for her, a woman who could mean nothing to him. And by way of thanks, she had almost accused him of being a bastard. As though it would have made any difference if he were.

To her chagrin, tears filled her eyes. She looked down, pulled a handkerchief from her pocket, and pretended to cough, wiping her eyes rapidly.

Julian reached across the table and touched her hand. "Please don't. You haven't offended me, Abby. Have I your permission to call you that? Am I being overly familiar?"

Momentarily distracted, she sniffed. "I would be hap-happy for you to do so." She looked at their linked hands and edged hers back. "Will this not make you—"

"Read your mind? Tell your fortune?" He laughed softly. "Not unless I concentrate. Do you imagine every time I touch someone I'm flooded with visions? I'd be a raving lunatic."

"Oh," she said in a tiny voice, then allowed her hand to drift toward his as though unaware of its actions. He responded at once, closing his fingers over hers in a strongly protective gesture. Immediately, she felt comforted. Cherished. And curiously bereft. There was also a sensation of excitement, or something like; she didn't know what else to call it. Holding his hand was pleasant in the extreme. And it was almost shockingly intimate. Again she drew back, half-afraid this time.

"Are you—are you doing that?" she asked.

Slowly he lifted his gaze from her hand, and she was stunned to see that in spite of what he had said, his eyes were black. While she watched, fascinated and more than a little afraid, his pupils returned to normal size. It was only then that he spoke, barely moving his lips as he did, appearing to be caught in a spell of some kind.

"That never happened before."

"What never happened before?" she whispered.

"I wasn't trying. My mind wasn't receptive, but I received a flood of emotions from you. Sorrow, regret, fear. And something else . . ." He looked into the distance, thinking. "Something essentially you. That essence of strength I sensed at the performance, perhaps."

Absurdly pleased by his final comment, she said, "I also felt a number of things that are foreign to me. It was . . . pleasant. A surge of power, of confidence. I thought I was imagining it. Or that perhaps you were sending me a message . . ." She felt suddenly joyful. *Had he been telling the truth all along?*

"No," he said, crushing her hopes a little. "I can't do that. At least, I never could before." He swallowed. "Can you?"

She looked at him incredulously. "Of course not!"

"But . . . it did happen."

"Yes," she agreed.

As one, their eyes fell to the table where lay their right hands, inches apart. His hand began to move toward hers. At the same moment, Abby reached for his.

"The horses are changed, milord," declared the coachman from the threshold.

Abby and Julian jumped. With a faintly guilty expression, the magician said, "Thank you, Bugbee. Have you eaten? Yes? Then we should be off."

With a hearty scraping of chairs, the diners filed from the room, Francis pausing to settle with the innkeeper. Moments later, they were on their way again.

Six

That same morning, summoned by a frantic message from Matilda Lyons, Philip rode to Sharonfield without eating breakfast, attending his toilet, or even paying his morning duty visit to his mother, who seldom stirred from the east wing of their house. When he arrived at Sharonfield, he sprang from his horse and flung open the door without knocking. Walters, who had heard the approach of hoofbeats and had only just unlocked the latch, was forced to jump out of the way to avoid being squashed.

Philip hastened toward the stairs, ready to bound up the steps three at a time, when he saw a sight that stopped his blood.

Matilda. Out of her bedroom.

Clothed in her usual white nightgown, robe and mob cap, she stood at the head of the stairs with one trembling hand gripping the rail. Jane, her fingers clutching the old lady's other arm in a firm clasp, hovered closely. Both women were ashen-faced.

"Have you found her?" Philip demanded.

"She is gone," Matilda answered, the life drained from her voice. "Gone, Philip."

"But where? How?"

She turned slowly. "Come to my room. I can't make it downstairs, can't stand any longer."

Philip raced upstairs, walked impatiently beside Matilda for a moment, then scooped her in his arms and hurried to the bedroom where he laid her on the settee. The lady was not too upset to appreciate this almost-forgotten pleasure, and her eyes twinkled a moment before going flat and dead again.

"The note is on the bed," she said.

Philip immediately crossed the room and snatched the letter. After scanning the brief message, the color ebbed from his cheeks, then flowed back like a tide. He crumpled the note and threw it on the coverlet.

Matilda craned her neck to look at him. "You see it's as I said. She has run away with that marquess's son. You've lost her, Philip."

He clenched his fists and marched to the window. "How can she think of marrying a man she's only just met? Is she mad? He won't wed her, not a woman so easily lured. Anything at all could happen to her."

"I know it! I know it well!" Matilda cried, stirred by the force of his anger. "After all my plans, all my work. Dear God in heaven, how could she betray me this way? And my maid, a viper in my own bosom whom I've fed for years, helped her and ran off, too! The idiot slattern!"

"The maid?" His gaze fell on Jane, who had stationed herself in the usual place beside the fire.

Feeling resentful, the servant opened her eyes. She looked forward to visitors calling, because it was the only time of the day she got any rest; but this time it appeared she wasn't to have even that. Upon seeing his thunderous expression, her resentment quickly changed to fear.

With a cowed look, she declared, "Not me, sir!"

"No, I can see that," he said cuttingly. "It was the other one. But you have rooms together in the attic, do you not? What do you know about this?"

"Nothing!" Jane sputtered, looking back and forth from her mistress to Mr. Demere, who were both staring at her as though she were an insect. "I don't know a thing!"

Philip drew closer. "You've shared attic space for years, and she didn't confide in you? You heard no sounds of packing, didn't see clothes strewn about?"

Jane shook her head frantically, tears bubbling to her eyes. "I didn't, sir. Most often I sleep in Mistress Matilda's dressing room in case she has need of me during the night. I was here all day and night yesterday."

" 'Tis true, Philip," Matilda said. "Leave her alone; I believe her."

Philip was not so certain. He continued to glare at Jane, who was too intimidated to look away for fear he would think her guilty. Jane could hardly bear it, returning a stare so full of wrath. She was used to her mistress's fleeting rages and crankiness, but this was a different order altogether. Mr. Demere's anger was much more intense and dangerous. Worst of all, it was undeserved.

But why was she surprised? She often took the blame for a lot of things she hadn't done. Her mistress loved to accuse her of misplacing fans and handkerchiefs and medicine bottles when it was herself who had knocked them beneath the bed or behind the table. Even Walters, who had known her for decades and ought to be her friend but wasn't, laid blame on her. Or expected her to do even more work than she already did, as if she were a lazy miss who leaned on her elbows and dreamed of handsome dukes all day. Like this morning. Telling her she had better clean cook's mess, because Charlotte Ann wouldn't be down.

Philip saw the change in her face and loomed closer. Jane bit her lip, debating. Would Walters protect her if their positions were reversed? He would not.

"Sir, you could ask the butler," she said. "Maybe he knows something. He said Charlotte Ann wouldn't be working this morning."

Philip turned and dashed from the chamber. Walters, who had been sitting on a bench in the hall doing nothing, stood and watched him run down the stairs with a feeling of impending doom.

Marcy Stewart

"What can you tell me about this disaster?" Philip demanded, when he had planted himself no more than a foot's span away. "Do you know where they are? If you have any knowledge at all, you had better say so, and quickly."

Lifting his chin and wishing he were taller, Walters assumed his most disdainful pose. "It was the mistress who received the note . . . *sir*. Why would you think I know anything?"

"Why?" Philip grabbed the butler by his lapels and lifted. "Because you told the maid the other one wasn't coming down this morning. I'd be interested in how you knew *that*."

Walters's thoughts slid rapidly as his feet left the floor. He cursed himself for that morning's slip, but then, how could he have known Jane would betray him? And now, if he didn't tell this madman what he knew he would doubtless be beaten.

Surely it wouldn't matter if he told. Miss Lyons had been on the road for hours; Demere would never catch her, even if he chanced upon the route they took. Therefore, a broken nose would serve no purpose at all.

He began to speak.

When he was no more than halfway finished, having just come to the part about his mental anguish over divided loyalties, Philip raised his hand in a halting gesture. "Hold. You're telling me Donberry is the magician who performed in town weeks ago?" When Walters nodded rapidly, Philip's cheeks reddened. "I knew it all the time! I knew there was something between them!" He began to pace. "After he whispered to her at the end of the program, Abigail said she didn't understand what he said, but it's obvious she did. She—she lied to me. Probably has been seeing him on the sly all along. It's *unthinkable!*"

He paced a few seconds longer. "But then, why would he make an appearance here under his true name—if true it is—if his intentions were not honorable?"

Philip stared at the butler without seeing him. Walters had slunk back to the bench and huddled there, hoping to be forgotten. Now, willing to appear helpful, he shrugged expres-

sively. Philip ignored him, whirled around and began pacing
again.

"He must think she's an heiress. In that case, it's as Abigail
expressed in her note; he means to marry her after all, and
they must be headed for Scotland." He became aware of Walters again and stopped. "What time did you see them in the
kitchen?"

"Close on one, sir."

Philip slapped his fist against his hand. "Too long. But . . ."
His face sharpened. "Tell your mistress that I am going after
them and that I intend to bring Abigail back. Oh, and send a
message to my mother that I'll be gone awhile. I can't say
how long." He started for the door, then turned back. "Is there
a pistol in the house?"

Walters face betrayed his shock. "Well, I—"

"You'd do best to speak truth. If I have to ask Matilda . . ."

The butler bowed. "There is the set of dueling pistols old
Mr. Lyons owned." When Philip made an impatient gesture,
Walters entered the parlour and returned a moment later carrying an embossed case. Two pistols lay inside, nestled on a
bed of red velvet. Philip examined the case for powder and
balls, found it well-equipped with both as well as cleaning
equipment, tucked the case under his arm, then swept by the
butler, heading for the door.

Relief at being let off so easily loosened the servant's
tongue. "I am terrible sorry, sir. So sorry for your misfortune."

Philip touched the doorknob, hesitated, then turned as if
recollecting something further he'd meant to say. But instead
of speaking, he lunged a powerful blow into Walters's eye. The
older man fell against the bench and clattered to the floor. The
force of his impact jarred the wall, which shook the peg-footed
Hepplewhite table and caused a century-old vase to shatter on
the tile.

"Do not speak to me of misfortune!" Philip spat. "You
should have stopped her!"

"Yes," Walters agreed weakly, holding his eye and wiping

the other one, which was watering in sympathy. "I should have." He struggled to his feet, adding with real regret, "I know that now."

But no one heard him; he was alone. There was only the sound of the door closing and Matilda's worried queries drifting down the stairs to keep him company.

By mid-afternoon, Abby had decided that England was too long a country. It wasn't that she didn't enjoying looking out the carriage window at rolling countryside that grew wilder and more hilly by the hour, nor that she disliked the villages and towns they skirted; it was only because she had too much time to think about what was going to happen to her. Things had moved so quickly in the past few days. The future, once such a dreary and certain prospect of marriage and continuing subjection, was now a vast unknown.

Increasingly she found herself thinking of Julian in relation to that future. Theirs was to be a marriage of convenience which would end as soon as he judged her safe. And then what? She tried to imagine how it would feel, not seeing his face, hearing his voice or touching his hand. In spite of the faint mistrust she still felt toward him, in spite of the frequent irritability of their encounters, she knew it would be a loss she would regret.

Charlotte Ann was growing tired, too, having been jostled into saying at one point, "If I was a churn of milk, I'd be butter now." It seemed even the turnpike roads, though better than the ones they used that morning, varied in their maintenance. Hundreds upon hundreds of turnpike trusts had come into being in the past fifty years, and the tolls were intended for the upkeep and repair of each section of road; but it was common knowledge that only half the funds were so used.

Part of her distress was caused not by the highways, but by the rapid pace they continued to maintain. No more did they pause for meals; only the briefest of stops were allowed, wherein the ladies would hurry inside for a moment while the horses were changed. At such times, Francis would purchase some tidbit to soothe their appetites: bread, apples, cheese. Julian apologized frequently for the inconvenience and promised the return trip would be more leisurely.

Abby accepted the tediousness of the journey without complaint. She knew Julian believed Philip would follow them. For that reason, and the lesser one of her reputation, it was paramount they have the marriage license as quickly as possible.

But she couldn't help wishing England weren't so long and Scotland so far away. It seemed a shame Fleet Marriages had been prohibited. Now one must go all the way to another country in order to be married quickly.

The ladies weren't the only ones who were tired. Julian looked increasingly weary as the day wore on, as did Francis, when she made so bold as to look at him. But both refused to rest inside the coach, saying the added weight would slow down the carriage.

And so the day passed, and night drew on. They finally stopped at an inn near Stoke. After a plain but filling meal of roast beef, vegetables, and peach tarts, the travelers, who had eaten together at one large table, stumbled off to their respective rooms. Abby fell asleep at once, dreaming of ivory satin wedding gowns, lace, and hands that sparked fire when they touched.

While she slept, Philip also dreamed. Once again, he and Abigail were on the stage in High Chipping, sitting side by side in the wooden chairs, the audience a mass of laughing and jeering animals all around. Hearing his name called, he looked toward the box seats and saw Harold, a set of bull's horns above his ears and a ruff of fur beneath his chin, pointing and screaming with hilarity. Beside him sat a faded old spider he thought at first was Harold's mother, but then saw it was

Matilda, her black eyes hard and shiny as obsidian, her face almost unrecognizable floating atop eight spindly, hairy legs. As he watched, she raised one appendage and shook it at him, shouting, "You have lost her! You have lost her!" He turned hurriedly back to Abigail, but she was gone—carried off in the arms of the caped magician, her fingers draped around his neck, her lips pressed to his in a lascivious kiss, her glorious hair streaming across naked shoulders like a wanton's; and when she lifted her head and glanced back at Philip, her dark eyes glowed with triumph.

Hurled into wakefulness, Philip sat up on the straw-filled tick, the blood pounding in his ears like a raging river. It was some moments before he oriented himself in the dark and recognized the humble room he'd rented, the sleeping, snorting, stinking bodies of the other men he'd had to share it with sprawled in little hillocks across the floor. They had been forced together because a prizefight in the district had oversold the rooms.

It would be a wonder did he not catch fleas or lice. A haystack would have been better, but he had been so tired and hungry that he'd been unable to resist the smell of singed pork as he passed the inn.

He thought back over the day's events; the persistent journey on horseback, though he was not so sure speed was of the essence—if the magician went through with his promise to marry Abigail and had taken her all the way across the border, speed was unimportant because he couldn't possibly catch them—and the confrontations that had brought him here, beginning with Matilda and ending with the owner of the Pendragon.

Cyril Tankersley had not wanted to tell him the charlatan's direction, of course. It was not the sort of information a responsible businessman meted out, particularly to someone who looked as hostile and dishevelled as Philip.

"Even if I knew his address, which I'm not saying I do, what do you want it for?" Tankersley had asked him, leaning back in a large wing chair that looked as if it belonged in someone's parlour; but it was in the businessman's office near the dressing rooms. The office was as plumply overstuffed and furnished as its owner, whose gold buttons strained between the edges of his vest and threatened to pop at any moment.

"You *must* have it. How else could you book his services?" When Tankersley started rambling about referral agencies, Philip thought rapidly. "He owes me a gambling debt."

"No, he doesn't," the other pronounced. "You're just saying that. Lord Merlyn didn't have a chance to form any bets. He was in and out of town like a bolt of lightning."

"How do you know? I might have known him before."

Tankersley squinted at him shrewdly. "Are you saying that little mentalism act was set up in advance? That he owes you for taking part? For weeks I've wondered how he did it."

"Yes, yes, that's it," Philip said, his fists itching to slam the self-satisfied smirk off the round face in front of him, but restraining himself, knowing he'd get nothing that way.

"Well, well, well," the owner said, heaving himself from the chair and moving to a cabinet behind him. "Another mystery explained. How disappointing." He bent, retrieved a file from the cabinet, straightened with a groan, and began leafing through the pages. "I must say I'm a little surprised at you, Demere. I wouldn't dream you'd be interested in doing something like that. I suppose times are hard all over, what?"

He pulled a sheet from the file, wrote something on a piece of letterhead paper from the desk, replaced his copy, and dropped the folder on the tabletop. Before he handed the sheet over, he contemplated it, pursing his lips and looking suspiciously at Philip.

"Are you certain you're not shamming me? The more I think on it, the more I remember how angry you looked onstage that night. It was most convincing. If you were acting, you could give Kemble competition."

Philip had no more patience to stretch. He leaned across the desk, snatched the note from the man's hand, and dashed

from the room. Tankersley's outraged cries followed him
through the halls and to the very threshold of the back door,
which Philip slammed.

Then he had ridden off on Pegasus, heading all day for an
address in Warwickshire, near Coventry. And having nearly
reached his destination, he'd paused here for the night. A mistake, admittedly, but there was no hurry unless Donberry had
lied to Abigail and taken her directly to his home. Either way,
the girl would no longer be the innocent he'd counted on. He
gritted his teeth, visualizing the scenes that might be taking
place at this very moment. His nightmare was mild in comparison to what he now imagined.

But it couldn't be helped. He had no hope of catching them
in time. His only sensible option had been to go to Donberry's
home—the home of Lord Merlyn, rather. Philip grinned in the
darkness. It was fortunate Matilda's butler had told him of the
dual identities. If he had gone to the marquess's home in Donberry, there would doubtless be many servants to protect the
man. And had the devil not been in residence, they would
never have told Philip his direction. So this was the best way.
He would arrive at *Lord Merlyn's* estate tomorrow. It should
give him time to plan his course of action.

However he gained her, whether married or ruined, he meant
to have Abigail. Wives became widows very easily. And
women who lost their virtue could regain it, after a fashion;
after proper repentance and punishment.

Abigail would be his wife yet. She belonged to him.

On the following morning, Julian awoke only when the sun
was high enough to shine forcefully through the windowshade
of his second-story bedroom at the Green Turtle. He sat up in
some confusion, ruffling his hair and yawning, his gaze raking
the room's whitewashed walls, its hunting tapestries and stur-
dily built furnishings, the popping fire in the fireplace, and
the man sitting in the chair beside it.

"Francis," Julian said, sounding surprised. "What time is it?"

"Nearly a quarter-past eight, milord," the servant replied.

"A quarter-past—" Julian hurriedly put his feet to the floor. Throwing off his nightshirt, he poured water from the pitcher into the basin and began washing. "This water is ice-cold. Why did you not awaken me?"

"Milord gave no such instructions last night."

"Do I normally give that kind of instruction when we travel? It has always been our custom to leave shortly after daybreak, has it not?"

"Milord is on his way to be married. Things change."

A smile creased the lather on the magician's face. "Yes. Speaking of weddings, where is Abby? Has she awakened, do you know?"

"She and her maid have breakfasted and are walking in the gardens at the back of the inn, milord."

Julian paused in his shaving to give the valet a curious look. "Milord, milord, milord. Why so formal?" The reflected Francis neither answered nor returned his gaze but continued staring straight ahead, his face impassive. "All right, Francis, what is wrong? Something has been bothering you for days."

There was a brief hesitation as the valet fought some inner battle. He took breath to speak, thought better of it and paused, then opened his mouth once more, his green eyes sparking to life.

"Have you told her about Miss Harriet?" Francis blurted at last.

The magician did not answer immediately but bent to rinse the remaining soap from his face, dried himself with the towel, and moved to the clothespress where the valet had neatly laid his clothing. Pulling on his shirt, he said, "No, I haven't. What would you have me say?"

Francis looked at him as if he had lost his senses. "You could start with what's between you two."

"Oh?" His voice was cool. "And what is that, precisely?"

"I don't know," Francis said resentfully. "You tell me. Many's the night I've heard her crying through the walls, and the next morning her eyes are all puffy and red. 'Tis nothing I've done to cause it."

Julian dropped his gaze. "It's not what you think, Francis. I've never promised her anything."

Francis struggled for control but could not disguise his bitterness. "She deserves better." His jaw moved angrily. " 'Tis too easy for you. Women watch you playing Lord Magic on-stage and drop at your feet. Well, you can't treat Miss Harriet like that. Not after all that's happened."

Understanding dawned in the magician's eyes. "You're right; she does deserve better. I'm sorry, old man; all this time I've thought you had no patience for women. I didn't know how you felt. I was aware you're fond of her, of course, but—"

"Don't know what you mean," Francis said rapidly, anger melting into embarrassment. Keeping his eyes averted from his master's, he reached out and straightened milord's collar over the fold of his cravat. "She's too far above the likes of me."

"I'm not so certain. You won't know unless you try."

Francis narrowed his eyes. "Now you're making sport of me and trying to rid yourself of Miss Harriet all at once." He pushed Julian's fingers away from the cravat and began tying it himself. For someone who could pull noodles through a sieve, the magician was woefully inept at tying knots. "I just thought your betrothed should be told, that's all."

"It has crossed my mind to do so, but how much does Abby truly need to know? I've told you our marriage is only one of convenience and will be ended shortly."

As he said the words, he felt a rift in the regions of his heart. Not to have those furious dark eyes tearing into him anymore? What kind of dull existence would that be?

"Yes, so you've said, but I've seen the way you look at her." Francis held out his master's silver-embroidered waistcoat. "When you're not shouting at her, you treat her like she's made of eggshells."

Julian shrugged into the vest. "She has been through much. She deserves kindness."

"Miss Harriet has been through a lot, too."

"No one knows that better than I," he said reproachfully, accepting the servant's assistance into a blue superfine frock coat.

"Yet you're marrying a stranger. One that latched onto you quick as a hawk swallows a rat."

Julian's eyes became frigid, and Francis stepped back a pace.

"Sorry, milord. Poor choice of words." He reached for the hairbrush, but the magician took it from his hand. Francis watched him comb his hair for a few quiet moments, then added, "What I can't fathom is that even though you're getting married, you're still having bad dreams. I know you had another one last night. Was it that new one, the one you had the other day and won't tell me about?"

Julian's stomach muscles clenched together. As much to convince himself as Francis, he said, "I just—I keep seeing her in danger, that's all. The wedding alone won't save her; it only provides me with a means of helping her without causing scandal. Demere is a determined man. We shall have to wait and see what transpires."

He dropped his eyes, unwilling for Francis to see the lies within them.

"Well, if and when he strikes, he's like to find you too weary to fight back, resting no more than you do," growled the valet. " 'Tis why I let you sleep late this morning, if the truth be known."

Julian clapped him on the back and led him to the door. "You're a good servant and an even better friend, but we had best get on our way." Forcing heartiness into his tone, he added, "Tomorrow is my wedding day!"

* * *

While Julian and Abby made their way north, Philip ate bacon and stale bread in a coffeehouse in Coventry. He gave little thought to the food or the noisy crowd of dirty farmers surrounding him. His mind was given over to the success of so easily finding the magician's residence, if the words of an old man with leathered skin and pouches under his eyes proved correct.

"Oyer, the wizard's 'ouse," the old man had wheezed. Uninvited, he had come to sit opposite Philip, and his nose dripped like a drainage spout. " 'Ee keeps to 'isself about five miles out. Nice place; uster live out that way mesel' afore I ran off to me life in the infantry." And then he launched into tales of old glory. Philip silenced him with a bottle of gin and stood. But while he pulled on his overcoat, the oldtimer sneezed directly in his face, an action that disgusted him so much he seized the bottle and crashed it against the wall. He left in a hurry after that; the looks on the farmers' faces were none too friendly.

Now he reined Pegasus off the main road onto the private lane that led to several estates, including Donberry's. When he arrived at the one with *Avilion Place* worked in iron at the top of the entrance gate, he peered through the bars and saw a Georgian house half-hidden behind spreading oaks. There was no gatehouse, but many trees; a virtual forest between the stone wall and the manicured garden surrounding the manse. Ample places to hide, if he could get past that gate and its lock.

He studied the grounds for a few moments; then, fearful someone would see him lurking about, moved on. About a mile down the lane, the trees thickened on either side. Philip led Pegasus deep into a thicket, tied the horse's reins around a tree trunk—he knew he could not trust the stupid beast to stay put—and retraced his steps.

Coming again to the walls of Avilion Place, he judged himself well away from the house and beside Donberry's forest. Taking a great leap, he tried to surmount the wall, but though he dug his fingers and boots into the stone, he could not hold on. Sliding down with bloody fingernails, bruised shins, and muttered curses, he looked around for something to stand on. There was nothing, but there were trees. He saw an oak farther down that hung over the wall and headed for it. In less than a minute he'd climbed the tree and dropped over the side.

Except for the fussing of meadow pippits and starlings, it was quiet in the woods. He would have to be quiet as well, for this was no wild forest but a well-groomed stand of trees; Donberry must have an army of gardeners to keep the undergrowth clear.

Philip felt another stab of envy. The villain possessed not only Abigail, but wealth, too. But not for long. Shortly, he would have nothing.

Philip knew he would have to keep his wits about him, but since he had eaten that bacon—greasy and rancid it had been, yet he'd been too hungry to stop—his stomach had rumbled and pained and was now flooded with nausea. After a gut-wrenching session behind a tree, he felt a little better and continued his exploration.

Within moments he came to a vantage point that revealed the house and a cluster of smaller buildings out back, including a cottage on the far side of a little pond. Nothing much seemed to be happening; the estate had an air of emptiness about it.

But someone was home; Philip saw smoke coming from several chimneys in the main house. A gardener appeared around the corner of the manse, his shears clipping the hedges that grew against the flat facade. The front door opened, and a woman emerged, spoke with the gardener a few seconds, then returned inside. Philip narrowed his eyes, his vision clouded by a blurring wave of nausea and cold sweat, his mind as hazy as his vision. At last he remembered. The magician's helper—what was her name?—Hilda? So she lived here, too. Interesting, but not particularly so.

It appeared that Abigail and Donberry were not at home, though he could not be absolutely sure. He would have to watch awhile to know how to act intelligently. Philip sat behind the cover of a patch of seedlings, his back pressed against a beech tree. He drew his arms to his grumbling stomach and prepared to wait.

But by nightfall, wracked by bouts of nausea and dizzied with fever, he feared something worse ailed him than mere food-sickness. There was nothing he could do here but get caught, curse his luck. With the greatest of efforts, he climbed the wall again, found Pegasus, and rode away. He needed to find an inn where he could recover, but not one inside Coventry in case Donberry heard of him. On and on he rode, the chilly evening air cutting through his clothes like knives. At last he settled for a farmhouse, barely keeping to his feet long enough to stumble past the door without knocking. A man and woman and several children looked up from the hearth in surprise.

"Sick," he said, and fell to his knees. "Help me. I'll pay."

The farmer jumped to his feet. The woman threw down her knitting. The last thing Philip remembered was the warmth of the fire and the sound of a child laughing and laughing, though whether at him or not, he could not tell.

Seven

Shortly after noon on the following day, Julian and Abby were married by the town blacksmith in the village of Gretna Green. It was not the wedding Abby had dreamt of since she was at her mother's knee. There was no chapel, no robed minister, no elegant wedding gown; just the most common of men to officiate, the plainest of rooms, and the jonquil gown she'd worn so many times before; and even that was wrinkled and spotted from their morning's travel.

The smithy used the Anglican wedding service, and Charlotte Ann served as one of the witnesses. Francis, disapproval shouting from every stiff bone, stood as the other. At the proper moment, Julian removed his gold filigree ring and placed it on Abby's finger. The circlet was a trifle large but seemed in no danger of falling off if she crooked her finger a little. When it came time to kiss the bride, the groom gave her a playful look and the briefest of kisses.

It could have been worse; could have been Philip she had married. But it was the fact that her wedding should have been so much more that caused her to grow quiet and pensive. She kept telling herself that at least Julian had not been lying about his intentions. He had not tried to sell her to a brothel. And since he had proven his trust in this matter, perhaps he was not lying or deluded about the other. Still, the doubts came.

Julian could not help noticing her solemn brown eyes and trembling lips. If he felt any misgivings himself over their recent actions, he hid them well. As soon as the ink dried on their signatures, he said cheerfully, "Did you notice that public house we passed outside Carlisle? It looked worthy of hosting a fine wedding luncheon. What say you to that, Lady Julian?"

Lady Julian. Abby had not once thought about the fact she would have a title now, too. She wasn't sure she liked losing her name, even if it only happened when she was addressed formally. It would take some getting used to, she supposed. But of course by the time she became accustomed to it, she and Julian would have dissolved their marriage.

Feeling lower than ever, she agreed to his suggestion about luncheon, and they returned to the coach. This time, Julian tied his horse to the back of the carriage—he seemed to take an inordinate amount of time in doing so—climbed inside and sat opposite the women while straightening his gloves and smiling secretly. Francis also secured his horse and sat outside next to Bugbee. Within moments they had crossed the Sark River and reentered England.

Abby and Charlotte Ann soon discovered the reason for Julian's enigmatic manner. "It will take us the better part of an hour to reach the inn," he said. "If you will excuse me, I shall remove my gloves and be more comfortable." He peeled off his right glove—rather ostentatiously, Abby thought—and placed it within his left hand. "In point of fact," he continued, pulling the left glove over the right, "I never liked these gloves overmuch. Too tight. I believe I shall rid myself of them."

Before Charlotte Ann could open her mouth to say she would like to have the pair for her brother, since they were of the finest cotton and in that York tan shade that was all the rage, Julian tossed them toward the closed window, and they disappeared.

Abby laughed. Charlotte Ann screeched and clapped her hands over her mouth. "Satan's work!" she cried between her fingers.

Seeing the maid was truly frightened, Julian said, "Not at all." He shook the end of his coat sleeve, and the gloves tumbled onto the floor. "See? Here they are."

Charlotte Ann's terror was replaced by comprehension, then grudging appreciation. "How did you do it, milord? I thought I saw them flying to the window, and then *poof!* Gone just like that."

"Ah. You *thought*. But the eye can deceive." He turned his attention to Abby and was rewarded to see a bright expression on her face. "I shall demonstrate my meaning. May I beg a coin, Abby?"

With some embarrassment, the young lady confessed she had not a shilling on her.

Wondering why things had come to such a pass that *he* should find it necessary to beg *them* for money, Charlotte Ann pulled her reticule onto her lap and said, "Here, milord. I have one." She plundered in its depths for a moment, then presented a coin to Julian.

He reached, but the shilling dropped through his fingers. "Oh, I'm so sorry." Moving his right hand to the floor, he scooped the coin into his fist and straightened, then appeared to transfer it from his right hand to his left. Glancing from Abby to Charlotte Ann and back again, he said, "Say a magical name."

"Don't know any," Charlotte Ann replied, watching his hands without blinking.

"Any name will do. Speaking will make it magic."

"Gretna Green," Abby supplied instantly.

"Francis," said Charlotte Ann at the same time, then flushed scarlet.

Julian hesitated a heartbeat and said, "Abby."

He opened first one fist, then the other. The coin was gone.

Both women grinned their delight, but when milord made no move to restore her shilling, Charlotte Ann's smile faded. "Where did it go?"

His eyes dancing, Julian looked at Abby. "Perhaps your mistress knows."

Abby thought fiercely, then pronounced, "It is in your boot."

A cloud of puzzlement passed over the magician's face. "My boot?" Doubtfully, he ran a finger around the rim of first his right boot, then the left, and shook his head. "Nothing there." His gaze fell on the lace at Abby's throat and sharpened. "Ah. Here it is." He appeared to pull the shilling from the froths of lace under her chin. "You had best watch your lady, Charlotte Ann. She has all the appearances of being light-fingered."

Both women giggled at this bit of nonsense, and the maid accepted her coin and restored it to her bag with some relief. Abby noticed that his eyebrows had moved expressively throughout his performance, particularly when he told them some little fabrication to mislead them.

All moodiness had now been forgotten. "It *was* in your boot, though," she said insistently. "You held your palm as though the shilling were in it, but it never went higher than your knees. Until you retrieved it from your boot and pretended to find it in my clothing, that is."

"I could not make a living were my audiences as observant as my wife," he said, then looked away, suddenly uncomfortable.

The words *my wife* seemed to hang in the air between them. It was an intimate phrase to describe two strangers, and for a moment no one said anything.

Abby could not bear the silence; it made her start thinking again. "I still cannot understand how you move so quickly."

"It's a combination of practice and distraction," he replied. "Just as a musician works at his instrument, a magician spends many hours learning his craft, adding new illusions, and keeping supple. But at the same time, he must be adept in diverting the audience's attention from what he is truly doing. As an example, one hand can draw the eye while the other does the work. A lovely assistant is also useful in this."

Abby had no wish to hear about lovely assistants. "Did your gift lead to your interest in magic?" she inquired, then rushed to add, "I hope you don't mind my telling Charlotte Ann about your ability. I thought it necessary to persuade her to join me."

When Julian's eyes met hers, Charlotte Ann glanced shyly at her shoes. "She would have heard soon enough in our household anyway. The servants speak of it, or so I'm told."

He crossed his arms and leaned back. "And to answer your question, I'm not sure my interest was fired by it. Rather, I became fascinated when reading about famous magicians in books and magazines. I was particularly taken with the American ventriloquist, Richard Potter, whose parents were a nobleman and his Negro servant. Potter was a consummate showman; he was a ventriloquist, a singer, a humorist, and a magician. And Pinetti of Tuscany; the Thumb-Tie trick which I do in my exhibition was one he used. He liked mechanical devices, too, including a talking head that answered questions inside a glass. There was also a swan that reversed its course as demanded. After reading about these men, I started attending every village fair I could find to watch the jugglers and illusionists and question them mercilessly. Before I was ten, I had a collection of magic books and practiced the illusions again and again."

Hesitantly, for she feared the subject might be a sensitive one, Abby asked, "Were your brothers amazed by the tricks you performed?" She hoped he would say it had proved a common ground, that he'd had some joyful times in his childhood. "I would imagine all children enjoy magic."

He had no time to answer, for at that moment one of the carriage wheels lurched through a deep pothole, and the passengers bumped about and rattled back and forth until the springs settled. Julian opened the window and leaned out, calling to see if there had been damage. Bugbee assured him that all was well, and they moved on.

The magician turned back to Abby. "You asked me something . . . oh, yes, about my brothers. Did they like my magic?" He narrowed his eyes, considering. "My oldest brother, Carl, professed to do so, but I'm not certain he wasn't just humoring a much younger brother. I must have seemed like a child to him. All four of my brothers are a good deal older; well, they are my half-brothers, actually. Carl was twenty when I was born, and the others followed at three- to four-year intervals after him. Their mother was the daughter of a local baron, and she died five years before the marquess met my mother."

"What are your brothers like?" Abby inquired, then flushed. She sounded overly inquisitive but couldn't seem to stop herself. Her interest in Julian's life was growing by the moment.

He didn't appear to mind; rather, he showed every sign of enjoying the interrogation; his posture was casual, his countenance relaxed. Charlotte Ann naturally said nothing and faded into the corner as a good servant should. But Abby thought that, judging by the avid look in her eyes, she was not missing a word.

"I shall have to tell you how they were ten years ago, remember," he said. "They may have changed, though I doubt it. People rarely diverge from their basic nature, or so I think. Have you found it so?"

Abby gave the question some thought, happy to be asked her opinion on something. Philip would have flatly presented his view as truth, and that would have been that.

She thought now of her grandmother's bullying and irritability; Philip's dominance and criticism; her parents' patience and quiet love; Grandfather's tolerance and playful slyness. She recalled several close friends she'd had in Kent; one was extremely bashful, another forever giggling and talking. Although none of them *always* acted in a certain way, none had strayed long from their characteristic traits, not in all the time she knew them.

Then she thought of herself. When younger, she'd been full of life, adventurous, trusting. After she had come to live with her grandmother, she learned reticence, compliance, meekness, and the ability to bury her own wishes in order to avoid war.

But in the past few days, she had agreed to marry a stranger and had run off and done so. And though she had periods of doubts and regrets, there was something new forming inside her, some wild, exciting thing bubbling and growing like a waterfall bursting through winter ice into new life.

Perhaps it wasn't new after all. Perhaps the old Abby was being reborn. And the man sitting across from her was responsible for it.

Julian watched her patiently while she ruminated, though his eyes were becoming more and more curious. "Yes," she said at last. "I think people change little, unless something very wonderful or very terrible happens to them."

"I'm glad to hear you say so. Perhaps I can give you an accurate portrait of them, then." He leaned his head back and fixed his gaze on the quilted ceiling of the carriage. "Carl as I said, is the oldest and my favorite, simply because he was more forgiving of a pesky little brother. He and his wife were almost like parents to me as I grew older. Edmond is a rather typical second son; he became a soldier early. Seth is the dreamer of the family; he might have had a career as vicar or curate if he hadn't such an eye for the ladies, and I use the term generously." He laughed. "A dutiful wife and family in a vine-covered parsonage would never have done for him, I'm afraid. The last I heard, he was painting nudes. None of my brothers had any time for me, other than Carl."

She waited a moment, then said, "You mentioned four brothers?"

Although he didn't move, Abby felt a darkness enter the carriage, an ache, an old hurt, that absorbed light and sound and brought a weight upon her chest. She looked at Julian, but his eyes were averted; she turned to Charlotte Ann, but she appeared to notice nothing.

Finally, he spoke, saying merely, "Oh, yes, I had almost forgotten my youngest half-brother, Michael. He was very close to my father, and I imagine he lives at home still. He married shortly before I left."

No more was forthcoming, and Abby did not pursue it.

Gradually the black spirit floated away. And then the coach turned and pulled into the yard of the inn. Julian opened the door and lowered the stairs for them to climb down. His hand touched hers for only the smallest instant of time, but she felt a rush of warmth, though it may only have been the kind light in his eyes, or her own gratitude for his attempt at cheering her. She met his smile with a genuine one of her own, and gladly accepted his escort into the inn for her wedding luncheon.

Eight

If her wedding was not what she had dreamed of, Abby thought the luncheon could not have been more convivial. At its end, she felt reluctant to climb aboard the carriage once more; fortunately, the combination of rich food and pleasing conversation led her to sleep the afternoon away.

Shortly before dusk, they drew into a large hostelry boasting a wide central section and two wings that flanked a paved courtyard. Even before Bugbee pulled the horses to a complete stop, the travelers became aware something was very wrong. The courtyard crackled with tension from clusters of people talking and gesticulating and looking grave. Servants ran back and forth distributing tankards and sandwiches and calling to one another. A gray-haired gentleman, his faded eyes awash in tears, shouted instructions to three men on horseback who fought to restrain their excited steeds. As Julian assisted Abby from the coach, another group of riders pounded across the pavement and drew on the reins of their sweating horses.

"Any word? Anything?" cried the old man.

"Nothing, sir," answered one of the young men. "I'm sorry. Not a trace."

The old man's face crumpled, but he recovered quickly and resumed giving orders. As Julian's party entered the inn, the fresh set of riders galloped away.

The atmosphere inside the Brittony Rose Arms was even more disturbing. Abby thought the oak-panelled walls covered with dark paintings and the flagstoned corridor must normally fill visitors with a sense of peace and restfulness. However, one could hardly feel so now, not with the sound of cries emanating from a room in the back.

"What's afoot?" Julian asked of the servant who came to greet them and take their coats.

The servant, who wore a wig and the livery of an eighteenth-century page, shook his head. "Ah, 'tis a sad turn of events. The grandson of Mr. Bartholomew Chawston has gone missing. The old man's a fine gent—a textile manufacturer he is—whose only son was killed at Waterloo, and Master Gordon is all he has left of him. The child's mother and grandmother are in a state, as you might imagine. 'Tis them and their retinue you hear in the back."

"How terrible!" Abby exclaimed.

Julian made no comment but followed the servant to the desk to sign their names. Francis sped after him, his arms full of luggage. Remaining in the corridor with Charlotte Ann, Abby saw Julian exchange a few words with his valet. She was surprised to see how irritated the magician looked. A moment later, he ordered Francis to follow the servant upstairs, then signaled them to join him.

The sounds of feminine distress grew louder as Abby neared the staircase. As her foot touched the first tread, she paused. "Perhaps I can do something," she appealed to Julian, who stood behind her.

"No, I think not," he replied; then, seeing her surprise, added, "There is little one can do to soften such sorrow. It's commendable of you to want to try, but interference at such a time may be regarded as an intrusion."

It could have been Philip speaking. Abby felt a crushing sense of disappointment but obediently continued to climb the stairs. Charlotte Ann had reached the top; Francis stood beside her, his eyes never wavering from his master's face. The inn servant, anxious to show the rooms, looked annoyed at their slowness.

Midway up the stairs, an idea struck Abby and she turned excitedly. *"I* may not be able to help them, but *you* might!"

Julian did not pretend to misunderstand. "No, Abby."

"But why not? What is such a gift for, if not to help someone in trouble?"

"You don't understand."

She felt as if the stairs beneath her feet were falling away. "Oh, do I not? On the contrary, I understand very well."

He stared. "I'm not certain I know what you mean."

"I mean that you have been lying about your so-called talent all along. There is nothing to it, is there, Julian? Why not admit it and have done with your trickery once and for all?"

"Abby," he remonstrated, then looked away from her accusing eyes. "It's not dependable. I cannot summon it as one calls a dog."

"But if it is there at all, you could try."

His jaw set angrily. "And how would I do that? Shall I ask for an item of the boy's clothing? Beg to borrow one of his breakfast dishes? Do you realize how strange such a request sounds?"

"It does not matter to me how it sounds. If there is the slightest chance you can help those poor people . . ." She studied his face and found it unyielding. Her new-found trust in him dissolved all at once. "Oh, never mind. I'm going to offer what little help I can, even if it's only a shoulder to cry upon."

Without looking at him again, blinking away tears, she fled down the steps.

Julian watched her disappear around the corner. His fingers gripped the handrail tightly. Slowly he brought his gaze upward to meet Francis's. An oddly defiant look came into the magician's eyes, and he turned and began his descent.

"No, milord!" Francis called urgently.

Julian, apparently having gone deaf, did not pause. Francis dropped the luggage to the carpet and hurried after him. Charlotte Ann gave the page a mystified look and followed, abandoning their bags to the irritated servant's care.

The cries of distress led Abby to a private parlour in the back where she was admitted by a harried-looking man who introduced himself as the innkeeper. A group of weeping, whispering ladies sat at a table behind him. She had barely explained her mission to the man when Julian nudged open the door and joined her. Although Abby's spirits rose tentatively, the innkeeper was clearly not pleased.

"Hullo, sir," he said, reaching out a hand and edging Julian backwards with gentle but persistent pressure. "I'm Ralph Swans, owner of the inn, and we're having a spot of trouble here. Nothing for you to worry about, sir; just need a little privacy for the ladies, you understand."

Abby, her face glowing, stepped closer to the innkeeper. "Please, Mr. Swans, this is my—my husband, Lord Julian Donberry. He only wishes to offer his help to the Mrs. Chawstons."

As she hoped, Julian's title softened Mr. Swans's resolve. "Oh, well, don't suppose it would do any harm." He stood aside and allowed the magician room to pass, but when Francis and then Charlotte Ann crowded into the doorway, he shook his head and led them back into the corridor, closing the door behind him.

Abby took the magician's arm and brought him to an older lady sitting at the head of the table. After ascertaining that she was Mrs. Chawston, Abby introduced herself and Julian. "We have come to offer what help we can to ease your sorrow," she concluded.

"I am grateful for your generosity, though I don't believe there is anything anyone can do," said the lady, whose elderly profile was beautiful despite the sagging flesh at her neck. In sharp contrast to the other women, her eyes were red-rimmed but dry. After drawing a shaky breath, she gestured to the young woman on her right. "May I present my daughter-in-law, Mary; her maid, Alice; and my abigail, Delores; on the other side of the table are my daughter, Fredrica Stone; her friend, Viola Barnes; and their maids."

The women were so lost in sorrow that they barely acknowledged the presence of Abby and Julian. The magician nodded to them, then looked curiously at a servant seated alone at the window seat.

Following his gaze, Mrs. Chawston said, "Oh, yes. And that is my grandson's nurse, Phoebe."

Phoebe responded to their attention by burying her face in a large cotton handkerchief and sobbing. " 'Tweren't my fault, I tell you!" she cried.

"Phoebe, you have been saying so all day," the elder Mrs. Chawston said sharply. "No one is blaming you."

Mary Chawston lifted her ravaged face from the table and looked resentfully at the nursemaid. "If only she hadn't fallen asleep . . ."

"Everyone needs to sleep," Mrs. Chawston chided. "You cannot expect a servant to stay awake twenty-four hours a day."

"But she knows how mischievous Gordie is. He often runs away and hides just to tease us. She should have been alert. Surely he made noise stealing away from his bed this morning. If she hadn't been drinking the night before . . ."

"I only had a glass of ale with me meal like all the servants did!" Phoebe wailed. " 'Twas nothing wrong with that, were there?"

Several of the women gave her condemning looks. Abby noticed the maids were the most censorious.

"We do no good arguing among ourselves," Mrs. Chawston declared. "Casting blame does not bring Gordie back to us."

Fresh wails greeted this remark.

"We should not have taken him," Frederica said. She had inherited her mother's regal nose, but a weak chin and scornful eyes robbed her of beauty. "He is too young to travel. Children belong at home."

"You say that because you don't have any children yourself," Mary snapped, rubbing her eyes with a scrap of lace. "You don't know what it is to be without your little one for a long period of time."

"A two-week excursion to the Lakes is not a long period of time," Frederica retorted. "And if Gordie means so much to you, why does he not sleep on a cot in your room instead of the nursemaid's?"

As Mary dissolved into a fresh wave of tears, Mrs. Chawston said imperiously, "Stop such talk this instant, Frederica. You are serving no good by it."

Viola saw her friend's face turn an ugly color and rushed to say, "I sincerely hope you will not be presented with a ransom note before the night is over. I fear kidnapping."

"So you have said, many times." Mrs. Chawston fixed the young woman with a quelling stare. "You are not serving us well by voicing that thought, either."

Viola lowered her eyes and murmured an apology.

"I cannot imagine what you must think of us, Lord and Lady Julian," the elderly lady said. "We are not usually at one another like this."

"Hmph," said Frederica, who dissolved into a fit of coughing when her mother's sharp gaze fell upon her.

"It's a difficult time for you," Julian said. "We don't mean to make it worse. My wife and I only wish to offer our assistance."

"Thank you, my lord." Mrs. Chawston dipped her handkerchief into a bowl of perfumed water sitting on the table, wrung it dry, and pressed it over her eyes. "I don't know what anyone can do now. Gordie's never run away for this length of time. I cannot help thinking he lies hurt somewhere."

"Have they sent dogs after him?"

"Yes, early in the day, but it rained last night. The beasts weren't able to follow his trail."

"Is it possible he's hiding inside?" Julian asked.

"The servants have searched the entire inn, top to bottom."

The magician could ignore Abby's shining eyes no longer. He gave her a brief look of conspiracy and said cautiously, "We happen to have a fine tracker with us. If you could lend us something of the child's—anything that he touched or wore recently—perhaps we will have better luck."

Mrs. Chawston blinked doubtfully, then waved her hand in the nursemaid's direction. "Fetch something of Gordie's, won't you, Phoebe? It's unlikely Lord Julian's animal will do better, but we would be foolish to turn down any offer of help."

Abby tore her hopeful gaze from the magician's long enough to press the older lady's hands. "Thank you. We shall do our best."

"I am certain you will, dear. We appreciate your thoughtfulness." Mrs. Chawston smiled briefly and rubbed the moist handkerchief along her face and neck.

When they reached the corridor, a grim-looking Francis broke away from Charlotte Ann and the innkeeper, who were seated on a bench outside the parlour. "I beg you, milord, don't become involved in this."

"But he must." Abby returned the valet's stare boldly. All in a moment she decided to be done with shrinking from him. He had not responded to her kindness, and she would be bound if she'd defer to his contempt any longer. Not when she was right, anyway. "If he can do anything at all, he must. They need him."

Julian's expression was rueful. "She is correct, you know. In the meantime, Francis, make yourself useful by finding a dog."

"A dog?"

"Yes. A stray if you can, and bring it to the front entrance."

Francis opened his mouth to question him further, but milord was already ascending the stairs, following Abby and the nursemaid. Charlotte Ann scurried after them.

"Why did you change your mind?" Abby whispered to Julian when he drew close to her on the steps.

He gave her a look that stirred her heart painfully. "You are forever underestimating your influence, Abby," he said.

She raced up the remaining stairs, ashamed to let him see the blush flaming across her cheeks. She was growing surprised at herself. The least compliment from him seemed to affect her in the most astonishing manner.

Master Gordie had been given a large room on the third floor overlooking the courtyard. Someone had straightened the boy's bed in spite of the day's confusion, but the nurse's cot was rumpled and forlorn-looking. Nurse Phoebe walked past it and knelt in front of a cedar trunk pushed against the wall. She pulled a chain and key from inside her bodice, opened the padlock and flung the lid backward.

"Don't know what you want," she said, her voice trembling. "Here's his little stuffed rabbit, and that there is his precious little shirt and pants what he wore yesterday. I hadn't had a chance to wash 'em."

Julian took the proffered items and sat on the edge of the child's bed. He held the clothing tightly between his hands for a full minute, then set it aside. Taking the toy, he touched it carefully, stroking it as one would a pet. After a long period of time, he sighed, looked at Abby, and shook his head slightly.

Abby felt a sharp pang of disappointment that had nothing to do with his inability to help the boy. Was he only pretending? Did he hope to fool her with this performance, then claim that this one time he was unable to sense anything? She might learn nothing more about him than she already knew.

Charlotte Ann, growing increasingly uncomfortable at the looks of these heathenish proceedings, backed from the room mumbling she would wait for them in the hall.

The nursemaid could contain her curiosity no longer. "What are you doing, milord?"

Julian ignored the question and Abby's downcast look. He patted the edge of the bed. "Sit down beside me, won't you, Nurse Phoebe?"

She frowned, glanced at Abby, then reluctantly obeyed. When he touched her hands, she balked and tried to snatch her fingers away.

"Easy now, nurse," he said. "I'm only trying to comfort you. I know your mistress has caused you distress in her accusations. I think if I were in your position, I'd find it hard to remember my own name. But now that we're away from them and in the quiet of your room, I want you to think very hard. Is there anything you know that might be useful in finding Master Gordie?"

The tension seemed to melt from her body. "It ain't right, them saying all those things. But you're nice, you and your lady. I wish I could think of something to tell you, but I already told them . . ."

As her voice trailed away, Abby looked at her curiously. The nursemaid's eyes had lost focus, as though she were daydreaming. At the same time, Julian's eyes darkened. Abby's heart began to pound.

"Yesterday you and the boy rode in the second carriage with the servants," he stated in a quiet, smooth voice.

"Yes, milord," Phoebe answered, speaking as dreamily as a little girl recounting a fairy tale. "The ladies was in the first carriage; the men rode horseback. We're a large party when we travel."

"You are indeed." He was quiet for a moment. "There was an argument in the servant's carriage, was there not?"

Her lips turned down childishly. " 'Tweren't no argument, really; just that awful Alice saying mean things to me like she always does. Just because she's a lady's maid. Thinks she's better than she is."

"What awful thing did she say to you?"

"Made sport of my best shoes, she did. Not that I was wearing 'em then—I had on my slippers what goes with the uniform—but she remembered what they looked like. See, we was all talking about clothes, and that's how it got started. Said a pig wouldn't wear my shoes in a rainstorm. I can't help it if all my money goes to my little sisters, now can I? I have to wear them old things on my day off, worn though they be."

"And what did Master Gordie say to all this?"

A smile broke across the nursemaid's face. "He took up for me like he always does, the little pet. Said he was going to buy me ten pair of new shoes and ask his mamma to throw Alice in the river if she didn't stop."

Julian smiled faintly and released Phoebe's hands. "Where is Gordon's nightshirt?"

The nurse rubbed her brow as though it ached. "He must of been wearing it when he left. Or got took. I haven't seen it since he went to bed."

The magician narrowed his eyes and glanced searchingly around the room. With sudden intensity he asked, "Has the bedding been changed since last night?"

"No, milord." The nursemaid looked bewildered. "I straightened it this morning but didn't put on fresh linens."

Julian snatched back the bedcoverings, placed one hand on the pillow, the other on the bedsheet, and closed his eyes. He remained thus for several long seconds, then began to speak quietly, almost to himself. "He is restless during the night. Can't sleep. Sits up, sees his nurse. Remembers. I will find pretty shoes for her."

Straightening, he ignored the slack-jawed Phoebe and walked toward Abby, who watched him with hopeful eyes. "Where does a little boy find shoes? There is no shop; he can't steal a pair of his mamma's, because she might wake up and find him out."

Acknowledging Abby with a burning glance, he passed her, leaned his hands on the windowsill and observed the scurrying figures in the darkening courtyard below. He turned suddenly, startling the nursemaid.

"The attics!" he declared.

Phoebe pressed her hand to her chest. "We already looked there."

"Nevertheless, let us try again."

A knock pulled their attention to the open doorway, where stood a handsome, correct-looking gentleman of young middle-age. "How do you do," he said. "I'm Nathaniel Stone, Frederica's husband. My mother-in-law told me you've offered to help search for my nephew."

Julian introduced himself and Abby, explaining they meant to begin with the attics.

"A waste of time," the other replied. "You would do better to join us outside. If your horse is fresh, we could use the added manpower. I noticed a fellow out there who must be your servant. Seemed to be dallying around trying to catch one of the yard dogs. Unless the man's a total idiot, we could use him, too."

Julian bit his lip and expressed his willingness to do so, but only after he indulged his admittedly strange whim to investigate the attics.

Moments later, the five of them—Charlotte Ann had rejoined their party, though she hung back uncertainly—stood inside the largest of the storage rooms. The center of the floor was free of clutter and swept clean, but boxes and trunks and shelves were stacked around the periphery. There was no window; only the feeble hallway light illuminated the room, which appeared sadly empty of little boys.

"See, I told you; a waste of time," stated Mr. Stone.

Julian walked slowly to the middle of the chamber. "The room is kept unlocked?"

"At all times, evidently," the gentleman said. "Swans says it's too much trouble to secure it with guests coming and going constantly. Seems to me he's inviting thievery." He eyed the magician impatiently. "Well, come on, what are we waiting for?"

"Please," Abby said, her gaze following Julian with a desperate hope. "Allow him just a moment."

Mr. Stone gave her an odd look, but nodded and fell silent. Julian stood motionlessly, his head bowed, then began ambling past the line of boxes and luggage. He paused in front of a large black trunk, his shoulders tensing. With agonizing slowness, he knelt in front of it, fingering the metal hasp which had fallen over the staple. Suddenly he exclaimed angrily, flipped back the hinged strap, jerked open the lid, and bent over the trunk. When he rose and turned back to them, he held the child in his arms.

Amid the subsequent cries of surprise and delight, Phoebe was the first to reach them, but it was Mr. Stone who took the unconscious boy from Julian.

"Is he—he's not—" Phoebe gasped.

"No, he breathes, thank God," Mr. Stone said.

Thoughtless with joy, Abby rushed to embrace Julian. He had not been lying! He had spoken only the truth from the very beginning!

Without hesitation, he folded his arms around her and leaned his cheek against the top of her head. Feelings of warmth and safety streamed into Abby's body, and something else besides; the sense of excitement she had felt that first day their hands touched so intimately. Was it happening again? That strange exchange of emotions? She relaxed her arms and lifted wondering eyes to his.

His face was alarmingly close. He gazed down at her, his expression registering equal wonder and a tenderness that snatched at Abby's breath. He appeared reluctant to release her. But caution drifted into his features, and he stepped back a pace.

They became aware of Mr. Stone at the same time. He stood close to them, the child still clutched tightly to his chest. Relief and ecstasy were fading from his countenance, and a suspicious light was dawning in his eyes.

"How did you know he was in that trunk?" he demanded.

Abby bit her lip as she watched the lines of the magician's face smooth into a mask.

"Your tone of voice puzzles me," he said quietly. "I was only searching for him as you've been doing. It just so happened I was more fortunate."

"Just so happened, eh?" Mr. Stone looked down at the child protectively. "We hunt all day and you find him in five minutes. Your good fortune seems unbelievable."

Julian straightened. "What are you suggesting, sir?"

Mr. Stone's eyes sparked, but after a brief staring match, s gaze fell before the magician's. "Nothing at the moment. or now I must inform the family and fetch a physician. But I want words with you later, as will my father-in-law, I'm re."

He rushed from the room. Phoebe stared wide-eyed at Ju-an, then ran after Mr. Stone and her young master.

"What is wrong with that man?" Abby asked indignantly. He should be grateful for your help."

"People often don't feel as we think they should," he said.

Stirred by the lack of inflection in his voice, Abby instinc-vely moved toward him. She was dismayed when he flinched ck, warning her away.

"Is that why you hesitated to help them?" she asked, sad-ned. "Because you knew this would happen?"

Francis appeared at the doorway. "Knew what would hap-n?" he asked grimly. "I see you found the child; I passed e gentleman on the stairs. Now that I've chased down a dog r you, are we about to be thrown out on our backsides?"

Julian smiled wearily. "I trust not. You may let the dog go w; it was to serve as my excuse for tracking the boy. Now won't need it; I've been found out. No one could have dis-vered the child so easily. The logical conclusion is that I put m in the trunk myself."

"I tried to warn you, milord."

"Yes, you did, Francis, but I never listen to anyone, do I? u have told me so often enough."

"You'll be lucky if they don't hang you."

"They most certainly will not!" Abby declared. "I shall tell em we are on our wedding trip!"

Julian's smile became genuine. "Thank you, my dear. That ould certainly stop them."

My dear. Intoxicated with a rush of joy, Abby proclaimed, f not, they will have to hang me as well, for I shall tell them played a part in it. After all, it's my fault you searched for m!"

Both men looked at her. The magician's eyes gleamed bril
liantly, and Francis's stern face softened. She was so confuse
and pleased by their regard that for several seconds she forgo
their dilemma entirely and dropped her gaze to the floor.

"They'll have to hang me, too," Charlotte Ann stated de
voutly, though with less enthusiasm. "I aim to be counted o
the side of the angels."

Julian quickly hid his amusement. "How kind of you, Char
lotte Ann, but I rather thought you, er—disapproved of m
ability."

"I did at first, thinking it was the devil's doings," the mai
replied, her thin lips quivering with emotion. "But I bee
watching you over the past few days, and you don't seem lik
a bad man to me. And after you found that little boy, I kno
you're not bad. Satan don't work against Satan, that's what th
good book says, and I believe it."

Julian kissed the maid's cheek, making her blush like
radish.

After retiring to their respective rooms to change clothe
the four travelers met for supper in one of the inn's man
private dining rooms. Julian had yielded to Francis's plea tha
they dine together "in case there was trouble." His prophec
seemed destined for fulfillment. They had not been eating lon
before a loud knock sounded at the door.

Abby began to tremble. Julian looked at Francis. The val
pushed himself back from the table and opened the door.

Mr. and Mrs. Chawston were admitted into the room, fol
lowed by Mr. Stone. Abby was relieved to see their expression
did not look at all threatening. Though Mr. Chawston appeare
past tired, he beamed at all of them, introduced himself, an
shook the magician's hand.

"Had to tell you how grateful we are for your help in fin
ing the boy," he said. "Don't know how you did it, but w
can't thank you enough."

Abby relaxed and exchanged smiles with Julian. It appeare
they would not hang after all.

"How is the child?" he asked.

"The physician says he'll be fine," Mrs. Chawston replied. He's suffering from exhaustion. The poor dear screamed and ushed against the trunk lid all day. He must have been asleep hen the servants searched the attic, for Gordie has no mem-ry of anyone entering and calling for him."

"He is such an adventurous boy, and all heart," Mr. Chaw-ton added. "Had some idea he'd fetch a pair of shoes for his urse, but when he got in the attic he found all sorts of things play with. After he saw that trunk without a padlock, he pened it, saw it was empty and went in, thinking he'd found new hiding place. Well, it turned out to be a fine hiding lace indeed, since the hasp fell over the staple and he couldn't r it off. If there hadn't been a few wormholes in the wood, ie boy would have suffocated, or so the physician said."

They all fell silent a moment, contemplating the tragedy iat might have been.

"The results could have been the same had you not found im when you did," Mrs. Chawston said. "He's already suf-ering from thirst and lack of food. By tomorrow he might ave been too weak to make any noise did anyone think to earch the attics again. That is why we're doubly thankful for our help."

The elderly lady cast a demanding stare in her son-in-law's irection, and Mr. Stone cleared his throat uncomfortably.

"I must offer my apologies," he said. "I behaved offensively ward you, and I hope you'll forgive me. It did seem unusual, our finding him so quickly."

His expression indicated that he still found it unusual and id not entirely trust Julian yet, but the magician chose to ccept the spirit of his words. "Yes, I was very, very fortunate. remembered how fascinated I was with attics as a child and iought it a likely place for him to hide."

"Well, we're happy you did," Mr. Chawston said, then har-umphed and wiped his nose with his handkerchief. "And now,

if you don't think it's out of order, I'd like to offer you a gif
to show our thanks."

"Oh, no," Julian said quickly. "I never—that is, thank you
but I cannot accept anything."

Mr. Chawston glared triumphantly at his son-in-law. " 'Ti
as I suspected. When my wife told me you were the son o
Lord Donberry, I immediately thought that no spawn of hi
would be looking for a reward. Or need to. Don't be offende
at my offering, though. There's some,"—his eyes rolled agai
in Mr. Stone's direction—, "that thought you'd jump at it, bu
I was sure the marquess hadn't raised any bounders."

Julian's eyes grew cool. "You know my father?"

"I should think so. Years ago he owned an interest in m
factory before I bought him out. Didn't get to see him per
sonally all that often, but had the best of dealings with him
He was a forward-thinking man and a shrewd investor. A forc
to contend with, I'd say."

The old man's face clouded, and he looked from Julian t
Abby and back again. "I must admit I was a bit surprise
to hear from the innkeeper that you're on your wedding tri
so soon after your sire's death."

A sudden, taut silence blanketed the room. The magicia
picked up his fork and set it down again.

"Did I understand you correctly? Did you say my father i
dead?"

Shock lengthened the old man's face. "Oh, my dear fellow
didn't you know? I wouldn't have been the one to break it t
you for the world! But then, you've been traveling and perhap
they couldn't get word to you. It happened about—oh, ten day
ago, I would guess, wouldn't you, Nancy?—heart seizure,
believe it was. 'Twas in the newspapers. But there, I've thor
oughly upset you after all you've done for us—here, here, le
us leave you alone."

Muttering embarrassed words of sympathy, the visitors hur
ried from the chamber, leaving a thunderous silence behin
them.

Julian looked ill; his face, even his eyes, had faded to a muddy color. Abby, frantically searching the corners of her brain for soothing words but finding none, reached out tentatively and placed her hand over his. Equally speechless, Francis watched him while Charlotte Ann covered her face with an edge of the tablecloth.

The magician looked uncomprehendingly at Abby's hand, then twitched his lips into a brief smile.

"Please excuse me," he said, and walked quietly from the room.

Nine

Abby watched the door close behind him with blurring eyes. The bowls of clear soup sitting on the table, the plates of half-eaten turbot and glazed carrots—all so appetizing a few moments ago—now seemed noxious. She sprang to her feet and moved to the door.

"He needs to be alone," Francis said, not unkindly.

Abby hesitated. Julian's servant knew him better than she did. But she understood the unwelcome loss of one's parents, and perhaps Francis did not. "That may be so, but I wish to at least make the offer of my sympathy."

The valet made no answer to this, and she continued on her way. After looking into the public rooms and the courtyard, she knocked at Julian's bedroom door, then searched the terrace at the back of the inn. She was standing in the darkness wondering what to do next when she heard her name spoken softly. Abby looked around but saw no one.

"I'm up here," Julian called from his bedroom balcony. "You should come inside. They have failed to light the lanterns tonight, and it's not safe there."

"I'm coming up," she said, and set her chin stubbornly when he protested. This time when she knocked at his door, she heard the sound of slow footsteps and the lock being pulled. She felt a mixture of dread and sorrow when she saw his face. His demeanor was not forbidding, but neither was it welcoming.

"Please, may I come in?"

"I'd rather you wouldn't."

She forced a twinkle into her eyes. "You're not afraid people will talk, are you? You are my husband now; it's not improper for me to join you on your balcony, is it?"

"No, I suppose not," he said wearily, and stepped aside.

She walked past him, saw no answering smile or twinkle in his expression, and tried not to cringe at her own boldness. What, after all, did she expect? He had only moments ago learned of the loss of his father. And no matter how long-separated they were, no matter how estranged, that loss must be devastating.

The lamps were not lit in his room, and she traced her way carefully among chairs, tables, and the bed to a pair of glass doors that led to the balcony. Glancing over her shoulder to make certain he followed, she walked outside and clutched the wooden rail, hoping to gather strength from it.

The night air brought sharp scents from the fields that surrounded the hostelry. The sky was exceptionally clear, and countless stars blinked around a crescent moon. It was easy to imagine she stood on the edge of the world, that the balcony was a captain's perch, and the railing beneath her fingers the pilot's wheel. A brief wave of dizziness strengthened the illusion, and she shook her head to dismiss the fantasy.

"I don't mean to intrude if you would truly rather be alone," she said hesitantly. "I've come to offer my condolences and will leave now if you wish." When he said nothing, she added, "I'm remembering my own parents' deaths, you see. I recall wanting to be alone, too, but certain of my friends wouldn't allow that. After awhile, I lost my resentment of them and came to appreciate how much their support meant to me."

"No one could resent you, Abby," he said gently.

Her eyes began to fill. Even now, even when his heart must be breaking, he had compassion for her feelings. "I am so sorry," she said, her throat thickening. "Hearing about your father this way must be terribly difficult."

He put an arm around her waist and leaned his other hand on the rail. *Who is comforting whom?* Abby thought helplessly.

"Do you know, it is difficult," he said. "I am surprised at how badly I'm feeling. I suppose it's strange. I've not set eyes on my father for some ten years. There has been no correspondence between us. It's not as though I'll miss him as I would someone more familiar to me. And yet . . ."

"He was your father," she finished simply.

"He was my father," he agreed. "And I suppose I've always hoped we'd reconcile some day. That can never happen now. It closes a chapter in my life I'd have preferred to have ended differently."

Before she could stop herself, she asked, "Why *did* you leave all those years ago?" In mortification she added quickly, "I'm sorry. It's sounds as though I'm prying." He remained embarrassingly silent. "It's only that—well . . . I have begun to know you a little, and, in spite of our disagreements, I believe you are a kind man. I can't imagine you having an enormous argument and leaving in a fit of anger, never to return, never to forgive."

He tilted his head, considering her with an oddly blank expression. "And yet that is exactly what happened. I am not so kind as you think."

A brief shudder ran through her body. His words were spoken ominously, as if some other Julian lurked behind his eyes. The fear dissipated almost immediately. She knew gentleness and consideration when she felt it, simply because she had lived so long with its lack. He was not Philip.

"I don't believe it," she said, and heard herself with surprise. A few days ago, she thought him capable of the darkest of deeds. But all that had changed now.

"You should." He removed his arm from her waist and leaned both hands against the rail, making her feel absurdly abandoned. "There are things about me that would surprise someone of your delicate sensibilities. Sometimes I surprise myself. I have been known to be cruel."

He took a deep breath and exhaled slowly. A night bird sang sadly from the bushes beneath them. Abby never looked away from Julian's face, but he would not meet her eyes.

"Perhaps it comes from being my father's son. The Donberrys have been aristocrats for centuries; long enough to force their arrogance and pride on generations of their supposed inferiors. Combined with my Gypsy side, it makes for an unpleasant mix."

She would not allow him to disparage himself. "You are speaking nonsense," she refuted.

He chuckled humorlessly. "Am I? My brothers didn't think so. Especially when I carried tales about them to my father. They would no sooner plan some boyish mischief before I would spoil it by telling what they meant to do."

"You were much younger than they. You probably felt left out of things."

"I did, but it took years for me to learn to keep out of their way. Father didn't appreciate my tale-carrying, anyhow. He felt it to be a sign of weakness. He thought I was finding my information by spying on my brothers, which disgusted him further." He hesitated. "You must forgive me, Abby. I am remembering all sorts of things tonight. It is as though I've become a child again."

If it were possible for her expression to grow more sympathetic, it did. After a moment of quietness, she said, "You have told me he ignored your gift. Perhaps he was secretly frightened of it."

"He never admitted it was genuine. I think the Gypsy element shamed him, especially after my mother died. Carl often told me Father was a different man while she lived. But as the pain of losing her lessened, I think the stigma of her being a Gypsy grew. Especially when he saw me daily in her place. I represented not only all he'd lost, but was the breathing result of what he considered an old man's folly."

Abby felt no surprise at the marquess's class-consciousness;

England was a carefully leveled society. But it made her furious that he blamed his son.

"Understand that he never spoke these feelings," Julian added. "It was something I sensed." He paused, but after a moment he pressed on, as if needing to tell someone, anyone willing to listen.

"I was able to learn a valuable lesson from his lack of understanding. When I was about nine or ten years old, one of our hunters was found dead in the stables. The dog had been mutilated. Tortured. It was not the only time an animal had been discovered thus on our property, but it was the first domestic one so treated. I touched the dog shortly after its death and had an overwhelming sense of Michael. When I told my father, he became furious and demanded proof. He ordered me to my bedroom until I could offer some evidence, which of course I could not do. It was not until a week later that Carl prevailed upon him to rescind his punishment. After that, I learned to keep quiet. In every incident save one."

Abby, whose breathing had quickened sympathetically at the long-ago plight of a misunderstood boy, whispered, "What incident was that?"

He straightened, leaned his back against the rail and crossed his arms. After giving her the swiftest of glances, he rested his gaze on the glass doors, or the dark room beyond them. "It was the event which precipitated my leaving home. But I'm not sure whether I should tell you. It's not a pretty story."

"If you don't," she said sincerely, "I think I shall die."

A grunt of unwilling laughter burst from his lips. "Well, we cannot allow that to happen. You are the most delightful creature, Abby."

While she flushed in pleasure, his face fell somber again. "As the years passed, there continued to be similar events— other animals were tortured and killed. There were odd disappearances of under-servants. I heard rumours that more than one stableboy had been beaten, then paid well to leave. My father closeted himself in his study more and more. I think he knew of Michael's sickness, or evil, or whatever it was that marked him, but couldn't confront it.

"You see, Michael was always his favorite. In the early years, Father often boasted he was the son most like himself. Michael is, or was, a man of great personal charm, as was Father when he chose to exert himself. I think my sire began to see the error of his judgment as time progressed. But still he wouldn't listen to the rumours, wouldn't pay heed to the cautions of his steward or even my brother Carl.

"I, of course, kept well out of the way. Until the chambermaid was discovered with her throat—" He blinked, seemed to come to himself, and looked at Abby. "Until the chambermaid was found dead."

Abby said nothing, but one hand flew to her lips.

His gaze remained locked with hers, though he seemed not to see her. "I discovered the maid in my bedroom lying on my bed. It was a tremendous shock, as you might imagine, a shock deepened by my affection for the child. She was only thirteen years old. I was seventeen at the time."

His words gained momentum, as if, now that he'd begun, he could not stop.

"The two of us had engaged in that kind of harmless flirtation which pretty young servants and lord's sons often do in country houses. It was no more than that, I assure you, though it might have been had events followed their course. I was no saint, and she was a lively, vital young girl. When I found her there—when the worst of my shock was over, I touched her face. Her body was still warm. I saw Michael as plainly as I see you now. I watched him trying to seduce Christine. I felt his anger when she rejected him. I saw him bending over her dead body and caressing her hair."

"Oh, dear God," Abby breathed.

"Yes. But that isn't quite everything. A moment after I discovered the girl's body, I heard Michael in the corridor outside. Carl was with him. It became clear to me they were coming to my room, that Michael was bringing my brother with the

intention of finding me there. And then the door opened, and
I stood revealed with Christine's blood on my hands. The knife
lay beside her on the bed. I saw it all in an instant. Michael's
hatred of me, his knowledge of my fondness for the maid. His
plan to accuse me of her murder before Carl, the brother I
loved. If you had seen Carl's face, Abby. The shock, the disgust. The sense of betrayal. It was really cleverly done, if such
a monstrous crime could be called such. And very like Michael. He is brilliant in his way.

"All of these things came to me at once. In my rage, I
grabbed the knife and attacked Michael. I see I've surprised
you. Perhaps you'll believe me now when I tell you I'm no
kind. At that moment I had nothing inside my head except
murder. But don't look so worried. I only cut the sleeve of his
jacket before Carl pinned me to the floor and took the knife
away.

"The scene that followed was as ugly as you can imagine.
My brothers hauled me into my father's study. I kicked and
fought all the way down the stairs, screaming that Michael
had done it. When my father heard all, he gave me a choice.
Confinement to the west wing of the house, under a physician's
care, or I could leave. The prospect of judicial punishment was
out of the question for such as I, of course. The girl's family
would be hushed with gold, and Christine would be buried
quietly.

"I chose to leave. I departed that very night, taking nothing
with me except the memory of Carl's disappointment and the
sure knowledge that my father knew I hadn't touched the
child."

"No," Abby said, her heart beating with outrage and sympathy. "Surely *that* can't be."

Julian's face was tightly controlled, but his eyes looked hollow and lost. "It can. He banished me knowing that Michael
killed Christine."

Numbed by his story, Abby was beyond tears. Her mind
echoed with emptiness. She could think of nothing to say that

was not trite or meaningless in the light of such injustice. Had she ever felt her life was hard? Could she ever feel so again?

"How can you bear it?" she asked finally, brokenly.

His eyes sharpened, and he seemed to recognize her with something like surprise. "My dear," he said. "Why have I told you all this? You are too tenderhearted to hear about such things. Don't feel badly. It all happened long ago. I don't normally think about it anymore."

She did not believe a word of it. All she could contemplate was giving him comfort, easing his pain. She walked closer and slipped her arms around his waist. She was being bold, bolder than she'd been in the attics when exuberance made her fling her arms about him. At that time she would have done so to anyone who had discovered the lost child. But now it was only him, only Lord Merlyn, Julian, her husband, even though he was a paper husband and not a real one.

And how sad that was. Since she had learned she could trust him, there was no denying the growing desire of her heart. Although she had only known him briefly, she wished his magical man was a forever-husband who would touch and cherish her, give her children, and grow lines in his face and silver in his hair at the same time she did.

The thought brought a sob to her throat, and she pulled him closer, not caring if she shocked him. He would understand; he knew he would.

He responded to her tightening embrace by clutching her even nearer, as though pulling her into himself. She could feel his heart racing beneath her own. Or was it her own heartbeat she felt? There was no knowing. Their hearts seemed intertwined, pounding an erratic duet. Whispering her name, he tilted her head upward to receive the kiss she had known was coming, had felt at the same moment he formed the impulse.

His lips pressed tenderly against hers. The balcony floor seemed to tilt beneath her feet. Irrelevantly, the imagery she had earlier of the ship floated into her mind. She almost laughed. One kiss and she was being swept out to sea. But

long before she wanted him to, he released her, turned awa
and gripped the rail.

"I have run mad. Forgive me, Abby. I shouldn't have don
that."

Truly, he must think her missish indeed—all that talk abo
her being tenderhearted and sensitive. She placed her hand o
his sleeve. "Please do not think I am shocked. I wanted yo
to kiss me, Julian."

He looked at the hand on his arm, then patted it as a broth
would. "You are being kind." His gaze moved restlessly acros
the field, as if he were looking for something, anything, s
long as it wasn't her. "I have taken advantage of your syn
pathetic nature, and I apologize." In a strained voice he adde
"I hope you will forget it ever happened."

She did not know whether to be amused or angry. "I don
want to forget it. No one has ever kissed me like that." A
soon as the words left her mouth, she wished them back; bu
it was too late.

Whatever he had been about to say died on his lips. "In
deed?" He smiled briefly. "I suppose you have had a grea
many kisses in order to compare them with mine." Clearly h
expected her to deny it.

Her chest became tight. She did not want to speak of Philip
embrace or her slight, weak pleasure in it. The entire memor
shamed her. "Oh, well, I—I have received the usual kisse
from relatives, of course."

He laughed shortly. "That is not what I meant and you kno
it." He took her chin between his fingers and forced her 1
look upward. "Who has kissed you, Abby?"

"No one," she protested, then dropped her gaze. He tweake
her chin gently. "Well, only Philip, and I did not want hin
to."

"The cad," he mumbled. "I *should* have called him out
She darted a look at him beneath her lashes and felt a rus
of warmth at the hard glint in his eyes. "I won't let it happe
to you again," he added fiercely.

She bit the inside of her cheek to keep herself from beaming like a gudgeon. "And what of you?" she asked archly. "How many ladies have you kissed?"

He looked surprised. "Me? Oh, I don't know. Can't remember."

"It must have been a great many if you can't remember."

"No, no." He laughed uncomfortably. "Why are we talking about this, Abby? None of it matters. You had best go off to bed now; we have an early day tomorrow."

"I am not sleepy in the least. And I don't want to leave before saying that you have no need to be jealous of Philip."

"Jealous? Of Philip?" He threw back his head and laughed—much too loudly, she thought with sudden irritation. "Of course I am not jealous of him. You know I want to protect you, but jealousy is a different thing altogether. It implies—well, you understand. Our marriage will be dissolved shortly. I don't want you to think I am growing possessive. You mustn't—you mustn't worry about that."

"Oh, I am not worried," said Abby, who could not have been more hurt had he stabbed her. "Do not think it for one moment. Or rather, think what you like. It is of no concern to me."

A tiny line appeared in his forehead. "I am happy to hear you say so."

"It is only the truth. I have never cared what you thought."

"That is excellent indeed, for I don't care what you think, either."

"Good! I see that we understand one another."

"Yes, perfectly."

"Perfectly and beyond any doubt." Abby folded her arms together and pressed them to her stomach. She blinked several times and added in a softer voice, "But Julian, I am sorry for your loss and for—for all the bad things that happened in your past."

He did not answer immediately but looked at her with eyes that glimmered brilliantly in the moonlight. "Thank you,

Abby," he said at last, then guided her inside, through his roo
and down the hall to the door of her own bedroom. He bow
over her hand without meeting her eyes, then beat a has
retreat to his chamber. Neither of them spoke another wor
as if nothing had ever happened.

Abby entered her bedroom and stared at the comfortab
furnishings with unseeing eyes, thinking perhaps nothing ha

Ten

Neither of them slept well that night, which was why they were late leaving the inn on the next morning. As Abby, Julian, and Charlotte Ann climbed into the carriage, Nurse Phoebe and Master Gordon, still dressed in their bedroom attire, ran out the front door and across the courtyard toward them.

"He wanted to meet you, milord," Phoebe said.

Julian immediately returned to the pavement, introduced himself, and shook hands. The boy, his hair sparking gold fire in the sunlight, gravely presented the stuffed rabbit the magician had tried to read on the day before.

"Thank you for finding me," Gordie said. "This is Pietro. Nurse told me you liked him." The child's high, clear voice wavered only slightly as he added, "You can have him."

"Why, thank you," Julian said, accepting the toy.

Gordie nodded, his gaze intent on the rabbit. His lips moved, then set in a firm, straight line.

"I like rabbits," the magician continued.

Gordie nodded again. Abby, watching from the carriage window, thought she saw moisture gathering in the child's eyes. Her heart twisted in amused sympathy. *Oh, Julian,* she thought, hoping he would look her way and read her face, if not her thoughts. *Don't be as beastly to him as you were to me last night.* But his attention was fixed on the toy.

"How nice of you to give me Pietro. You have had him since you were a baby, haven't you?"

"How did you know? I guess nurse told you."

"No, Pietro did."

Gordie looked at the rabbit with stronger interest. "He did?"

"Yes. Why do you look surprised? Doesn't he talk to you?"

The boy's face relaxed, and he almost smiled. "Sometimes. But I didn't know he talked to anybody else."

"Well, he does. If the truth be known, he told me where to find you yesterday." The magician's eyebrows twitched a little at the lie.

"Truly?"

"Truly." Julian cocked his head at the rabbit, then looked at Gordie. "A moment, please, he is speaking to me now." He brought the toy closer to his ear, and his face lengthened in shock. "Do not say so, Pietro!"

The little boy danced from foot to foot. "What did he say, what did he say?"

"It is the most surprising thing. He has become quite rude, and I know it's not like him. Pietro says it is his duty to watch over you, and that if I take him away, he will bite me."

"*Did* he?" Gordie breathed, his face a portrait of delight. "He is being very naughty."

"Well, yes, I suppose so, but he's terribly fond of you. Much as I'd like to have him, I really think I should leave him with you so he won't be unhappy."

"I s'pose you should," Gordie said tiredly, a bedraggled parent used to his child's foibles. He took the rabbit, nestled it against his chest, then turned back to the inn, scolding Pietro as he walked.

Phoebe started after him, then stepped back to Julian. "Thank you, milord. Still don't know how you found him, but we'll never forget you." The magician tipped his hat, and she curtseyed and hurried after her charge.

When Julian reentered the coach, Abby knew her thoughts were written plainly across her face. She made no attempt to hide them, but he did not look at her. He was probably too modest to accept her admiration. This was the man who had said terrible things dwelt in his heart. She tried to imagine Philip showing kindness to a child and nearly laughed out loud.

At that moment she forgave him for his behaviour on the night before. He had done nothing wrong. She was at fault for investing too much meaning in a kiss. Her heart had run away with her head. There was no reason to think he must fall in love with her just because she felt that way. He was preserving her from a terrible fate with Philip. He didn't have to love her, too.

How bleak seemed a future without him, though.

As the coach sprang into motion, her thoughts tangled and knotted until she felt a headache coming on. None of her companions appeared more willing to talk than she. Even Charlotte Ann, pale with weariness, appeared unwilling to speak. Finally, after a meagre luncheon at a farmhouse, Abby settled her head against a cushion and prepared to nap like everyone else.

She slept lightly, fitfully. When Julian cried out, she sprang to immediate wakefulness. For a moment, she thought she'd imagined the noise, or dreamed it. He was still asleep, his head leaning against the interior carriage wall at a bruising angle, while Charlotte Ann sat stiffly upright, her mouth hanging open and spawning moist snores.

Just as Abby closed her eyes again, she heard the sound a second time, a low, visceral groan that seemed torn from Julian's chest. Prickling needles sped up her back, and she shivered at the utter despair of the cry. His forehead creased and uncreased; his eyes moved back and forth beneath his eyelids; his face was damp and pale.

"Julian," she said quietly, shaking his arm. "Wake up."

He continued to dream for an instant more, then his lids slowly opened. Black eyes stared at her without comprehension. Dark, dark eyes, empty eyes. Abby felt a momentary imbalance, as if she stood on the edge of a deep, bottomless well. Fear washed over her; a fear born of superstition and irrationality. For one brief fraction of time, she thought, *I don't know this man. I don't know him at all. What is he?* And then it was gone, replaced by compassion as he sat erect and re-turned her gaze, his blue eyes still befuddled with sleep.

Abby forced her lips into a smile. "You were dreaming."

He scraped his fingers through his hair, then took a hand-kerchief from his waistcoat and wiped his face. Apparently he was not going to answer.

"What did you dream?" she persisted.

He shook his head and looked out the window. "I don't know. I don't remember."

"You are not telling the truth, Julian."

He stiffened. "I beg your pardon?"

"Your eyebrows moved up and down. I have noticed they do that when you tell untruths."

"Have you?" he asked faintly "How interesting."

"Won't you tell me what you dreamed?"

"Why do you want to know?" he asked, exasperated. "Dreams are only tricks of the mind."

"That may be so for most dreamers, but not you."

He snorted. "I have nightmares like everyone else, and silly dreams. Meaningless." He seemed to be trying to convince himself.

"But your eyes . . . they were dark when you awoke."

"Were they?" A pained expression flickered across his face and disappeared. "You are very observant."

"It always means something important when your eyes darken like that, doesn't it?" When he remained silent, Abby's breath grew short. "You dreamed about me, didn't you? About Philip. What did you see? Tell me."

"No, no, Abby, it wasn't about Philip." He gave her a trou-bled look. "Please don't ask me anymore."

The intensity of her questions had brought her forward until their knees touched. Now she shifted her weight backward, all the way against the back of the seat. Charlotte Ann flopped against her arm, and Abby pushed her in the other direction without waking her.

"All right," she said between tight lips.

He smiled in relief. "We should be stopping for the night soon. I apologize for not taking time to show you the beauties of the north. I fear I'm treating you shabbily, not pausing to view the mountains properly. Have you seen the Peak?"

"No," she said crossly.

"Oh, well, perhaps someday you can. And we really should visit Wedgwood's Etruria at least; it is so near. But I confess after a three-month tour of smoky playhouses and indifferent lodgings, I'm weary of traveling and long for the comforts of home."

Abby made no answer to his chattering. She was too irritated to answer; unbelievably irritated at his refusal to satisfy her curiosity. But as she thought more upon it, she decided she *had* intruded into his privacy. There was no reason to think he'd dreamt of her. Maybe he'd had a vision that was scandalous in nature, albeit frightening for some reason. She had better not allow her growing independence to evolve into obtuseness. Not if she wanted him to love her as much as she loved him.

It was almost dark when the carriage gave a sudden jolt and lurched to a teetering stop. Both Abby and Charlotte Ann fell toward Julian, and all of them crashed against the door. When Francis rushed to open it, only his quick footwork and capable muscles kept them from tumbling to the road.

"Dear Lord have mercy!" cried Charlotte Ann, who had been dreaming about a certain valet clad only in his pantaloons carrying her up the slope of a glass mountain. "God forgive me!"

"Are you all right?" Francis asked. "Anyone hurt?"

Julian struggled to remove the brim of Charlotte Ann's bonnet from his eye, then scooped her off his lap toward Francis. When the servant lifted her, squealing, to the ground, Julian and Abby disembarked. All of them paced away to stare at the coach, which was tilted toward the left front wheel.

"Wheel broke," Bugbee announced unnecessarily as he checked the team and harnesses. He patted the flank of the wheeler nearest him, then spat into the bushes. "Must of been that hole in the road t'other day. Must of cracked the wheel, and now it's broke clean through."

"Didn't you check the wheels?" Francis accused.

"Couldn't see nothing wrong with it." Bugbee's eyes narrowed. "And just so you'll know, I allus checks everything top to bottom, while others are feeding their faces and burning their legs by the fire."

"Well, nothing can be done about that now," Julian said. "We should be near the Highwayman, which is about five miles up the road if I recall correctly. Abby, if you and Charlotte Ann will ride double with myself and Francis, we will go on ahead and take our rooms. Bugbee can stay with the coach."

Charlotte Ann pressed her heart. "You can all go, but please please do not ask me to get on a horse. Once I was near trampled by one and I can't abide the beasts."

"You'll be safe with me," Francis said.

The maid looked at him longingly. "I can't; I just can't. I'll die if I do." As if to prove her statement, she began to pant loudly.

"Never mind," Abby said, moving to pat her maid's hand. "I'll stay with you. We won't have long to wait, surely."

The magician sighed. "Very well. Bugbee, take my horse and go with Francis. Bring a cart or gig or something so we don't have to wait while the wheel is repaired."

Bugbee's homely, stubbled face brightened as he contemplated Julian's black. "Thank you, milord." Rubbing the horse's mane reverently, he eased into the saddle. "Don't forget there's a blunderbuss in my box."

"Hopefully we won't need it," Julian said irritably, waving them on.

"Don't I know it!" Bugbee called over his shoulder, grin

ning. "You're the worst shot in three counties! Er—sorry milord!"

"He is becoming overfamiliar," the magician muttered as the sound of hoofbeats died away.

At the mentioning of the gun, Abby's eyes had widened. Now she looked around nervously. A bottomless silence enveloped them. Woods stretched into the shadows on either side of the road. No lights from nearby cottages beckoned warmly through the chill air. Clouds covered the moon and stars, and she could hardly see the faces of her companions.

"Do you think it's safe?" Charlotte Ann cried. "You don't reckon Mr. Demere is out there somewhere, do you?"

Abby waited for Julian's answer, but he only mumbled and began moving restlessly around the carriage, running his hand along the panels, talking to the horses, and rummaging in the boot. Abby and Charlotte Ann watched him, hugging their arms across their chests and stamping their feet to dispel the increasing chill.

"What are you doing?" Abby asked.

"Looking for the tinderbox so I can start a fire. Search for some branches, won't you? But don't wander far."

They obeyed willingly enough, and before long a fire was crackling just beyond the edge of the road. Julian pulled a log close to the warmth, and all three of them sat on it with their hands stretched toward the flames.

After a moment, Abby began to laugh.

The magician looked at her curiously, his eyes reflecting the humor he saw in her face. "What amuses you?"

"Oh, I have just thought we must look like three magpies sitting on a fence."

He smiled. "I had rather be a raven, if you don't mind. There is slightly more dignity in the image."

"Very well; three ravens, then."

Charlotte Ann heaved a great sigh at their foolishness. They fell quiet again, and Abby watched the flames with a growing feeling of peace—a peace that was soon shattered by the maid.

"I hear something," she said, her head rising like a dog scenting game.

Abby heard it, too. Hoofbeats, but coming from the wrong direction to be Francis and Bugbee returning. When Julian rose to peer down the road, she rose, too, and stood as closely to him as she could without stepping on him. Charlotte Ann became a shadow behind her.

The rider soon came into sight, and they relaxed. He was no more than a lad of fourteen or so, and his steed was a worn old mare looking to have only a walk or two left in her. The boy wore the simple attire of a farm laborer, yet the material of his shirt and trousers was new and clean. He appeared delighted to see them.

"Guess you broke down, eh?" he asked in a surprisingly deep voice. Before they could answer, he continued, "Hadn't seen a cat moving this way, have you?"

"No, no cats," said Julian. "Who are you, may I ask?"

"My name's Lawrence Tushley, and you must have passed our farm a ways back. This is my time of the day for learning whittling with my grandpa, but instead I'm trying to find the cat for me mam. She's got one leg missing and is a lot of trouble."

A puzzled look came into Julian's eyes. "I am sorry to hear it, but should you speak so about your mother?"

"Hunh? Oh! Me mam don't have her leg off, it's the cat!" When Abby began to giggle, the boy looked at her and grinned. "Her name's Melissa. The *cat's* name is Melissa. If you ain't doing nothing, I wish you'd help me look. See, our dogs caught scent of a fox this afternoon, and off they go with the cat behind 'em. Thinks she's a hound, Melissa does. Now Mam's worried she hadn't come home."

Abby's expression became rapt. "Julian . . ." she appealed.

He glanced at her, then looked a second time. "You cannot be serious."

"But it would be so easy for you."

Waving his arms theatrically, he looked at the sky. "Do you

believe I was born to ensure the happiness and well-being of every creature in the world?"

"No, only that of those who cross your path."

He dragged his irate gaze away from her condemning one, stalked back to the fire and sat down. "I am not calling forth the beast to search for a flea-bitten, three-legged cat."

"Oh, she's that all right," Lawrence called merrily. "I don't know what kind of beast you have, and I guess you're not going to help; so I'll be on my way. I might be out here all night and never get to whittle. I could fall sick and die, too, since it's so cold, but that's no grief of yours!"

"I'll help you," Abby declared. "I'll look in the woods until our ride comes back."

"Will you? I'm obliged! If you find her, just yell and I'll come fast." Since he wore no hat, he pulled his forelock and clicked the horse into forward movement, calling for Melissa all the while.

After he disappeared into the darkness, Abby gave the magician a defiant look and turned toward the woods. When she saw how gloomy it was inside them, she said bravely, "Come, Charlotte Ann. Let us see if we can find this poor, lost creature."

"Not me," the maid said firmly, and went to sit on the log beside Julian. "I'm scared of cats and even more scared of woods at night."

"I'm beginning to think you are frightened of everything," Abby said irritably. As she eyed the forest, her vexation increased. But she could not back down now, not while Julian watched her with so much amusement. She set her teeth and plunged into the woods.

The going was difficult; at every step she had to push aside tangles of dried vines and thick undergrowth. Many of the branches were leafless now and hard to see in the dark; moreover, their spiny points could take out an eye if she weren't careful.

When she heard the noise of someone approaching behind,

she looked back in relief. Julian was coming with a makeshift torch in his hand. She had been certain he would not leave her to walk in these woods alone. Well, almost certain.

"I knew you would want to help that boy."

"I'm not here to help him but to keep you from trouble. I've never used the beast to find an animal and I don't intend to start now."

She began walking again, peering upward into branches and stirring the bushes with a stick she found. "I wish you would stop calling your gift a beast. It seems . . . ungrateful."

"I *am* ungrateful. I've told you before that I'd rather not have this . . . aberration. Nothing good comes from it. Nothing."

She turned to stare at him. The flaming branch he held illuminated the anger in his eyes. Well, she was feeling more than angry herself.

"Tell Gordie that, why don't you?"

"All right, that one time it was useful. But had the child been unable to tell what happened to him, we could have found ourselves in the gaol."

Abby did not know what to make of his bitterness, so she pushed on, calling the cat's name over and over again until her throat felt raw. To her fury, Julian began to echo her cries, mimicking the inflection of her voice every time. It was all beginning to seem quite hopeless, yet she was too stubborn to call a halt. But she had to stop, finally, when a sudden, agonizing wrench to her head made her gasp in pain.

Julian, who had dropped a few paces behind, rushed to her side. "What is wrong?"

"My hair! It—it is tangled in the branch."

He held the torch above her face and grinned. "So it is."

She struggled to free her hair but seemed only to make it grow more tightly wrapped around the limb. "Help me, Julian, don't just stand there watching!"

"I don't know if I should, Lady Absolom. Francis will tell you I'm no good with knots."

"Julian, please!"

"All right. Here, hold the torch and I'll use both hands."

He began to work busily. Of necessity he stood very close to her. She tried to be unaware of his nearness but could not help it; his breath tickled her skin. Only inches away, his cheeks were reddened with effort, and his eyes glinted with the light of total concentration. Oh, he was trying so *hard*.

At last she was free; but when he lowered his arms with a triumphant flourish, she did not move but kept her gaze pinned to his. She watched the victory in his eyes transform to something warmer. For an endless moment they remained thus; then Abby let the torch slip from her fingers to the ground. Hesitantly she lifted her arms around his shoulders.

For a heart-stopping instant he did not respond. Just when she thought she must die, he clasped her to him. And then, with great reluctance, he brought his lips to hers.

"Julian," she whispered as he traced a slow pattern of kisses on her eyelids, her cheeks, and the tender flesh at her throat. "Julian." She began to kiss him back while threading her fingers into his dark, dark hair. All her anger and hurt from the previous night faded away. He was so beautiful. She caressed his temples, his cheeks, the strong chin.

In her ecstasy, the words flowed unbidden from her mouth. "I love you, Julian," she said.

The moment she heard herself, she knew she should not have spoken. She sensed the change in him before she felt the hesitation in his kisses, the slight stiffness of his body. It was that mysterious exchange of feelings again, she supposed. If so, if the whole thing was not an illusion born within two oversensitive hearts, he must at this moment be receiving the shame and embarrassment pouring from her soul.

As if he had, his arms tightened around her in a final hug, then he slowly released her. She felt like a child being given a sweet to soothe its hurt feelings. Abby bowed her head so he could not see her face, her humiliation. But he was having none of it. He forced her chin upward and ventured a smile, looking no more secure than she felt. There was a barrenness, an emptiness in his face. She could not read his expression, and he was being careful not to touch her anymore.

"Abby," he said. "I love you, too."

Immediately, her heart flew to her throat and shone from her eyes. She leaned toward him, but he put up a restraining hand. She was nonplussed. This was not how she'd imagined a scene of tender declaration: the two of them standing a foot apart, she wanting to embrace him, he forbidding her to come any closer.

When he spoke, his voice sounded tight, as though he were strangling. "I've lost my head again. Forgive me."

"No. You will not do this to me a second time, Julian. You cannot declare your love and kiss me in one moment, then push me aside the next."

The torch near their feet was glowing fainter, and it cast haunting shadows across his features. He rubbed his head as if to wipe away an ache, then dropped his hands. "Abby, there is something you're going to have to know, though God help me, I don't want to tell you. But I can see it will be worse if I do not."

She waited breathlessly, wondering if she would be able to hear him over the pounding of her heart.

"Do you remember how you told me not to regard my ability as a beast? Well, I'll be interested in knowing your opinion in a few moments." He backed up and leaned against a nearby tree as if he needed support. "I have been having dreams during the past days. Dreams about you. New ones since we ran away together."

She had a sudden desire to cover her ears but knew she must be strong. "You had one this afternoon in the carriage, did you not?"

"Yes." He curled his fingers into fists, then relaxed them. "What would you say if I told you that you must never marry; never have a real marriage, I mean, for the sake of your life?" When she only stared at him, he went on, "Abby, you cannot know how it pains me to say this. It seems you are fated to die in childbirth."

For one moment, her knees felt as if they would give way. She replied in a hoarse whisper, "But that was my future with Philip. Not with you."

"Yes, well . . ." His expression clouded with embarrassment. "It appears I may have done Demere a small injustice. In my vision, I *did* see him brutalize you, even during your pregnancy. Naturally I attributed your death to his violence. But now . . ."

"But now?" she prompted, her teeth aching from clenching them so tightly.

He grew pale and very still, pulling into himself. "You recall I told you I cannot see my own future unless it intrudes into someone else's? In my dreams, I am holding a sleeping infant in my arms. You are lying in bed with a sheet pulled up to your chin. Your eyes are closed and someone is weeping. I hear a voice crying, 'She is dead! She is dead!' I don't recognize the voice until I awaken. The voice is mine."

A lengthy silence fell between them, a silence Abby broke. "You said you were wrong about Philip killing me. Perhaps you are wrong about this vision, too."

"No. I want to be wrong, but I don't see how it's possible."

He looked vulnerable standing there with his hands shoved into his pockets and his head bowed. She wanted to pull him closer and kiss away the worry lines creasing his forehead.

"But what of your interpretation of the dream? How do you know you have made the correct one this time? Perhaps it was not I who died, but the poor babe. Or someone else entirely."

He looked startled, then considered it. A light wind rattled the brown oak leaves above their head and scattered a few to the ground.

"No, I don't think so. There was a heavy feeling of sorrow. I know it would be terrible to lose a child, but I can't imagine such grief for a newborn. Everyone knows how precarious the life of an infant is. And I certainly don't feel that strongly about anyone else."

She continued to think rapidly. "Well then . . . how old was I in the dream? Perhaps this was my tenth child, or my twelfth. I never wanted to live to a great age, anyway."

His face softened into tenderness. "Dearest, I have no way of making my dreams tell me more than they do."

Pressing a finger to her lips thoughtfully, she stepped past the circle of dying flames at her feet, then swirled around. "Perhaps not your dreams. But if you touched my hand . . . ?"

He stared at her blankly for several seconds, then a meagre look of hope entered his eyes. "Perhaps. It's worth trying." Under his breath he added, "One more time. Just this last time." He pushed away from the tree, took her hand, and kissed her palm. "For luck," he explained. Then he wrapped his fingers around hers and looked into the darkness.

Abby kept her gaze on his. When his eyes became black, she trembled with expectancy. The moments lengthened. Finally, he looked at her and smiled briefly before releasing her hand.

"What did you see?" she asked breathlessly.

He looked down at his shoes. "Nothing. Oh, I felt what you're feeling as I always seem to when we touch; but other than that, absolutely nothing. Not a hint of your past or present or future."

Her shoulders sagged in disappointment. When he lifted his eyes, she was shocked to see the joy in them.

"Don't you know what that means?" he asked. "It was like trying to read myself. You've become so close to me that you're inside whatever this thing is that guides me. Don't look sad, Abby! It's a curse to be given hints of your beloved's future, especially if it's something bad and you can do nothing to prevent it."

"I suppose," she said doubtfully.

"These dreams began as soon as I believed you intended to

accept my suit, before I knew I loved you. Perhaps I wouldn't be having them now if I'd known that sooner."

"I wish you hadn't been so slow about loving me, then," she complained.

"No. This warning is good. Now I know how to avoid losing you." The brightness in his eyes began to fade. "But there is this, Abby . . . even though we love each other, we cannot stay together. I am not strong enough to resist you. Every time I see you, I want to carry you off to bed. And sooner or later . . ."

She felt the blush rising but was pleased at the desire she saw in his eyes. She wanted to lie in his bed, too, though she wasn't sure what that involved in spite of whispered confidences with her girlfriends in Kent. All she knew was that she wanted his arms around her forever. But he was telling her that wasn't possible.

"There must be a way," she began. "I—I don't want to leave you."

"And I don't want you to leave me, either. But the important thing is that we love each other, isn't it?" He sounded as unsure as she felt. "Many people never have that much."

Lifting a hand toward her hair, he smoothed a tangled strand behind her ears. Then, as if even that had been too long to touch her, he withdrew his fingers with sudden briskness and looked away, straightening his cravat and smoothing his waistcoat with extraordinary absorption.

"We had better get back."

"But—"

"There isn't anything more to discuss except getting out of these woods."

Abby's lips tightened. Evidently her opinion on the subject did not matter. As her feelings darkened, she noticed the woods had grown even darker. "The torch has gone out!"

"I suppose we're fortunate it didn't start a forest fire. Come, Abby. Francis has probably returned by now."

He took her arm and began leading her forward very slowly.

The trees were like great hulking shadows around them. It was easy to trip over unseen roots and logs, and they did so often.

Her thoughts were so distressed that she accepted his leading and didn't notice their direction at first. But after several moments there could be no denying the wrongness of it all.

"Julian, where are we going? The coach is back the other way."

He stopped, looked around, then shook his head. "No, I'm certain it's straight ahead."

"No." She pulled her arm away from his. "I don't recognize these trees."

"Recognize the trees? Abby, we are groping around like blind men. How can you recognize any of the trees?"

"I just can. And I am going *that* way."

He watched her move off, then began to follow. "Are you certain? Now that I think about it, it seems to me we came from over there." He pointed in an easterly direction, one which Abby was positive they had not yet set foot upon.

"You are *lost,* Julian," she said, disguising all but a trace of scorn in her voice. "How can anyone who finds wayward children become lost?"

"I never claimed to have an ability as a direction-finder," he said shortly. "Besides, I am not yet certain it is *I* who am lost."

"Well, follow me and you will soon see who knows where they are going and who doesn't."

She could not restrain a burst of pride in being able to take command, even in this small way. But after they had picked their way through the undergrowth for some time and appeared to be getting no closer to the road, her cheeks began to grow warm.

"I am waiting anxiously for the scent of our fire," he said finally, a dangerous edge in his voice. There came a sound of smacking and rustling behind her, then a muffled grunt of pain. "And I'll thank you not to slap branches in my face."

"Sorry. It slipped from my grasp."

"Very likely. Admit it, Abby, you can no more find our way

out of this wood than you could find that cat. Francis will have to call a search party for us."

Abby was trying to think of a stinging retort when she heard a piercing scream. "That's Charlotte Ann!" she cried, and began struggling toward the sound, which was coming from a direction they had not yet tried.

A short while later they emerged from the wood breathing hard and looking tattered. Charlotte Ann had stopped screaming, for Lawrence now held Melissa, who had found the maid and taken a fancy to her. Francis and Bugbee were waiting with a cart, and two other men stood ready to help with the wheel.

Julian's eyes began to twinkle. "I believe we must thank the cat for our rescue."

Seeing his smile, she could not help responding despite his annoying behaviour in the wood. Besides, he had done much that had not been annoying. Had he not said he loved her?

When he saw the warmth in her expression, he looked a little taken aback. "I—I'll go see if they need any help."

She watched him hurry to join the men, her lips twitching. *You'll not be rid of me so easily, Julian Donberry,* she vowed.

Throughout the next two days, her eyes returned with helpless frequency to Julian's face. She could not stop. Since she had been so bold, so forward, so crass as to declare herself to him, she could think of nothing but her love for him.

All she wanted now was to make their joining real in every sense of the word. She didn't want to annul the marriage, to live by herself in some suitable city. Childbirth or no childbirth, he was not going to slip away from her. She wanted to be with this wonderful man forever.

Unfortunately, Julian hardly looked at or spoke to her anymore. When their eyes met, he looked away ashamedly as if he regretted everything he'd said to her. Well, he would have to recover.

She realized she was being presumptuous. He had originally

only meant to help her, not shackle himself to a stranger for life. But had he not said he loved her, too? If he didn't mean it, he shouldn't have spoken the words. And somehow she would make him forget this nonsense about them not living together as man and wife.

For whole hours at a time, she was able to forget the reason they married was to avoid the danger Philip represented. He seemed a distant threat now, especially since Julian had discovered Philip was not going to kill her, at least not in the way that was first thought. Besides, how could Philip find them? He didn't even know Julian and Lord Merlyn were one and the same man. And should he discover that fact, he'd have no way of searching out their location.

She was happier than she could ever remember being. Life was full of possibilities, and every one included Julian.

On the final morning of their journey, she glanced at the perfect face across from her—though just now its owner was being difficult, pretending to sleep so he wouldn't have to talk—she wondered at herself. Had she truly fallen in love with a man she'd met only weeks ago?

Yes, yes, indeed she had.

He was such a good man. The first man since her father whom she trusted entirely. Fortune had smiled upon her the night she attended Julian's magical performance. She did not deserve his regard, could never repay him for what he had done for her.

As they continued to travel, her anticipation at being out of a moving coach, her desire to see his house, all worked to lighten her mood further. She was tired of traveling. She felt as though she had *always* been in this carriage, had been born in it, raised in it, and with all probability would die in it. If their marriage journey had been an apprenticeship, she was ready to *be* a carriage now; she knew exactly how to rumble and bump and cast her passengers against the sidewalls until their heads rattled.

She never wanted to sit down again.

Julian made polite, impersonal conversation during the rest of the trip. He pointed out local landmarks and promised to take her to tour Warwick Castle. But as they drew closer to his home, he seemed to become more and more uncomfortable. Several times he started to say something, then stopped. She could not help feeling a growing disquiet. When they pulled into a hostelry for an early supper, even Francis contributed to her unease. The valet was solicitous toward her, and the frequency of his glances made her nervous. She could not understand why now, now that their journey was almost done, everyone except Charlotte Ann and herself seemed reluctant to arrive after all.

Men must not grow as weary of traveling as women did. It was the only answer that made sense.

They arrived at Avilion at sunset. Abby viewed the iron gates with pleasure, her anxiety dissolving. While Francis unlocked the padlock—Julian explained the gates were not ordinarily locked, but he had ordered them to be secured because of the unlikely event of Philip finding the estate—she craned her head to see the house and grounds. There was nothing that did not please her. They drove through the gates and pulled to a stop before the yellow-stoned manse. Its proportions were symmetrical and solid-looking. Comforting. Safe.

As Bugbee sounded the horn, the front doors flung wide, and two menservants came from the house to assist with the luggage. A stout, middle-aged woman dressed in black emerged to stand at the top of the steps, beaming; the housekeeper, beyond a doubt. She was followed by a little man, also dressed in black. And then, as Abby accepted a footman's assistance from the carriage—Julian had rather curiously exited the coach first and disappeared around the side of it somewhere—she looked up in time to see a woman walk gracefully from the interior and join the others on the steps. The lady was dressed in a cream-colored dress, the lines of the gown accenting the voluptuous curves of her body. She had great quantities of red hair and was more beautiful than anyone Abby had ever seen.

Hilda of Silverwaithe Farms, she remembered instantly, poking at the straggling hairs that had escaped her pins, brushing at the dust and tea stains on her old green dress. She had no idea why her spirits should suddenly plummet; it was only natural that Hilda would live here with her employer. Julian no doubt provided housing along with wages for his workers. He was like that; generous to a fault. There was no reason why the woman's sensuous walk down the stairs and the purposeful way she approached her master, then leaned her head closely to his as though whispering secrets, should bother her. And surely she had only imagined the amused glance Hilda cast in her direction.

But Abby knew she did not fabricate the way Julian refused to look at herself, nor could she conjure up Francis's sympathetic eyes. Days ago she would have been glad of the servant's support, but now she hated him for it.

Yet those were the least of the surprises awaiting her at Avilion.

"Is he there yet, Mamma?" cried a disembodied, childish voice from somewhere nearby.

"He has arrived," called Hilda, laughing.

A small girl ran around the corner of the house, her arms full of wildflowers. She made a charming picture in her crisp white dress with her red hair streaming behind, her brilliant blue eyes shining. Abby struggled to smile at the child's evident joy in seeing them. Perhaps she had few visitors and lived a lonely life.

"Papa! Papa Julian!" the little girl cried, and threw herself into the magician's arms.

I am not so kind as you think, he had said. *I have been known to be cruel.*

Abby felt the world spin. The yellow walls of Avilion darkened to black, and she fell to the ground like a downed bird.

Eleven

Philip fought to open his eyes. He was hot and thirsty. Every breath knifed pain through his chest. Had someone nailed his lungs together? *He could not breathe!*

A tow-haired child of indeterminate age came to peer at him. Philip decided it was a boy, though one could not be certain with these farm people. He had a sudden, feverish recollection of seeing this smudged face before, and others like it. All of the inhabitants living here were dirty and slovenly and probably stunk to heaven, if he had the nose to smell them. But he could not breathe; he was choking for God's sake, and they would not help him. He was going to die in this primitive hovel on a bed of straw. What an ignominious end for someone who had always tried to live decently, to look well, to mind his estates dutifully, and it was all Abigail's fault!

Now the odious boy was touching his sleeve with hands that were sticky and filthy, and he could not prevent him, was weak as a newborn kitten. He could feel the child's warm breaths on his skin, see the fascinated look in his eyes. The little monster began dancing a straw man up his arm and across the blanket under his chin. Bits of hay flaked from the home-made toy and fell across his face.

He must be in hell.

"There now, Tootie," said someone nearby whom he could not see. Apparently the room was so small, everything in it was near. "Leave the gennulman alone."

Philip's throat worked mightily. "Help," he croaked.

"Oh, you be awake again," said the voice. A scrawny-looking woman shuffled to his bed. Her stringy hair and vacant eyes seemed familiar.

"Fetch . . . physician," he panted. "Sick. Have money."

She laughed, reminding Philip of the honking of a goose. "You say that ever time you wake up, mister. You are some piece of cake."

"Please. Can get more. If not enough. Money."

She patted his shoulder. He hadn't the strength to cringe away from her black-encrusted fingernails. "Don't fret. We took a little to pay for the doctor and for food. You be right enough in a few days."

"Doctor's been here?"

"Why, yessir, he has. Twicet. You don't remember?"

Gasping, Philip moved his head slightly against the straw.

"Never mind, then. You keep still. That's what he said to do. I got soup on the fire. Lemme go get you some."

"Wait." He took several shallow breaths. "What's wrong . . . with me?"

"You got the Devil's Grip. Ain't nothing to do but lie it out. Lots of folks got it hereabouts. Since you came, my Harold's down with it, too." Resentment flashed across her features, then disappeared. "But that ain't your fault."

Philip thought he could hear someone coughing near the fireplace, but he hadn't the strength to look. "How long?"

"Guess you been here four or five nights. Don't remember exactly. Oh, you mean how long afore you're on your feet? Probubbly a week, if you don't die first. But don't worry. I'll take good care o'you."

A week. If he didn't die first! And what would Abby be doing in the meantime? Abigail and her noble husband. Or lover. He grit his teeth. A wave of heat reddened his skin.

"Easy," said the woman. "I know it hurts. I'll go get you something to eat, then you sleep. 'Tis the best thing."

Another child, an older, feminine version of the first one, loomed over him. "Mamma," she whined. "I don't feel good."

"Oh, lord," the woman said, sighing.

Oh, God, thought Philip, his feet moving restlessly on the straw.

Sitting beside the marble fireplace in her bedchamber, Abby stared dully into the flames. A part of her mind was aware of Charlotte Ann moving about the room, straightening it; another part felt an objective, distant appreciation for the luxuriousness surrounding her.

The room was modern with Egyptian accents. The walls were tinted yellow, and the furnishings were crafted of dark woods ranging from a mahogany sleigh-bed to a curule armchair made of black-japanned beechwood. Colorful, glazed urns graced the floor on either side of the large window, and a carved sphinx sat upon the dresser. The doors were bordered in gold leaf, even the despised one that connected to his bedroom. What she had seen the night before—the *little* she had seen—of the public rooms downstairs were decorated in a similarly exotic manner.

She allowed her observations to soothe the ragged edges of her mind. When other, more dangerous ruminations threatened to surface, she quelled them. She preferred it that way, preferred to remain numb.

Her fingers tightened around her shawl. In the fire's glow, Julian's ring sparked and drew her eyes. Why was she still wearing it?

Across the room, Charlotte Ann was trying to make the bed while watching her worriedly. "Aren't you going down to breakfast, Miss Ab—I mean, Lady Julian?"

"No," Abby replied dully. "And please don't call me that."

Charlotte Ann grimaced. Seeing her mistress huddled in that odd chair, her shawl drawn around her like an old woman, folded the maid's heart into knots. Without asking permission, she abandoned her work and sat on a footstool in front of the fire.

"You don't think—" Charlotte Ann swallowed. "You don't believe that woman is his real wife and he faked your marriage, do you?"

Hearing her worst fears voiced, Abby clenched her fists. "I don't know. I have no idea what he does, or why. I have no understanding of anyone or anything."

"Oh, now, miss—my lady—I don't know why I said that. They couldn't be married. She must be his—you know. Lots of men have such, though I must say not many keep them under their own roof. But don't worry; the good Lord will punish him for it. Don't carry on so."

"I'm not carrying on. You don't see any tears, do you?"

The maid saw no tears, but her mistress's pretty brown eyes looked empty, like someone had blown out the light behind them.

"Men are animals," she condoled.

Abby nearly smiled. "I don't believe you mean that. I've seen the way you look at Francis."

"You have?" Charlotte Ann's eyes grew round.

"Don't be embarrassed. I'm not saying you were obvious about it. I'm sure no one else noticed."

The maid's mouth turned down at the corners. "I think they did. I think *he* did. See, he started out being friendly to me. But when I got friendly back, he began to act standoffish. Real polite, but like there was a maypole between us, except for when he offered to take me on his horse; but he couldn't help having to do that. I'm too ugly for the likes of him, and that's the truth of it."

"You're not ugly!" Abby exclaimed, struggling to avoid looking at the servant's ears.

"Well, that's as may be, but I can see he's got better things in mind for himself. It shouldn't be that way, though, should it? Men ought to look on the inside of a woman. But a pretty face wins over a kind heart every time."

Abby did not mention it had probably been Francis's pretty face which had attracted Charlotte Ann to *him*. Instead, she

eached over and patted her hand. "You're right. Men are animals."

"I still can't believe Lord Julian treated you that way,
though. He seemed so nice."

"Yes." Abby leaned back and pulled the shawl tighter. "He
did, didn't he? But it seems it was all an act."

"Maybe we're thinking wrong, my lady. Maybe she's a
friend or relative."

Abby's eyes darkened with scorn. "A friend whose child
just happens to call him Papa?"

"She said Papa Julian. Maybe that means something."

Abby's mouth twisted. "It might if the girl didn't look so
much like him. Did you see her eyes?"

Charlotte Ann sighed and shook her head commiseratively.
He should've told you about the child. But what I can't un-
erstand is why that woman would put up with you being here.
She didn't look surprised when you got out of the coach. Just
waltzed up to him like she'd known you was coming. That
on't make any sense to me. What mistress would go along
with such doings?"

What mistress indeed? Abby regarded the maid with-
ut visible emotion. The shawl slipped from her shoul-
ers. She sat a little straighter in the chair, recalling the
old expression in Hilda's eyes. Had there been a hint of
esperation there?

"Yes," she said slowly. "That is rather strange, isn't it?"

"I guess it's like you said before; there's no understanding
ome people."

Fire ignited in Abby's eyes. She stood up abruptly, her bones
creaking as if she were a hundred years old. What had she
een thinking, sitting there so long? What she needed was
xercise. And food. She was starving.

"See if you can remove the travel stains from my yellow
ress," she commanded. "I'm going down to breakfast."

* * *

By the time Abby arrived downstairs, the others were gath ered around the table. She had been unwilling to venture fror the bedroom until Charlotte Ann had done her finest work i dressing her hair. Abby knew she had never looked better, nc even on her wedding day. It was not a remarkable accomplish ment, since she was wearing the same dress now that she ha then. But it was her best one, the only one she owned that di not have something wrong with it.

Thus she knew she had nothing to be ashamed of when sh walked into the dining parlour and saw Julian ignoring hi newspaper and chatting familiarly with Hilda and the chil over plates of food. And yet, the cozy domesticity of the scen pierced her like thorns.

At her entrance, he became hospitality itself, exclaiming he name and hurrying to escort her to a chair directly opposit him. "I hope you're feeling better this morning. It was hear less of me to push you ladies for so long without making mor frequent stops on our journey. No wonder you collapsed wit exhaustion. I myself slept like the dead last night."

The motion of his brows and the shadows beneath his eye belied the truth of this statement, but Abby felt no empath for him. Moreover, he knew it was not tiredness which cause her to faint. Perhaps he was trying to spare her further humil ation, but it was past time for such measures.

"Traveling is deadening, isn't it?" drawled the woman b his side, her hazel eyes sparkling cynically. "And Julian i always in a hurry. In all the years we've toured together, in a the places we've been, he promises and promises to take more leisurely pace the next time and the next, but he neve does. I can understand why you would swoon." Affectin heavy concern, she added, "I trust you won't become ill."

"I won't," Abby said firmly. "I feel quite recovered today.

"I hope you didn't faint because of me," said the gir "Tommy told me I look like a ghost in my white dress. I gues you don't know Tommy. He's the muck-boy and is always sa ing silly things. Did I frighten you?"

"No, of course you did not," Abby said.

"Oh." The child's face fell.

Julian replaced his teacup in its saucer, making a loud clatter. "My manners have deserted me. Abby, may I introduce my assistant, Harriet Snell, and her daughter, Colleen."

So they were not married. Abby could not decide whether to feel relief or distress that her own wedding had not been an act of bigamy—unless, of course, Julian had more beautiful ladies hidden at Avilion, one or several of whom would prove to be his wife, or wives. One never knew.

While she exchanged nods with her new acquaintances, Julian rang the bell beside his dish. Immediately, a sturdy-looking footman entered through the service door and offered to serve Abby's plate. She accepted a boiled egg and toast. While the servant filled her teacup, she noticed Harriet studying her. Something nasty stirred within Abby's breast, and she smiled sweetly.

"I shall have to be careful not to call you Hilda, for that is how I first knew you," she said. "I suppose you don't like using your real name on the stage, since such an occupation is . . . unusual for a woman."

"Oh, you may call me anything you like," Harriet returned, laughing lightly. "Only do not call me Harry, for that is Julian's particular name for me."

Abby ducked her head as if she had been struck. She tried to disguise the motion by sipping her tea. The scalding liquid was hot enough to boil chestnuts. She pressed her lips together painfully and vowed not to be disparaging in the future.

Into the uncomfortable quiet which followed, Colleen said, "I have something to show you, Papa. Are you finished with the newspaper?"

The magician's eyes widened. "I'm almost afraid to say yes."

"I promise not to spill anything. I've been practicing and practicing, and besides, there's no water in this trick."

He slid the newspaper across the table. "Very well then,

you may have it. But count yourself warned, Abby. Quick movement may become necessary."

Colleen threw him a look of disgust and lifted the newspaper. After tearing off one sheet, she halved it, gathered the fragment and her empty water glass and walked to the end of the table. Standing on the chair, she wrapped the paper around the glass, leaving only the mouth and an inch below it uncovered. She then pulled a button from her pocket and placed it on the table.

"Do you see this button?" she intoned. "I am going to push it through the table."

"Impossible," Julian declared loudly.

Colleen grinned. "You shall see." She covered the button with the upturned glass, waved her hands over it, then pushed. Breathing deeply in concentration, she lifted the glass, stared at the button which still remained on the table, and frowned. "Oh, dear!" she cried, apparently in great distress. "Something has gone wrong!"

Harriet's mouth twitched. "No! And you have practiced so hard!"

"Perhaps you should try again," the magician ventured.

"Very well," Colleen said tiredly. "Whatever you wish."

Puzzled, Abby watched as the child again placed the glass over the button and pushed. To her astonishment, the newspaper collapsed flat.

"Goodness!" Collen exclaimed. "Now I have pushed too hard and the *glass* has gone through the wood!" To prove her statement, she brought the water glass from her lap and set it on the table, then dissolved into giggles.

"Well done, sweetheart!" Harriet enthused, clapping her hands.

"It's evident we shall have to add you to the tour before long," said the magician.

"You're very young to perform so well," added Abby, impressed, as she tried to ignore the look of fatherly pride in Julian's eyes.

Colleen frowned as she returned to her seat. "I'm eight."

"Oh, I hadn't realized you were that old," Abby amended, smiling. "But even so, I couldn't learn to do such a thing, not at any age."

"Yes, you can," the girl said expansively. "I'll teach you how. Would you like to learn after breakfast?"

"That's good of you," Julian said. "But Abby is scheduled for a session with Mrs. White, and later she may want to explore Avilion or rest."

"Oh, you're to have some new gowns," said Colleen. "Mrs. White is the best dressmaker in the world, isn't that so, Mamma? She makes Papa Julian's costumes, too. She stitched this dress I'm wearing. Do you like it?"

"Yes, I do," Abby replied. "The sprigs match your pretty red hair precisely." Her expression cooled as she turned back to the magician. "However, I need not trouble your Mrs. White. I'll hardly be here long enough to warrant new clothes."

Before Julian could reply, Colleen bubbled, "Oh, do you think my hair is pretty? Tommy says red-haired women are mean and ugly and have nasty tempers."

Harriet's nostrils flared. "Miss Shelley is allowing you to spend entirely too much time with the stableboys."

"Oh, Tommy doesn't mean you, Mamma. Everybody knows *you* are kind and beautiful." She stirred her porridge sadly, leaving them to draw their own conclusions.

"But you are beautiful as well," Abby declared reassuringly.

At the same instant, Harriet said, "You are far prettier than I, sweetheart."

The women exchanged startled glances. A grateful light flashed in Harriet's eyes, then disappeared. Abby felt a brief kinship with this woman who so obviously doted on her child.

The moment passed.

Julian cleared his throat. "There is not a lady at this table who is not lovely. But I must insist on the dress-fitting, Abby, since you were unable to bring many clothes with you. Besides, we don't know how long your stay may be."

Abby placed her knife and fork in her dish and nodded for the footman to remove it. She glanced at Harriet and her daughter, then lowered her gaze. "If you have a moment, I would like to speak with you."

"Is that terrible man still after you?" Colleen asked. "Mamma said you and Papa were pretending to be married so he couldn't hurt you."

The magician rose so abruptly he almost knocked over his chair. "If you are finished, Abby . . ."

She nodded and followed him from the room. Behind her she heard Colleen asking, "Did I say something bad, Mamma?"

Abby pretended not to hear, as did Julian. He led her to a parlour across the hall and gestured toward a pair of chairs separated by a low table with legs carved to resemble snarling dog's heads. Staring at the table, she sat in one chair while he took the other.

"Now, about the dressmaker . . ." he began.

With difficulty she tore her gaze from a vicious-looking set of canine fangs and looked at him. "How can you speak to me of dresses? I believe there are more important things to discuss."

"The only important thing is keeping you safe."

"Indeed. I thought a great deal about that last night, and I have come to the conclusion that I am safe enough already. Philip must believe we are married and will have abandoned any plans for interfering. If it were otherwise, we should have seen him by now. Therefore I'm confident the best course for me is to journey to a new city, find employment, and have our marriage annulled. If we *are* married, that is."

"If we are—Abby, what do you think the past week was all about? Why did we go to Scotland?"

She averted her eyes from his bewilderment and forced herself to speak calmly. "I cannot say with certainty. Since we've come to Avilion, I have learned the most surprising thing about you; in particular, that you are capable of hiding information that even the most inconsiderate person would give

Nothing you do shocks me now, so perhaps you will understand my doubts concerning the legality of our wedding."

He leaned toward her beseechingly. "Abby—"

She motioned him back. "Don't waste your concern on me. I will not weep or faint anymore so that you may inflate your opinion of yourself by pretending to help me." Her words gathered heat. "How I must have amused you, throwing myself at you as I did. One might believe you would have mentioned a mistress and daughter to me, but that is only how *I* think. It appears that *you* possess a different thought process altogether."

She stopped, breathless. Her blood pounded at her boldness—she had not intended to tell him how she felt, had planned to act cool and indifferent—but how astonishingly right it seemed. He'd deserved every word she'd spoken. The sight of his closely reined distress did not subtract one whit from her sense of vindication.

Or if it did, it was only the most niggling amount.

"Very well, Abby," he said quietly. "It shall be as you say, but I beg you to allow at least a fortnight to pass before you leave. We should know Philip's mind by then."

She was surprised to feel a rush of disappointment. She had not expected him to give in so easily. And had she detected a glimmer of relief in his eyes? Well, he was a man for playing games, wasn't he?

At the very least he could have offered an explanation for his behaviour. A portion of her heart had hoped desperately for him to deny that Harriet was his mistress. She wanted to hear him say it was only a coincidence Colleen resembled him, and that she called him *Papa* because she liked him so much. Since he appeared disinclined to do so, she raised her chin and stood, not daring to risk speech now.

He escorted her into the hall. "You must, however, spend the morning with Mrs. White. To be brutally honest with you, I have grown tired of your yellow and green gowns, and that

brown thing you wear offends me. Please, for my sake, allo
her to work up a few alternatives."

Abby's eyes flamed with renewed indignation. Witho
speaking, she turned and mounted the stairs, leaving him
watch her in eloquent silence.

A short while later, Powell, the butler, brought a salver lade
with correspondence into the parlour. He was a little man—
midget, in truth—who had been discovered by Lord Julian
a fairgrounds sideshow during the early days of his caree
Powell made up for his lack of stature by a natural gracefulne
and a great affection for the man who had rescued him fro
the hard life he'd been leading.

Powell hesitated a moment when he saw his master sitti
and staring at his boots. Softening his tread, he approache
him and whispered in his high, compressed voice, "Your ma
milord."

"Thank you, Powell. Just leave it on the table."

"There's a lot of it. You've been gone a long time."

Julian glanced at the pile. "Yes. I'll look at it in awhile."

"Miss Harriet wouldn't let me give it to you last night. Sa
you'd be too tired."

"She was right. Get off with you now, I want to be alone

Undeterred, the butler continued, "Did I tell you how sor
I am about your papa?"

"Yes, yes, you did."

"Last night when Francis told us, we were all sorry, th
whole household was. I hope you're not feeling bad about hir
Miss Harriet said you didn't want any fuss, that we're not
go into mourning."

"That's right, she's always right. Now go before I make yo
disappear."

Powell snorted. "You'd cut off your right arm before you
let anything happen to me."

"I wouldn't depend on it." He waved him toward the doc

"I'm leaving, I'm leaving. But at least the mystery's solved now."

"Mystery?"

"Yes, about the black-bordered note in your mail. It came right after you left. Don't mind telling you it worried me. Now I know it must be about your papa's death."

Julian looked up. "Black-bordered note?"

"Yes, milord," Powell said, adding in an aggrieved voice, "It's in your mail over there. I've been trying to tell you."

The magician jumped to his feet and began scattering letters in all directions. Within seconds he found the missive, an elegant page of stationery that was sealed with the Donberry crest. While the butler bent to retrieve the castaway mail, Julian walked a few paces away and broke the seal with shaking fingers.

Moments later, he said in a flat voice, "Fetch Francis."

Powell had never seen his master look so lost. He ran to obey.

Julian was pacing when Francis arrived. "The most surprising thing has happened," he said without preamble. "I have received a letter from my father's steward. It's the first letter from my birthplace that I have ever received. In it he tells me the most astonishing news. Did you know my family has had my location all these years and never once attempted to contact me?"

Francis stood silently, knowing there was no answer to his wrath.

"My father had me followed, it seems. Lord Merlyn and Avilion have never been a secret to any of my family. Nor were the early years, the years when I nearly starved. None of them lifted a finger to help me. Perhaps they found it amusing that I struggled to earn my living performing magic. I wonder what they made of it. I wonder what my father thought."

He clenched the note and brought it close to his face in helpless rage. "And now I shall never know! I shall never speak to my father again, nor to Edmond, nor Seth either, for they are all dead! All! And now Carl is ailing, and the steward suspects foul play. He does not state it openly, but his suspicions are between the lines: *Michael*. So I am to abandon the life I have made and rush to Donberry Castle to settle things. I am cut from my father's will and my brothers' affections, you understand, but only I can help! Well, what think you of this, Francis? You, who are more brother to me than any of my natural ones. What say you?"

Francis allowed none of the compassion he felt to show in his face. "I think we're in for another journey."

Julian's breath exploded through his mouth. He turned abruptly and stalked to the window. "You're right, of course. Start packing at once, Francis. Powell, tell Bugbee to see to the carriage."

Both men hurried to obey, but before Francis left the room, Julian called him back. "You'll need to inform Abby and her maid that we're traveling again. I am too much of a coward to do so myself."

"They won't be happy," Francis replied.

"I know, and I'm sorry for it; but I'll not abandon her to be caught by Philip Demere." As Julian charged past his servant, he added under his breath, "Will nothing in this world ever be right again?"

Twelve

Over the next three days of hard traveling, Abby's deep silences and her maid's accusing looks drove Julian to ride outside the coach with Francis. The chill winds and unceasing rain of late autumn satisfied the darkness of his mood. It seemed a fitting punishment for his actions, though looking back he knew he could have done nothing differently.

He did, however, think Francis might be more understanding. The valet scarcely spoke to him during the whole of the journey. Finally, when they were drawing near to the Donberry border, Julian had had enough. He urged his horse to a trot and motioned for his servant to follow. When they were some distance from the coach, he slowed his mount to a walk.

"We're almost home," he called through a veil of drizzle, then shuddered. What childish yearning had prompted him to name the castle home? Not wanting to think about it, he shifted his weight on the saddle and sent a piercing look to the valet, who appeared to be lost in a stoic daze. "Why don't you speak your mind, Francis, before we arrive and I have other things to occupy me besides your ill temper?"

Francis kept his gaze on the road ahead. "There's nothing wrong with my temper, milord."

"No? This morning you allowed me to tie my own cravat, and you see to what results. You avoid looking or speaking to me and act on the whole as if I've grown another head. I suppose you're still angry about Harriet. Well, let me assure you we shall soon return to our former lives."

Green eyes regarded him stonily. "You've hurt her."

"You weary me, Francis. We have been over and over it. There is nothing to be done."

"I'm not talking about Miss Harriet, milord."

Julian looked at him a moment, water dripping into his eyes. "Oh." His mount slithered into a patch of mud, and he tugged on the reins, then returned his attention to Francis. "You surprise me. I thought you had no great affection for my wife."

The servant shrugged. "At first I believed she was only after your title and wealth. Now I know better. She's a fine lady." *Better than you deserve,* his eyes said. "Fond of you, too, for some reason. Why don't you tell her the truth?"

The magician's jaw tightened. "I haven't lied to her."

"That may be, but you're letting her think some things that aren't right. What would you call that, if not lying?"

"Her safety and well-being are always foremost in my thoughts," he said evasively. *Especially her safety from me.* "Not how she perceives my life."

Francis's lips tightened into a thin line. "You could make her feel better if you'd talk. It pains me to watch her. She can't hide her feelings like Miss Harriet."

The weight across Julian's chest sank a little deeper. "Thank you, Francis. Thank you for telling me what I already know. Did it never occur to you there might be a reason for my silence? Perhaps you don't understand everything as you seem to think."

The valet eyed him speculatively, then grunted. "I'll tell you what I think. You're a devil to go on letting her feel like she does when a simple word or two could change all. Milord."

Without looking at him again, Francis turned his horse about and rejoined the carriage.

Julian watched him through narrowed eyes, thinking angrily, *Pack your bags and leave, tyrant.* But he knew he'd never speak the words. What was worse, Francis knew it, too.

An hour later, they ascended the final hill leading to Donberry Castle. Julian had continued to ride some distance in front of the carriage. It was necessary to be alone when he saw his birthplace for the first time in ten years.

And there it was at last; the proud, ancient structure he knew so well, set among a vast expanse of rolling pastureland and clusters of woods with a river shining in the distance. In the early afternoon light, the edifice seemed to float among the hills like an earthbound cloud-castle. No folly this; the castle had been held by the Donberry family for centuries. The crenels and merlons were authentic, and real iron and stone missiles had been thrown more than once through the machicolations. Or so the family legends went. He saw that a black flag waved above one bartizan; the family crest from another.

Pulling his horse to a stop, he stared until the carriage almost caught up with him. Hearing it creaking behind him, sensing Francis drawing near, he stirred forward again. He had no patience for his valet—his friend's—condemnation, nor did he desire his sympathy. What he wanted was to be alone. No, rather, he wished to turn around and retreat to the security of Avilion. Perhaps that would settle the hammering in his chest. But he moved on.

The walls which once surrounded the castle had long since crumbled to an ineffective, though interesting, ruin. Julian and his party moved through the gates without impediment and pulled into a cobblestoned courtyard worthy of the largest inn.

The magician dismounted, handed his reins to Francis, and moved slowly toward the shallow steps that led to the front door. Before he touched the knocker, he looked back at the carriage and saw Abby watching him from the carriage. Her dark eyes were solemn, her face pale. At the moment he saw no hurt or resentment in her features, only anxiety. He gave her what he hoped was an encouraging smile, but his lips moved like wood.

With a surge of anger—his anger was not far beneath the surface these days—he clanged the metal ring against the door two times, slowly. It was the family knock, the knock they used when late hours or unexpected arrivals caused one of them to stand upon their own doorstep waiting for admittance. After all these years, he had used it without thinking. Feeling a kind of horror at himself, he lifted his hand to knock a third time, and perhaps a fourth. But the door swung open before he could do so, and a tall, silver-haired butler looked at him inquiringly.

"Good day to you, Dickens," the magician said.

It was difficult not to be amused by the procession of emotions which crossed the butler's face: aloofness, surprise, then incredulity. "Lord Julian," he said in an amazed voice. " 'Pon my soul!"

"I suppose you never expected to see me again. You are more stout than I remembered, but you carry it well. But where are your manners, Dickens? I am melting in the rain. Are you not going to admit me?"

The butler's face became a study in conflict. "My lord, I . . ." He looked behind him, as if to find an answer in the hall. "I'm sorry, I don't know if—"

"Dickens, my father is dead. It was he who banished me, not my remaining brothers." When the black-clad servant still wavered, he added, "Even if you refuse me, surely you cannot deny shelter to my wife, who is beyond weariness?" He paused. "And given to swooning, I might add."

Dickens peered at the carriage, then came to a decision. "Come in, my lord. You may rest in the hall while I speak with Lord Michael." His features looked pinched, as if he feared the outcome of such an interview.

Dread seized Julian. Was he too late? "Shouldn't you rather consult with Carl? He's all right, isn't he?"

"Lord Donberry is too ill for visitors today. Lord Michael has been acting in his stead."

Julian relaxed. After waving for the occupants of the carriage to join him, he turned back to the servant. "To speak truth, I should like to see the steward first. Is he on the premises?"

"Mr. O'Reilly is in his office, my lord. I will fetch him."

While the butler disappeared into the interior, Julian raced down the steps and offered Abby his escort, which she took willingly enough, though she would probably have been happy to accept anyone's. At this moment she looked woebegone and overawed, her gaze wandering the length and height of the castle in undisguised astonishment. When they crossed the threshold, she stumbled a little, too taken with the dizzying three-storied ceiling of the great hall to mind the uneven stones of the floor.

With her hand gripping his arm, he suddenly saw the castle through her eyes—its vastness, its coldness despite colorful tapestries on the walls, rugs beneath their feet, and a roaring fire in a hearth big enough to roast a horse. Emotions flooded from her into him. He imagined what she imagined. Rushes on the floor. Crude torches projecting from the walls. Crowds of roughly dressed peasants gnawing joints of meat and throwing the bones to the dogs. She was not seeing what was really there—the improvements his father had made, the comfortable furniture groupings, the expensive wooden tables and flowers. Donberry was as homelike as a castle could be, but she was frightened to the quick by her gothic imaginings. He wanted to crush her to him and kiss away every fear. Instead, he led her to a settee near the fire and dropped her arm.

"Remember your father's interest in architects and buildings," he counseled in a low voice. "Donberry is only a pile of stones."

She looked at him in surprise. He smiled reassuringly, but she did not respond. He was glad to note, however, that the terror had faded from her eyes.

Charlotte Ann rushed to sit beside her, intent on preventing anyone else from doing so, namely him. He gave the maid a faintly reproachful look, but he'd not planned on joining Abby. It was far too dangerous.

In the center back of the room was a wide, stone staircase that separated halfway up and led to the two wings of the castle. As he moved to speak with Francis, he heard someone descending the stairs behind him with a quiet, unhesitating step. He knew that sound as surely as if he'd heard it yesterday. Blood pounded in his temples. Something in his face caused Francis to respond with a forward movement, but Julian shook his head slightly. He forced his features into a calm mask, turned and walked a few paces toward the steps.

"Hello, Michael," he said.

Lord Michael paused and looked at him. Puzzlement passed across his face, then a flare of recognition. The faint pink in his cheeks drained away, leaving his skin sallow and slack. Then, with a recovery the magician could only admire, he smiled tightly.

"Why, hello, Julian. What an unexpected pleasure." He descended the remaining stairs and shook his brother's hand, releasing his grip almost immediately. "You've changed since I saw you last."

"Have I? You look precisely the same." And it was true. Michael had been a man when Julian left but had aged well. With a rush of shock, Julian realized how much alike they now appeared. Save for his brother's lighter hair and heavier frame, he could almost be looking into a mirror.

"To what do we owe the pleasure of your visit after all this time? Not that I'm unhappy to see you, of course." Lord Michael's features took on a solemn cast. "You know we have lost Father. Is that why you've come?"

"Yes, partly. I thought a visit to my remaining brothers was long overdue."

"So it is, so it is. Then you must have heard the terrible news about Seth and Edmond as well. Such tragedies. Our family has been living under a cloud these past two years." His glacial blue eyes warmed with interest. "As a matter of curiosity, who told you?" When Julian shifted uncomfortably, he added, "Was it Carl?"

Julian inclined his head noncommittally.

"Ah, I thought so. Alas, now poor Carl has taken ill, too. You see it's as I said. We live under a cloud. But such things often happen in families. People go on happily enough for many years, then tragedy strikes again and again." He clasped his hands together loudly, then looked at the group nestled around the fire. "And you have brought friends with you, I see."

Julian followed him to the others and performed introductions.

"So you are married," Lord Michael said, viewing Abby with sharp speculation. "This is a new development, for I had not heard of it." He turned with evident embarrassment to Julian. "You'll forgive me, I hope. Father informed us of your whereabouts and activities from time to time."

"Yes, so I've been told."

Lord Michael's gaze lingered on Julian's face searchingly, then wandered back to Abby. "But how charming she is, how lovely. Would you allow me to escort you to my wife's chamber, Lady Julian? I am certain she will be delighted to meet you. Or would you rather rest first?"

In a strained voice, Abby said, "I should like to meet her." It was apparent she was afraid to say otherwise.

"Good, good. And will you join us, Julian?"

"I regret I must delay seeing Nina; I need to speak with my servant regarding the horses."

"Ah, yes, it's Francis, isn't it? I remember you. Well, come then, Lady Julian. To be truthful, I'm glad my brother doesn't join us. Nina is often overcome if several visitors attend her at once. Another time, then, Julian."

The magician squared his shoulders and took a quick breath. "Do I understand you will permit us to remain a few days?"

"My brother," said Lord Michael with a large smile, "I can think of nothing that would please me more."

"Lord Seth was the first," Calvin O'Reilly said to Julian a short while later in the small, dark room that was the steward's office. "Happened well over a year ago. Shot by his own pistol while he was cleaning it. Least that's what was put about."

"But you think otherwise," Julian said, staring intently at the short, ginger-haired man sitting behind a desk crowded with maps and books. Incomprehensibly, there were several boxes of earth on the desk top as well.

O'Reilly snorted. "Who wouldn't? Lord Seth scarcely ever handled a gun in his life, let alone cleaned one. Only thing he ever touched was his paintbrushes. Except for his women, that is. He handled plenty of them."

The steward pursed his lips. "I wouldn't have suspected Lord Michael if it hadn't been for the other things he'd done. There were all those times with the servants. You remember from when you were here. And then that little maid . . ." He dropped his gaze and pushed one of the boxes absently with his fingers. His knuckles were swollen and arthritic. "I never believed you had anything to do with that girl's death."

Julian swallowed. "It's good to hear you say so, Calvin. Even now."

"Yes, well, I was too afraid in those days to speak up. Lord Donberry was a powerful man, though he changed mightily after you left."

"Did he?" Julian asked in dispassionate tones.

"He did, my lord. I'm thinking he knew what was what, but a more stubborn man has never been found. Couldn't admit it to himself or anyone else that he'd made a mistake. And then, he always had something against you. None of us could understand it."

The magician shifted uncomfortably and returned to the subject at hand. "What happened to Edmond?"

"His reins broke and he fell off his saddle!" exclaimed O'Reilly with indignation. "You remember what a horseman he was, don't you? A fine soldier, too. For him to fall off his beast and crack his skull on the fence . . . Well. Seemed unfair, somehow, though he died instantly and didn't suffer."

"It sounds like a terrible accident."

"If it weren't for my suspecting Lord Michael, I'd have thought so, too. But there I was, mourning Lord Edmond—don't mind telling you he was always my favorite of you boys, a real man's man he was—and next thing I know, I'm looking over his saddle and gear, just wondering. That's when I found his reins had shallow cuts in several places, as if somebody was taking no chances he'd come out of his morning jumps alive."

Julian rubbed his temples; he was getting a devilish headache. "Do you suspect Michael of my father's death, too?"

"I'm not so sure about that. Lord Donberry had a heart seizure about, oh . . . two or three years ago. Afterwards he was an invalid, lying abed all the time. Those were bitter days, I have to say. He was not a good patient. Looked like it was going to go on that way forever. But after the two boys died, the old man took a downward slide. Still, he was as stubborn about dying as he was everything else, and it surprised me when he finally did go. Peaceful, it was; in his sleep. Lord Michael was fairly done up for a while, so I can't say I suspect him there.

"It's Lord Carl that I'm worried about. Guess I should call him Donberry now, though there's not been enough time for the title to be his officially. Anyway, one minute he's hale and hearty; the next, sick as a dying dog. He's been that way since the funeral."

"Is there a chance grief has made him ill?"

"Not a bit of it. He and your sire were never close, leastways not after you left. Lord Carl always knew him for what he was."

Once again Julian wished he hadn't come. O'Reilly was dealing in speculation and had little proof. Even Edmond's cut reins could be caused by the natural deterioration of leather. And though it wouldn't surprise him if Michael had turned his murderous impulses toward his own family, he found himself oddly reluctant to believe it. As he pondered, his gaze fell to the desk top, where O'Reilly continued to fiddle with the boxes of soil.

The steward saw him. "Soil samples," he explained. "From our east and west fields. I plan to send them off to the Board of Agriculture for their recommendations. I've been studying Thaer's work and Humphry Davy's, too. We've been using compost, lime, and marl. Wheat production's up to an average of twenty-two bushels an acre, but I'm hoping to do better."

"You've always been an excellent steward," Julian said, his eyes glazing.

Bristling with pleasure, O'Reilly waved his hand modestly. "I can't claim the estate saw all that in profits. We had a blasted invasion of rats get to the grain, but the problem's controlled now. Got rid of the ugly creatures, I did."

Sensing the man was ready to explain more on the subject, Julian blinked and added quickly, "Why have you asked me to come? What do you think I can do?"

O'Reilly looked at him as if he were a simpleton. "I'm hoping you'll stop Lord Michael before he becomes the new marquess."

Stunned, Julian stared back. That was it, of course. Michael and his twisted plans. He meant to have the title and all that went with it. Unless, of course—

"Did none of my brothers have sons?"

Shaking his head, the steward leaned forward, making his chair squeak. "You know Lord Carl married late. He and Lady Carl had a son; I guess that was after you left. But the boy died young of a wasting disease. Their daughter—you remember Louise—is in finishing school. Lord Edmond now, he was married two years before his little bride died; and marriage never appealed to swoony-eyed Seth. And, not that it matters to his succession, Lord Michael's wife has had three stillbirths but no live children. I guess it's possible they still have a chance, though Lady Michael is getting on now."

"So only Carl stands in his way."

"That's right, my lord."

Julian opened his hands helplessly. "What can I do, Calvin? You have no proof. Do you think a magistrate would investigate on the basis of our suspicions?"

The older man appeared reluctant to answer. He rubbed the stubble on his chin and looked into the distance. "Well . . . to speak truth, I thought you might use your magic." When Julian's eyes narrowed, O'Reilly explained, "I know your family gave you trouble about it, and a lot of the servants were afraid of you; but I never felt like the others did. Seems to me if the good Lord gives you something special, you should use it."

"I wish," Julian said slowly, "you had said that to me then."

"I wish I had, too. It's been on my conscience all these years. But I didn't want to lose my position. I have a wife and five children. Fear can make you do bad things. I never forgot you, though. That's why I wrote. You've made a life for yourself as a stage-magician, but I'm asking you to use your real magic. You can do something, can't you?"

Julian gave him a measuring glance, wondering how far this intelligent man's patience would stretch. Judging by the eagerness in his eyes, not far. "It's not possible for me to predict. The ability I have is not always dependable. Ordinarily, I must touch either the person involved or an object that he has touched in order to learn anything, and even then I might see nothing." He stared at his boots. "And to speak truth, I don't like to use it."

"Oh," said the other dully, scratching his ear. "Surely you'd be willing for such an important reason. But I thought you could look at him and know what he was going to do next, like a fortune-teller."

"No, it's not like that. Most of what I read has to do with events in the past, though occasionally I catch a glimpse of the future."

Suddenly thinking of Abby, he shivered. He would give all not to know—but no, he did not mean that. *Don't think of it.*

Crossing one leg over the other, he continued, "Reading

Michael's intentions would be difficult. I need more than an instant to form a bond, and he knows it. You should have seen how quickly he ended our handshake awhile ago. I know he won't permit me to touch him for an extended period of time."

O'Reilly continued to watch him hopefully. After a long, uncomfortable moment, Julian sighed. "All right, I'll try, but I think I'll have more luck with the objects than I would with Michael. What about Edmond's reins; do you have them? And Seth's gun?"

O'Reilly nodded and rose with arthritic painfulness from his chair. He withdrew a key from his pocket, stepped to a wall of cabinets beside the desk, and unlocked one of them. He handed the items to Julian.

The magician held first the gun, then the reins, for a long time. Try as he would, he could feel only sorrow and loss. "It's no use," he said at last. "Perhaps it has been too long since their deaths. Or too many people have touched the objects."

The steward struggled to hide his disappointment. "There must be something you can do. Maybe you could speak with Lord Carl."

"Yes," Julian replied slowly. "Perhaps I should."

Abby wanted to go home, if only she had a home. Any place would be better than Lady Michael's sitting room and the maddening strangers within it.

"Lady Julian is shaking with cold," Lord Michael said solicitously. "Why don't you offer your seat to her, my dear?"

Without looking at her husband, Lady Michael rose immediately from her chair beside the fireplace. "Of course," she said meekly, her blank eyes finding Abby, then lowering. "Please, sit."

"Oh, no, that's not necessary, thank you. I am perfectly comfortable on the loveseat, and it's almost as close to the fire as your chair."

Unheeding, the woman continued to stand in front of her. When Abby thought she detected a brief, pleading spark in the lady's eyes, she said in exasperation, "Oh, very well," and exchanged places. She darted a resentful look in Lord Michael's direction. He appeared to misinterpret it, for he smiled graciously and inclined his head.

It had not taken long to sense the order of things here. In his treatment of his wife, Lord Michael reminded her sharply of Philip; only Michael was much worse. According to Julian, his brother had committed murder, perhaps more than once. It was possible he had even killed members of his own family.

She had been afraid to come, afraid to leave the relative safety of Avilion and throw herself into this hornet's nest. But Julian had been certain he could protect her, that she was in no danger. Now she wished for the hundredth time that she had left him for parts unknown. It would have been a safer course. But the force of his will had persuaded her, just as Philip's so often had.

And now, observing Lord and Lady Michael, she understood the futility of constantly subjugating oneself beneath the desires of another. Lord Michael's wife, Nina, had been a beautiful woman—could still be beautiful, did her features have any spark of life in them at all—but had faded into a mouse. Brown hair, gray eyes, an elegant figure within an expensive rose silk gown, but no soul, no will of her own.

Abby surreptitiously looked for bruises on her arms but saw none. Perhaps all her bruises were hidden, if not beneath her gown, then under her bones. The deeper ones, she knew, were more painful.

Her ire grew by the moment. The fear she had felt in Lord Michael's presence had almost completely gone, to be replaced with increasing wrath. He was like a magnet drawing her disappointment and rage. How different was Michael from Julian, really? And how different was Julian from Philip? She could trust no one. Not any longer.

It would be a happy day when she walked from all their

lives forever. The only person she would regret not seeing again was Colleen, who in only an hour had utterly charmed her. It was unconscionable the child's father had been unwilling to marry her mother.

And why hadn't he? she wondered, staring into the flames and trying to attend Lord Michael's patter. Julian had married her, a stranger, in order to rescue her from a terrible fate—or so he'd said, though she couldn't think of any other reason why he would have done so. Why, then, had he not wed the woman who carried his child? It seemed alien to his character to behave in such a manner.

But then, perhaps he had no character worth mentioning. Perhaps he acted only on whims, like a weather vane spinning in a gale.

One corner of her mind cried, *How can you think so about Julian?* She tried to stifle it.

"Lady Julian, you are tired," Lord Michael said in an amused voice. "I have asked you twice how it was you and my brother met, and both times you have only stared at me."

"I'm sorry," Abby said, stirring to attention. "We met at one of his performances."

He laughed toward the ceiling. "How like Julian. I'll warrant your parents were horrified at having a magician calling on their daughter. I'm sure it was necessary for him to give his true name before they allowed him to pay his addresses to you."

An inner prompting cautioned her to tell no more than was needful. She shrugged her shoulders delicately and smiled. Turning to Nina, who sat with her hands folded in her lap, she asked, "How did you meet Lord Michael?"

The lady glanced at Abby, then back at her hands. "I—"

"She is the daughter of a squire in northeast Donberry," Lord Michael interrupted. "Her father visited here frequently to seek the expert advice of our steward on farming. Because of those visits, he has a thriving vineyard now. As time passed, it was natural to invite him to dine with us, and our fathers became friends. Soon the families were exchanging visits, and so we met."

Abby spared him the briefest of looks, then directed another question to Nina. "What things do you do to occupy your time?"

"Nina does fine needlework, don't you, dear? Do notice the crewel-work on the dining chair cushions tonight, and you'll see her handiwork."

"I look forward to it," Abby snapped. "Perhaps tonight, Nina, you will explain how you stitched them. Unless, of course, your husband knows that as well."

The room fell silent. Mindful of her rudeness yet glad of it, Abby kept her attention on the other woman. Nina did not lift her eyes, but her interlaced fingers tightened until the knuckles turned white.

Lord Michael laughed suddenly. "I am reproved!" he cried. "Julian has found a spirited wife, I see. How I envy him! But alas, dear lady, Nina does not often join us at table. She is far too retiring to enjoy company, and prefers her meals served in her rooms."

He rose abruptly. "I think it's time we left now; you'll have no wish to tire her. And I'm certain you'll want to rest before dinner. Allow me to escort you to your room."

Abby took her leave as graciously as she could and followed him into the wide corridor. To her discomfort, he bundled her arm into his and set a slow pace.

"Dear Lady Julian. Do you have a Christian name of your own, by the by, and may I address you as such?"

"You may call me Abigail."

"You sound eager to do away with your beloved's name. Has the romance worn thin so quickly?"

She made no reply but could not disguise the blush on her cheeks.

"Alas, have I hit upon a tender spot? Forgive me. I suspected Julian was unworthy of so lovely a lady. And, from the looks of things, yours was a hasty wedding. If you'd had more time, you wouldn't have made such a mistake."

At her questioning look, he grinned. "How did I know? Why, your ring, of course. Julian has not troubled to supply you with a proper wedding band, and you are forced to wear the childhood ring his mother left him. I couldn't help noticing you've had to wrap a ribbon around the band to keep it from falling off. My brother is such a romantic."

She glanced at the ring, then slowly lowered her hand until it was hidden among her skirts. "I have only told you my given name as you asked. You are making too much of a small matter."

"Oh? Perhaps I've misunderstood. Shall I have a single bed chamber prepared for the newlyweds, rather than an adjoining suite?"

"No!" she cried. "That is, I mean . . . the suite will be more suitable."

He gave her a sympathetic look and patted her arm. "Say no more, my dear. I understand these things perfectly. Before marriage, one's prospective partner can seem the embodiment of every romantic dream ever envisioned. Afterwards, the faults, the misunderstandings, the deceptions—all these steal away the attractiveness of that idealized person. I know what you are enduring. I've gone through the same disappointment myself."

"I have not said—"

"It was not necessary; I see it in your eyes. He has disillusioned you. No, do not protest. You are still loyal, and I find that admirable. But if ever you need a shoulder to lean upon, I am here."

She stared up at him, appalled. In the dimming light, his eyes—eyes so like, yet unlike, Julian's—glimmered with brittle concern.

"I meant that in the most respectable way, of course," he added. "You have misinterpreted my words as something unseemly, though I must say the thought is diverting. It would not be the first time Julian and I . . . How shall I phrase it? To offend you would devastate me. Allow me to say it would not be the first occasion when my brother and I have shared the same . . . interests. How does Harriet and her little daughter, by the way?"

She could not mistake his meaning. Abby jerked her arm from his and stepped backward. She glanced frantically at the bedroom doors bordering the corridor and bumped into a table behind her.

His face lengthened. "What, did he not tell you about Harriet? Doesn't she still live in her little cottage behind—what is it called now, it is something fanciful; ah, yes—Avilion?"

"Where—which one is my room?" she asked in a strangled voice. He had better tell her soon, for she was going to be sick.

"You seemed shocked, yet you must have known about Harriet; he would never expel her from that cottage. Not with the child. Not *he.*"

He began to breathe rapidly, a sudden storm of rage building within him. But the swiftness with which he calmed himself frightened her more than his wrath had done. Within seconds, he smiled briefly and touched his cravat as though checking for wrinkles.

"I perceive Julian has lied to you. Forgive me for being the one to tell you."

Abby's mind began to move again. "A moment," she said, pressing her arms against her stomach. "If you—if you and he . . ." Her mouth worked soundlessly. "Which one of you is Colleen's father?"

A startled light came into his eyes, then disappeared. Slowly, a smile spread across his face. "Oh, my dear." His voice dripped with concern. "I would tell you if I could, but . . . who can say?"

Dark spots floated before Abby's eyes. "Dear God." She turned her back to him. "Why did neither of you marry her?"

"My sweet Abigail, it was impossible. I was already married, and so was Harriet, to some ne'er-do-well who ran off to sea." With lively interest, he studied her face a moment longer. "Otherwise, I'm certain Julian would have wed her. He was quite mad about the girl."

Thirteen

When Abby reached her bedchamber at last, she closed the door on Lord Michael's profuse and insincere apologies. Leaning her back against the heavy oak door, she stared sightlessly into space.

Charlotte Ann looked up from her unpacking and shivered at her mistress's expression. "Lady Abby? Are you all right?"

Abby stepped to the center of the room. She plunged her fingers into her hair and clenched her scalp so tightly hairpins began to fall. A moment later, she dropped her hands, and several dark curls unwound and fell to her shoulders. Her wild eyes gazed uncomprehendingly at the large-scale furnishings, then focused on Charlotte Ann for the first time.

"I am leaving this terrible house." She sniffed and dashed tears from her eyes. "Do you go with me?"

The maid blanched. "Leaving? Do you mean now?"

"Yes. Immediately."

"But it's raining! And we have no horses, or money, or—"

"We have our legs to carry us, and the public road is no more than a mile away. Something will come along. As to money . . ." She stalked to the door which she hoped led to Julian's bedchamber and knocked. When no answer was forthcoming, she slipped into the room and began searching through drawers, mumbling to herself and flinging undergarments and handkerchiefs and cravats in all directions until she found a small money bag. While the maid observed in horror, she removed several pound notes and sovereigns.

"I'll pay him back when I find employment," she said. "If you'll fetch paper and pen, I'll tell him so."

Charlotte Ann brought the required items. Abby scribbled a few lines and folded the note into the bag. As she did, Julian's ring came into her line of vision. She yanked until the ring came off, then tried to unwind the narrow ribbon which had tightened it to her finger. The task proved too painstaking for her mood, and, heaving an impatient sigh, she bundled ribbon and ring together in the bag.

"Now. Let us depart."

"But—your clothes. I'll need time to pack them again."

"I don't care about that." She raised her chin, which was wobbling so much she could hardly talk. "My gowns are old and ugly anyway. Or so I've been told."

"Well . . . I'd like to have *mine,*" said the maid, who knew what it was to be cold in winter.

"Very well. You stay and pack. As for myself, I refuse to linger another moment in this wicked castle. Words cannot describe how evil this place is, and its people." She stalked toward the door, then turned suddenly. "You do want to come with me, don't you? I can't promise a position, so I'll understand if you wish to remain."

Charlotte Ann looked as if she were seeing a dark pit opening at her feet. She gazed into Abby's dark, troubled eyes and said brokenly, "I should have known it would turn out like this. God is punishing me for running away." She swallowed and wrung her hands. "What would I do here? I'll come."

"Good. It's probably for the best we're leaving separately. I'll tell the butler I mean to stroll the grounds before dinner. You take only what's necessary for you and hide the bag beneath your cloak. When you're ready, inform the butler you intend to fetch me. I'll be waiting at that little farmhouse where the road meets the drive."

"Yes, my lady," Charlotte Ann said weakly. But her thoughts were spinning in another direction.

* * *

Neither the footman nor Carl's personal servant wanted to admit Julian to his brother's chamber. Finally, it was Lord Donberry's wife who heard the disturbance in the sitting room and came to investigate. Her expression was outraged until she became aware of the magician's identity. As recognition dawned, she pushed the servants aside and embraced him.

A smile was on her face when she pulled back, but tears floated in her eyes. "Dear, dear Julian," she whispered. "How glad I am you're here. You're precisely what Carl needs."

He looked at her with a mixture of emotions. How well he remembered Lady Donberry's plump face and form, her generous spirit and ready laugh. Her hair was almost completely gray now, but few lines marked the piquant features that had captured Carl so long ago.

He had felt close to her in those days. Yet after he was so ignominiously exiled, she had never written, never made an attempt to mend the rift between the brothers. Seeing her brave and sorrowful face now, though, he could not find it in his heart to feel resentful.

"Are you certain, Sophia?" he asked. "You don't think I'll disturb him?"

She pressed his hands and swallowed hard. "I'm afraid we're past worrying about disturbances."

He flinched. "Do not say so."

"Pray God I'm wrong," she said, her breath catching on a sob, "but I fear I'm going to lose him."

He pulled her into another embrace. After a moment she broke away and patted his arm. "Allow me to prepare him for your visit. Be careful not to betray your shock when you see him."

While she disappeared into the bedroom, he waited impatiently, ignoring the irritated glances of the valet. Less than a minute later, a weak, masculine voice called his name. He hurried forward. And was nearly undone in spite of Sophia's warning.

His brother Carl had been the tallest and strongest one of them all. Now his body scarcely lifted the bedcovers. His skin, deathly pale, hung loosely over his bones; his eyes were lifeless sapphires buried in rock. Yet he smiled at the sight of his youngest brother, and one hand struggled from the covers to reach toward him.

Julian clasped it immediately and sat on the edge of the bed. In a rush of affection, he brought the hand to his chest. The years dissolved. He saw Carl leading him on his first pony. Teaching him to play whist. Defending him against his other brothers. And then, unbidden: *forcing him into his father's study, believing he had murdered Christine, trusting Michael instead of him.*

He dismissed the thought, concentrated instead on his brother's hand and what it might reveal. To his relief, a vision seemed to be forthcoming. His heart began to race. Carl, Sophia, and the familiar old furnishings of the room faded until he could see only darkness. In the center of the darkness, a hazy light dawned; forms moved and took shape. He watched the images for an unknown length of time.

Gradually he became aware that Carl was speaking to him, had been calling his name repeatedly in a breathless voice. Swallowing his disappointment—for he'd only received forebodings of death, concerns for Sophia, and nothing about Michael—he released Carl's hand, which had begun to flutter in his like a butterfly seeking freedom.

"Still as fey as ever," Lord Donberry whispered, his alarm fading now that Julian had finished.

"I'm sorry." He considered fabricating an explanation, but decided against it. "There was a small hope I'd find the reason for your illness."

"And did you?" Sophia asked anxiously, sitting on the edge of her chair.

"No. He is too full of love for you to think of anything else."

To his dismay, she buried her face in her handkerchief and wept.

Lord Donberry laughed weakly. "There, there, darling. It's a good thing for me he said so. What if he'd found I was thinking of some old love or one of my mistresses? Then you would have real cause for weeping."

Her shoulders shook, but she did not lift her head. "You have no old loves or mistresses," she mumbled into the cloth. "You have never loved anyone but me."

Lifting his shoulders in a tiny shrug, the marquess winked at his brother. "She is never wrong." Suddenly, his face twisted in pain. When the spasm passed, he took several shallow breaths. "Thank God you're here, Julian. If anything happens to me, I want you to help Sophia. Michael is not capable. He grows . . . he grows more erratic with every passing day."

Julian spoke carefully. "I have no wish to upset you, but I must ask the question. Do you think Michael played any part in Seth's or Edmond's deaths?"

Blotches of color appeared on the marquess's cheeks. "I've heard the rumours. I'm also aware there are those who think my sickness is attributable to him. I refuse to entertain such notions. I know he's unstable, but his violent tendencies have never run toward the family." He stopped as another wave of pain assaulted him, then gasped, "I can't believe it of him now."

Lady Donberry stroked her husband's arm, her face mirroring his pain. "Do not forget Nina, my love."

"He has never hurt her," the marquess rasped.

"Perhaps not physically, but the poor woman is so browbeaten she's afraid to venture from her room."

Lord Donberry moved his head on the pillow. "I don't wish to discuss Michael. My youngest . . . and dearest . . . brother is here at last." He extended his hand a second time, and Julian again seized it. The marquess laughed faintly. "Promise not to tell my fortune anymore. You frighten me when you do. Always did. For a long time, I thought you were the mad one, not Michael. Time has proved otherwise." He moistened his lips, and his eyes became damp. "I beg God every night He will forgive me for believing the wrong brother so long ago. I beg that you will. Have you . . . have you come to forgive me before I die, Julian?"

"You are not going to die," the magician said fiercely. "I won't let you."

"When you are as old as I am, you'll realize how very little control we have over our destiny."

"You're not old, Carl. But to answer your question, of course I forgive you." He loosened his brother's hand and lowered it to the blankets. "But I must know something." Unwilling to tire his brother further, he hesitated. Yet there might not be another opportunity. "If you—if you came to believe me after Christine's death . . . why did you never contact me?"

Lord Donberry lowered his lashes. When he looked at Julian again, his eyes were haunted with guilt. "Because in matters dealing with Father, I lacked courage. Sophia and I had to live here with him. Had we gone against his wishes . . ."

"He would have made life difficult," Julian finished.

"Impossible is a better word," added Lady Donberry.

The magician sat quietly a moment, wishing his brother had communicated with him anyway. How different the past ten years would have been. How free of bitterness.

The marchioness saw his distress. "Carl did what he could Who do you think arranged matters for your first performances as a magician? Didn't you think it odd so many houses were willing to book an unknown young performer?"

Julian's expression lightened dramatically. "You? You booked them for me, Carl?"

Smiling crookedly, Lord Donberry said, "Don't make too much of it. You must be good at what you do; otherwise, no amount of wrangling could have gotten the bookings that followed. I only opened the door."

Julian could think of no words that would express his feelings without maudlin sentimentality. He locked gazes with the marquess and smiled. Somewhere within his heart, gaping old wounds began to knit together.

He shifted his weight slightly on the bed, taking care not to unsettle his brother. "The last few moments alone have made my journey worthwhile; but I've come for another reason, and that is to help you. I know you don't want to discuss Michael's hand in your illness, so we will leave him out of the discussion. Yet I understand your symptoms could be attributed to poison. Can you think of something only you have drunk, or eaten, that might have caused your illness?"

"No, there is nothing. You sound like my wife." He turned his head weakly. "Did you ask Julian to come? Speak truth, now; I won't be angry."

Lady Donberry denied doing so. "Though I wish I had, long ago," she added. "Had Julian been part of our lives, perhaps none of this would have happened."

"It was Calvin O'Reilly who wrote," Julian said.

The marquess grunted. "I should have known. When I first became ill, he asked me the same question. We went over the list of things I ate and came up with nothing that only I ingested."

"Nevertheless, it would be wise if Sophia monitors everything you eat or drink from this time forward."

"That I will do," she said, her eyes wide and worried.

Lord Donberry made a dissenting motion with his hands. "You should know the physician says my disease could be caused by a number of things."

"Dr. Stalworthy does not know everything," Lady Donberry pronounced. She rose and straightened the front of her skirt. "You are growing weaker every moment, dearest. We should leave him for a while, Julian. He will never rest so long as you are here."

Julian stood and reluctantly took his leave. The marchioness accompanied him to the anteroom, her control slipping as soon as the bedroom door closed behind them. "What think you, Julian? Do you suppose there is any chance he will recover?"

Whatever he might have said was lost as sounds of a dispute in the corridor brought them both to the hall door. Julian was surprised to find Charlotte Ann arguing with the footman and valet much as he had done a half-hour before. When she saw him, her solemn eyes brightened.

"Oh, milord, she's gone. Lady Abby's gone, and expecting me to join her. I wish you'd bring her back because I can't, and no good is going to come from two females on their own without money." After a brief, conscience-stricken pause, she added, "Or without much money."

Julian bid the curious marchioness adieu and hurried Charlotte Ann toward the stairs. After learning Abby's direction, he ordered the maid to return to her room and ran for the stables, shouting for a gig to be brought. He watched the stableboy shuffle off to do his bidding, then impatiently began to assist.

When he finally set off, he had to set a slower pace than he liked, because the gig had an annoying tendency to become bogged in the mud that streaked the gravel road. But it was all right; with a clanging of emotions, he saw Abby's hooded figure in the watery distance. She would not get away, no matter how determined her step, nor how wrathful her heart.

Her escape struck him with compassion and regret. What had he done now to cause her to run away from him? He longed to hold her until their uncanny rapport filled them both with mutual understanding. But it was impossible.

Hearing his approach, she turned suddenly. Her mouth formed an angry circle of surprise, and to his exasperation she began to run. For an instant he imagined riding alongside her, reaching down and scooping her up like a knight rescuing a maiden. Their bodies would melt together on the seat and . .

Ridiculous. The gig would overtip and land them in the mud.

When he was within ten paces of her fleeing figure, he pulled the horse to a stop, jumped from the gig and ran afte her. She was no match for him with her shorter legs and narrow gown. When he caught her, he tried to spin her around to face him; but to his shock, she fought like a hell-cat, her fists pounding his shoulders and chest rapidly yet harmlessly, her face contorting into a mask of frustrated rage.

"Release me at once!" she screamed. "Do not touch me, you devil!"

He dropped his hands and stepped back. She froze for an instant as though not believing her good fortune, then spun about and resumed running. For several seconds he watched in bafflement. When he caught her the second time, she dragged her arms downward, trying to slide from his grip. She nearly succeeded in plunging them both into the mud, but he caught his balance in time and pulled her back onto the road.

"Stop it, Abby!" he cried.

"Unhand me and I will!"

"I'll release you if you promise to stand and tell me what has disturbed you enough to run off like a child!" Water drained into his eyes. "And in the rain, too. Have you lost your senses?"

"No! I have become sane for the first time in my life!" She glared at him with undisguised hatred, her body shaking with rage. Her gaze dropped scornfully to the hands clutching her arms. In a calmer, chilly voice she said, "If you were anything of the gentleman you've claimed to be, you would let me go. Since you are not, you have my word I will not run—for the present time, at least. But I give you fair warning I will not stay with you at the castle."

He pounced upon the only part of her speech that made sense to him. "Do you mind the castle so much, then? I did not realize. We can remove to an inn. There is a small one nearby."

"It is not the castle which bothers me; it's the people within."

"Meaning me, of course. What's wrong, Abby?" His voice softened as he dropped his hold on her. "What has happened?

I know you have been upset for several days now, and much of that is my fault. But you haven't tried to run away before. What has changed?"

His tone gentled her somewhat, but her eyes continued to move with restless, despairing energy. "What has changed?" she asked hollowly. "Only everything."

He looked at her sadly. "Everything, Abby?"

She turned and moved a few paces away, startling him into thinking she intended flight again. But she only crossed her arms and gazed at the sodden fields. He had the impression she did not see them, that she was far away in some terrible landscape of her own.

"I trusted you more than I ever trusted anyone," she said finally, her voice breaking on a sob. "And now I've found that trust was misplaced. What is more, you know the reason for it and are pretending ignorance."

Beneath the indignation, the brittleness of her words, he sensed a vast emptiness and loss. Julian felt a gulf open inside his chest. The pain of it was deep, far deeper than the megrim tearing through his forehead.

"This is about Harriet and Colleen, isn't it?" he asked quietly. His question brought a startled look from her, a look she quickly masked. Taking this as confirmation, he nodded. "I have done you an injustice. I've let you think Harry is my mistress, and Colleen my child." She shot him a vicious glance, and he flinched. "I had my reasons for doing so, but I can see nothing justifies the hurt I've caused you."

He approached tentatively, but she shifted away and he stopped. "Colleen is not my child, Abby. She is Michael's."

Instead of greeting this news with surprise and relief as he hoped, she looked at him with disdain. When she spoke, her words were heavy with contempt.

"How do you know?"

He felt the blood drain from his cheeks. The hammers in his head pounded with greater fierceness. Rain dripped down his face like tears.

"And what is the meaning of that question?" he asked coldly.

"You know perfectly well that I am referring to . . . oh, I cannot say it." She covered her face with her hands, then lowered them angrily. "Don't bother pretending you don't know. I am referring of course to the ungodly manner in which you . . . you and your brother . . . carried on with Harriet."

For a long space of time he regarded her silently. Something in his face startled her, but still she did not speak, nor did he. And then, with surprising suddenness, he turned and began walking back to the gig.

After an instant's pause, she ran after him.

"You have nothing to say to that, do you?" she hurled, breathless in her attempt to match his steps. "Now your easy explanations have ceased!"

"There is nothing I can say," he replied angrily. "You have been listening to Michael, with whom you've been acquainted for only two hours and already know to be a murderous liar. Anyone willing to accept the word of a stranger over that of someone she's known much longer and has, one would hope, more reason to trust—anyone like that is beyond hearing reason.

"But it does not matter," he added with growing venom. "Such has happened to me before, and with those who have more cause than you to trust me. Michael has a way about him of inspiring belief. No matter how mad his ravings, there is always the ring of truth to what he says. And when I try to justify myself, I sound like a naughty child offering pathetic excuses."

They had reached the gig. He started to climb aboard, then looked at her inquiringly. She appeared to debate a moment, then put out her hand. He assisted her to the seat and joined her.

"I'm willing to listen to your justifications," she said in a small voice.

He turned the gig about and drove awhile before answering.

When his words came, they were clipped and spoken without emotion.

"I've known Harry all my life. All of us have. Her father was the village vicar. She and I were close in age, but our paths crossed infrequently; Harry was a rather gawky-looking girl and attracted no one's notice. Yet on several occasions we had interesting conversations. She made an excellent audience for my magic tricks, and I taught her a few illusions. That was how things stood when I was thrown out. I neither heard nor thought about her again until three years later, when she came to me backstage after a performance seeking help."

He pushed a lock of wet hair from his eyes. "When she told me what had happened to her, I could not refuse to offer my assistance. She was destitute. And like me, a victim of Michael."

A frown etched little lines beneath his eyes. "She was not a woman of loose morals, Abby. As she matured into a beauty, my brother became attracted. She had no interest in a married man and spurned his attentions. Michael was furious. He forced himself upon her. To make a bad matter worse, after it became apparent she was increasing, her father threw her from the house in shame.

"Harry sought help from Michael, but he laughed and denied siring the child. After she threatened to go to his wife, he relented and arranged for one of the footmen to marry her. Harry felt she had no choice; she married. But her new husband was disgusted with what he called damaged goods. He ran off with the small settlement Michael gave them. When Harry made a fresh appeal to my brother, he had her removed from the castle forcibly.

"She drifted about after that, trying to find a position that would allow her to keep the child with her. It was only by chance she saw my lithograph and attended the performance. When I saw Colleen, I realized at once the babe was part of my family. I could not deny Harry what she needed to exist.

Eventually she was able to earn her wages by serving as my assistant. It has been a fortunate arrangement for us both."

He clamped his lips together, darted the briefest glance at her, then turned his attention back to the road.

They were drawing closer to the castle, but the horse was very slow in the rain. The saturated animal put one hoof in front of the other in apparent misery. Abby rested her eyes on the beast, looking as miserable as he did.

"How tragic. Then you and Harriet . . ."

"There has never been anything between us, Abby. I won't deny there have been times when marrying her seemed the perfect solution for Colleen's sake. But I've never been able to forget that Harry is the mother of my brother's child. And there was the problem of the husband, you see. We have only recently learned that he is dead."

Abby grew very still. "Then Harriet is a free woman." She pulled the hood of her cloak closer to her face, and he barely heard her next, woe-filled words. "Now you will be able to marry her, if you wish to."

He looked at her quickly. The pressure inside his head began to lessen. "There is one major impediment to that course of action."

She peered up at him, blinking away the rain. In a hopeful voice she asked, "Harriet is like a sister to you?"

"No," he blurted, images of Harry's countless overtures playing through his mind; but it would break all the rules of gentlemanly behaviour to mention them. Still, he must erase the growing alarm in Abby's eyes. "The problem is that I do not love her. Not in that way. And she's been through enough. She deserves more than a man who cannot give her all his heart."

A ghost of a smile played at Abby's lips, then faded. "I believe you, but I don't understand why you told me nothing about Harriet and Colleen before we reached Avilion. How could you allow me to think what I did?"

"I warned you that I'm not kind."

"Oh, stuff. I have found you to be considerate upon occasion."

One eyebrow raised ironically. "You overwhelm me."

"You are welcome. Now answer my question, please."

He sighed deeply. "All right. I thought if you were disillusioned, you would not persist in wanting to remain with me." He glared into her eyes, but it was evident he was not angry with *her.* "Now, do you still think I am considerate?"

She studied him in silence. The sound of the courtyard cobblestones beneath the wheels startled her. She had not noticed they were almost at the stables.

"I am beginning to think you will do anything to be rid of me."

Knives plunged fresh wounds into his head. He pulled the gig to a halt within a hundred yards of the stable. One of the grooms came to watch them curiously from the shelter of the building.

"That may be true, but do not doubt, do not *ever* doubt, that I love you."

She began to speak rapidly. "When you touched my hand onstage that first night we met, you said you saw great strength—a lion's strength—in me. No one ever spoke to me in such a way. I fear it has turned my head. I find myself saying the boldest things to you; things I would never dream of saying to anyone else. And now I tell you this. Put aside your fears for my safety. Let us live the lives we have been given as joyfully as we can."

Her eyes were so hopeful that he wanted to groan. Putting an arm around her shoulders, he said, "We need not be in a hurry to make decisions of this importance. We have ample time." But he knew there could be only one decision.

"Of course," she said faintly.

Forcing a twinkle into his eyes, he clucked the horse into motion. "You'll be glad of a warm bath and fresh clothes after this adventure. And I'll thank you to put my ring on again."

She attempted to imitate the lightness of his tone. "I wil

and at the same time I shall return the funds I've borrowed from you." When his eyes widened, she hurried on. "Speaking of fresh clothing, I look forward to the results of Mrs. White's needlework. She took my measurements before we left Avilion and promised to send a few things before the week's end."

"What fortunate news," he said, pulling the horse to a stop in front of the stables. He handed the reins to the groom, climbed down and assisted Abby from the gig. "Does that mean you will never wear that awful mud-colored dress again?"

"Your interest in my clothing surprises me, my lord," she bantered bravely, walking beside him to the castle. "I thought gentlemen were unconcerned with such trivial matters."

He gave her a playful look. "When a lovely lady is forced to hide her beauty inside a dismal garment, any gentleman would cry foul."

There was a moment's silence. "You always know what to say, Julian," she replied, no longer able to feign jocularity. "In nearly every instance."

He questioned her with his eyes, but she did not return his look nor speak again, not even when they entered the cold walls of the castle and climbed the stairs to their rooms.

Fourteen

Although Julian's explanations had soothed Abby's wounded feelings, her relief rang hollow during the next few days. Weeks ago the prospect of setting up her own establishment would have delighted her. Now her heart was too deeply entangled to contemplate such an existence.

Julian continued to treat her kindly, but it was a distant kindness. He never touched her except by accident, nor did he sit beside her by choice. His aloofness continued to scorch her. She longed for his kisses; she hungered for his arms to encircle her. Night after night, she stared at the door connecting their bedchambers with a feeling of incompletion and loss. More than once she imagined herself walking past the door and into his bed. But every instinct warned he would reject her, and she knew she could not bear that.

When their paths crossed, Lord Michael observed Abby and Julian with amusement. He often tried to separate her from the other family members, but she contrived never to be alone with him. He seemed fascinated by her revulsion. Whenever she was present, he missed no opportunity to criticize the servants or throw jibes at Julian or Nina. But to her he was gentility itself. She could no more sit down than he would rush to bring a cushion for her back and an ottoman for her feet. Only the best portion of meat could be placed before her, and woe to the footman who did not drain her vegetables properly and serve her the largest trifle or pudding. Every topic raised at table must include an opinion voiced by Abby. And always,

always, his eyes regarded her with a solicitousness that hinted something secret and indiscreet lay between them.

Abby did not imagine he was attracted to her; she believed he treated her so in order to provoke angry reactions from Julian or Nina. But neither rose to the challenge, probably because his lack of subtlety did not mislead them either. Only when Lord Michael flew into a rage over some mundane matter would Julian step in to calm him. She was surprised the magician could do so easily; he need only move toward Lord Michael to make him shrink away. She could almost feel sorry for her brother-in-law, if it were not for the delight he took in creating mischief.

As the days passed, she came to realize her first impression—that Lord Michael and Philip were much alike—was in error. There was a meanness, a small and petty viciousness behind her brother-in-law's behaviour that hinted at madness. She was more afraid of him than she had ever been of Philip, who, now that he no longer seemed to be a threat, appeared harmless and sane in comparison. At least her almost-fiancé's possessiveness and overbearing ways had been born of frustrated love, if such could be called love.

Lord Donberry took a turn for the better during the next days, though he could not move from his bed. Julian visited him daily, sometimes taking Abby with him. She rapidly became fond of the marquess and his wife, a fondness they returned in kind. Lady Donberry especially seemed someone with whom she could grow close, and that lady entertained Abby with several lively conversations about Julian's boyish escapades

Abby wished she could feel an equal affinity for Nina, but Lady Michael's stifled, meek manner put her off. Abby told herself it was because she exhibited many of her own tendencies. Had Abby married Philip, she would doubtless have behaved in the same fashion.

But none of that was Nina's fault. Ashamed of her prejudice, Abby made every effort to be congenial. However, a week following her attempt to run away, she could not disguise her consternation when Nina knocked at her door.

The lady held several gowns in her arms. When Abby admitted her, Nina said softly, "I've noticed you weren't able to pack many clothes, so I thought you might like to borrow a few of my gowns while you are here. We are much the same size, and I don't think alterations will be necessary."

"How kind of you," Abby gushed, feeling dismay. *Were* they the same size? A quick glance in the cheval glass beside the door confirmed the fact. Somehow she had felt much taller than this poor, bland woman. "Julian has been complaining about my dreary wardrobe. But I'm afraid your generosity is unnecessary because I received several new gowns from Avilion this morning. I've just finished trying them on. Would you care to see them?"

Nina placed her dresses on the sofa and said she would. Abby instructed Charlotte Ann to bring the garments from the wardrobe one at a time, and all three women commented on the various merits of each.

"I fear Mrs. White must have sewn night and day to make four gowns in this length of time," Abby said. She smiled contentedly. "Two for day wear, and two for evening. I haven't had so many new clothes at once in—," with a pang she recalled giddy buying sprees with her mother, "—in years."

"You must wear the lavender muslin today," Nina replied, her mouth barely opening as she formed the words. "Purple is Michael's favorite color."

Abby looked at her in surprise.

"I like for him to be pleased," Nina explained

"So I would imagine," Abby said fervently.

Nina fingered the fabric of the lavender gown. "He's been a sad man since his father died." She dropped her hands into her lap and knitted her fingers together restlessly. "That loss devastated him more than anyone knows."

Glancing up suddenly, she looked at Abby with determined eyes. "We must all try to do our best to help Michael fee better. He is a good man, a deserving man. I see how Julian watches him with suspicion, how he never allows him to visit Carl alone, and I tell you, it should stop. I don't like to think he's turning the marquess against him. It is very upsetting to Michael."

Nina was breathing hard and blinking, obviously trying to gain control of her emotions. Abby watched her speechlessly. Charlotte Ann cleared her throat, rolled her eyes, and jumped to restore the gowns to the wardrobe.

"I don't mean to offend you," Nina said after several uncomfortable moments. "It is only that Michael means everything to me. I want him to be happy." Her lips tightened. "How long do you remain with us?"

Shocked at the lady's rudeness, Abby stiffened. "I truly cannot say. Julian has not mentioned a departure date yet."

Nina nodded once, slowly, and stood. She walked to the sofa and collected her gowns, then took her leave with a minimal exchange of words. When she had gone, Abby turned to Charlotte Ann.

"Pinch me; I must be dreaming," Abby said. "How can she possibly be so besotted with Lord Michael when he treats her as he does?"

"Takes all kinds," Charlotte Ann commented sagely.

During the remainder of the day, Abby tried not to think about her strange interview with Nina. Instead, she gloried in the feel of her new day dress—she chose the ivory one with an overlay of old lace, *not* the lavender—and the compliments it brought.

After luncheon she persuaded Julian to walk with her in the park that surrounded the castle walls and told him of the morning visit. He did not seem as surprised as she.

"Sometimes people learn to side with their oppressors," he said. "It happens in war; why should it not happen in domestic situations? Although I must admit I'd not expected a spirited defense of anything from a timid woman like Nina."

"Have you ever obtained a reading from her?" Abby asked. When he admitted he had not, she added with a smile, "Perhaps she hides great strength. She may be a lioness in disguise."

"You are the only lioness I care to know." The light in his eyes made her feel she had been embraced. She swayed toward him, but he moved back almost imperceptibly, his boots scraping the brick walkway.

Of course, Julian, she thought painfully. *It wouldn't do for me to touch you.*

As if to make amends for his coldness, he inquired, "Have I told you how lovely you look in that new dress?"

Her smile wavered back to life. "I don't remember," she teased, pushing aside her hurt. "Would you like to do so now?"

That evening before dinner, Abby dressed in her favorite new gown, a deep blue satin cut in the fashionable Greek style with high waistline and low decolletage. Tiny jewels were sewn across the bodice and hem like fairy dust. Mrs. White had sent along decorative blue feathers which Charlotte Ann pinned into a bandeau and interlaced among Abby's upswept curls. Her only jewelry, other than Julian's ring, was the locket containing her parents' miniatures.

The others were gathered in the hall when she descended. Julian was reading a magazine, Lord Michael paced in front of the fireplace, and Nina sat some distance away, embroidering flowers on a piece of white linen.

At Abby's entrance, Julian glanced up from his magazine and set it aside. As he stood, his gaze moved over her appreciatively. A slow smile crossed his face. Abby blushed and felt herself growing warmer and warmer. She could not look away from him. He was devastatingly handsome in his black evening clothes and white linen shirt. The intense blue of his eyes was casting a spell over her. She was bewitched. She wanted him to cross the room and take her in his arms.

But it was Lord Michael who rushed to her side. "I have never seen anyone so lovely in my life," he said eagerly, then took her hand and led her to sit on a satin sofa near his wife. "Look at her, Nina. Take note of the simplicity of her dress, the purity of its color. You would do well to imitate such a style, though naturally Abby's beauty and youth cannot be copied."

Abby cast a distressed look in Nina's direction, but the lady's wan smile remained in place, her head tilted in a half-bow. For the first time, Abby found her meekness chilling. But she dismissed it from her mind when the dinner bell sounded, and they moved into the dining room.

Abby could never enter this room without thinking of a cave, or a chapel. The chamber was impossibly long and narrow, the ceiling appearing higher than the room's width. A series of stained glass windows yawned along the outside wall. The table was at least twenty feet in length; and though the four of them sat at one end of it, proximity could not make them cozy, nor could the attentive servers, whose shoes slapped the stone floor with echoing importance.

As always, Lord Michael led the conversation, chattering about the estate, Napoleon's exile, the shameful condition of veterans, and any other subject that entered his head. Abby's mind wandered. Once she caught Nina's eyes upon her, but the lady's gaze quickly returned to her plate.

"I think Carl is much improved, don't you?" Lord Michael asked loudly. "He'll soon be well enough to join us downstairs, I think."

"Do you?" Julian asked mildly. "I hope you're correct."

Lord Michael frowned. "Well, you saw him when I did. He was able to eat a full meal today, the first in a fortnight. Don't you think it a good sign?"

"I do if nothing further happens to make him ill."

"Are you implying something, Gypsy?"

"Not at all. Why? Should I?"

Lord Michael laughed. "If you're trying to be subtle, Julian, you're not managing very well."

Leaning back to allow the footman room to serve his plate, Lord Michael's eyebrows suddenly pulled together. "What is this, Grimsdorff? It looks like salmon, but that cannot be. No one would bury salmon in cream sauce with peas and carrots and mushrooms. And by my soul, can this be celery?" His face darkened. "Well, don't leave it in front of me, man! Take this monstrous concoction back to the kitchens! If Spurrows can't poach the fish properly, he will soon find himself sacked!"

Without visible emotion, the footman bowed and removed the plate.

Lord Michael turned to Abby and said with sudden gentleness, "Would you like to return that dish, my dear? You don't have to eat it."

"The salmon looks perfectly delicious to me," she said primly. Her brother-in-law's tantrums were increasing as the days passed. His childishness both frightened and embarrassed her.

Her rejection appeared to disturb him. "I am going to visit Carl," he said suddenly, and pushed back his chair.

Julian's voice crossed the table like a whip. "Not now. He and Sophia are having their dinner."

"What does that matter? Carl is always happy to see me."

Nina turned toward him but kept her eyes lowered. "You've not eaten, dear."

A peevish look stole across his features. "Have Grimsdorff bring my meal upstairs. I'll dine with my brother." He rose and walked toward the door.

Julian threw an apologetic glance at Abby and stood. "I'll join you."

"No!" Lord Michael turned back, his cheeks suffusing with color. "For once I wish to see Carl alone! Since you came, you have attached yourself to me like a leech, and I am heartily sick of it! It's my right to spend time with him; do not forget it is I who am his only true brother, not you!"

Abby's eyes widened as Julian rushed around the table. To her relief, she saw no anger in his face, only tight control. When he reached for Lord Michael's arm, the older man jerked away.

"Don't touch me! I know what you are, and you'll not taint me with your evil!"

He ran for the stairs. Julian paused only long enough to excuse himself and followed.

Silence descended. The remaining footman turned his back to them and quietly began lifting and replacing lids on the dishes arrayed at the sideboard to no apparent purpose. Abby stole a look at Nina. She did not seem unduly upset, had not even paused in eating the despised salmon. Abby attempted to imitate her and lifted her fork.

Lord Michael had been right; the food was tasteless. After a moment, she replaced the utensil and put her hands to her face. Her cheeks felt hot.

"Do you know, I am no longer hungry," she said. "Would you excuse me? I think I'll make an early night of it."

Nina looked up from her dish. "I hope Michael hasn't upset you. It is only his way."

"Er—no, of course not." Abby could scarcely control her features at the woman's complacency.

"I know what will make you feel better. I have a bottle of one of my father's finest bordeaux in my room. Why don't we share a glass before you retire?"

The last thing she wanted was to spend time alone with this strange woman, but there was no graceful way out. "Thank you, Nina," she said. "That sounds delightful."

When Julian rushed into the marquess's bedchamber, he found the valet serving dishes of salmon to his brother and sister-in-law at a table pulled near the window. The sight of

Carl sitting apart from his bed struck him with joy, but he was surprised to see no sign of Michael.

"He hasn't been here," Lord Donberry told him, looking puzzled.

"Perhaps he changed his mind when he discovered I meant to accompany him. He insisted on seeing you alone, and I find that disturbing."

"As do I," Lady Donberry said. "There's no denying how much better Carl has become since you've joined Michael on every visit."

"That's because I'm tough as old boots," the marquess said gruffly. "My recovery has nothing to do with Julian stopping Michael from killing me, which I still maintain is a preposterous notion."

"Well, whatever the reason for it, I'm glad of your continued recovery." Julian straightened his waistcoat and glanced at their plates wistfully. "I suppose I'd better leave you to your dinner. I've abandoned the ladies downstairs."

"Oh, don't go, m'boy. Stay awhile. Sophia is growing tired of my solitary company anyway."

After giving her husband a mild look, she turned to Julian. "He's absolutely right. The two of us are fighting like cats and dogs. Do stay, dear, and give my tired eyes and ears a rest from his incessant complaining."

Lord Donberry slapped his thigh and snorted. "Pull up a chair, Julian, I command it!"

He complied easily enough. It was good to spend time with his family, or what was left of it. His relationship with Carl had evolved beyond what it had been on the best days of the past. Julian reveled in the ease of their companionship. The old resentments were fading away.

They chatted for some minutes on matters regarding the estate and the steward's plans for alternating crops. When the marquess noticed Julian staring longingly at the second remove—roast chicken and stuffing—he ordered the valet to bring another plate.

"Do you know what I'm thinking would be excellent with this fowl?" Lord Donberry demanded of the servant after he had served Julian. "That little bordeaux Nina sent up from her father's orchard. 'D'you remember, Pike? She brought a couple of bottles and we broke one open shortly before I became ill. I haven't thought of it since. Go fetch the unopened one, won't you?"

Pike moved hesitantly toward the anteroom. "In the cellars, is it, my lord?"

"Well, I would think so unless someone has drunk it already. Where did you put it?"

The valet's eyes shifted back and forth. "Don't know, my lord. Can't remember." He puffed out his cheeks. "Guess I was too overset by your sickness."

Lord Donberry waved his hand dismissively. "A paltry excuse if ever I heard one. Well, if you don't find it, bring us a bottle of port."

Julian had grown very still. He did not stir when the servant left but kept his gaze fastened on Carl. "You drank the wine before you became ill?"

The marquess glanced at him and sighed. "Julian, surely you're not thinking—" He shook his head in exasperation. "Sophia, can you account it? Now he believes Nina is in on the plot to do away with me. Dear God! All my brothers are mad!"

"Not Nina necessarily—" Julian began.

"I should think not," the marquess huffed. "The dear lady shared her father's latest vintage with me to see if I might wish to place an order. She and I sat right there in the sitting room and shared drinks from the same bottle. Now, Lord Suspicious, what make you of that, since she ain't dead or dying?"

Julian's posture slowly relaxed. He gave his brother a look of wry embarrassment, shrugged his shoulders, and forked a bite of chicken into his mouth. Lord and Lady Donberry exchanged amused glances and began to eat.

"We don't mean to laugh at you," Sophia said. "But the very idea of Nina—well, it is too ludicrous to contemplate.

She is so quiet and gentle and gracious. Her concern for Carl has been touching. Since he's been ill, she has even made a special soup for him from time to time. And before you become excited again, yes, she partakes of the soup and even offers it to me. Of course, I don't eat it, for the soup has leeks in it, and I can't abide leeks."

Julian nodded and smiled faintly. The meat seemed to grow larger and drier as he chewed. He washed it down with several swallows from his water glass and replaced the crystal goblet on the table with exaggerated care.

He had left the women together in the dining room.

There was nothing to worry about. But he needed to see Abby. He needed to see her immediately.

"Excuse me," he mumbled, and bumped the table in his hurry to exit, startling Lord and Lady Donberry.

While Julian conversed with Lord Donberry in the west wing, Abby gazed at Nina's room with interest. It was her second visit, but the first time she had been too weary from traveling to notice anything. Now she saw that framed needlework covered the walls from floor to ceiling, breathing life into the pale stone. Brilliant Turkish rugs were layered over the carpet, and dried flowers nestled into every corner. Ceramic children laughed and fished and posed coyly on the dresser and chiffonier. If there were more patterns and hues than met Abby's taste, she could not deny the room was homelike and cheerful.

"Your bedchamber is charming," she said. "Is all the needlework your own?"

Nina emerged from her dressing room carrying the bottle of wine and two glasses. "Yes," she said proudly. "All of it Michael thinks it's too much, but it suits me. His room is much simpler. He has no liking for clutter."

She motioned toward a round table flanked by two chair near the fire. Abby followed and seated herself. "I hope th bordeaux hasn't gone flat," Nina continued. "I opened it last night and stored it on the windowsill, which is almost as chilly as the cellar. I trust you'll like it."

"I'm sure I will, though I confess I've not drunk much wine in my life and am no expert." While Nina filled their glasses, Abby eyed the tablecloth which had been embroidered in overlapping vines and rosebuds. "This must have taken forever to stitch!" she exclaimed.

Nina lifted her glass and pressed it to her cheek. "I've discovered that anything meaningful takes time," she said, and sipped. She watched Abby carefully over the edge of her goblet. "Have you found it so?"

Abby started to drink, then paused, reflecting. "I suppose." She recalled the long years at her grandmother's house, the interminable, endless days. "But sometimes I think *everything* takes time, even the bad things."

"Yes." A dry smile stretched Nina's lips. Abby had the sudden notion that every gesture the lady made was little, as if she tried to attract less notice that way. What a sad mouse of a woman she was. But she was speaking again, and Abby forced herself to attend the soft words. "Everything *does* take time. Even *you* seem to be taking a lot of time before trying my papa's bordeaux."

Abby glanced at the sparkling, clear liquid and laughed. "Forgive me; you are wanting my opinion." She brought the glass to her lips. But when a brief knock at the door startled her, she lowered it untouched and turned curiously.

Nina's maid, a plump, nervous woman of middle age, burst into the room. A spasm of annoyance wrinkled Nina's brow. "What is it, Della?"

"I'm sorry to bother you, my lady, but there's a messenger from your sister. Her birthing time is come and she wants you."

The lady looked at Abby and sighed. "Tell the man—no, wait. I'll speak with him." She stood and patted her hair. "Please stay, Abby, and drink your wine. I'll not be tending my sister; I don't think Michael can spare me tonight. I shall return as soon as I tell the messenger." She excused herself and left.

Abby waited until the door was closed, then set her glass back on the table. It was a shame she didn't enjoy the taste of wine; she'd only accepted Nina's invitation as an act of kindness. And now she had been left alone.

She stirred from the chair and began examining the needlepoint pictures in more detail. Each design was of a floral nature and looked excruciatingly intricate. Nina must have the patience of a spider.

The connecting door smacked open suddenly, making her jump. To her dismay, Lord Michael entered the chamber.

He beamed when he saw her. "Bless me if it isn't Abigail! I thought I heard voices. But where is my wife? Don't tell me I've caught you snooping in here all by yourself."

"She invited me in and was called away for a moment," Abby said uncomfortably. "But I should be going."

He stepped into her path, blocking her exit. "Nonsense. If she's returning, she'll be disappointed if you leave. Please stay. I won't hurt you. You're not afraid of me, are you?"

The expression in his eyes seemed to beg her to say *yes*. She struggled to keep her features composed. "No, no. But I *had* better depart. I'm growing tired."

"Surely you jest; you look too fresh and beautiful to be tired." He moved toward her, but when she stepped back, he veered and paced to the fireplace. "Remain awhile. Talk with me. I don't want to be alone." His voice softened, and he stared at the floor. "Things happen to people when they are alone."

Abby's heart skipped a beat. His fear drifted toward her like smoke. Why was he afraid of being alone? Had he seen something? She had never been fanciful before coming to this castle which she could not make herself like, but now it was easy to imagine ghosts lurking around every corner.

"What sort of things happen?" she whispered, swallowing

He looked past her to the window and the darkness beyond

it. "Terrible things. Voices. Sometimes there are noises that can't be explained. Have you heard them?"

She saw at once their imaginings were of two different orders; hers were born of reading too many florid romances; his must be traced to some darker, deeper source. Her fear melted into sympathy. He sensed it and shuddered as if to throw his delusions and her pity from him. When his gaze fell upon the table, his face brightened.

"You were having a glass of wine with Nina. Is this the famous bordeaux her father keeps boasting about?"

She smiled faintly. "I believe so."

"Well, you are fortunate indeed, for I've not been accounted worthy enough to try it yet." He walked jauntily to the table. "But I shall now."

He lifted one of the glasses and swallowed rapidly. "Not a bad little wine. A trifle sweet for my taste." He refilled the glass and began to sip. "Won't you join me?"

Still drawn by a compassion she'd not suspected she could feel for this man, Abby reluctantly approached the table. But then the glass fell from his hand and shattered to pieces on the carpet between them. His face twisted in agony, and he clutched his arms to his stomach. Bending double, he began to retch violently.

Abby froze. His suffering was so intense, she could not think.

He lifted desperate, wild eyes to hers. One hand clawed at his throat. "Can't—breathe!" he wheezed. "Help . . . me." He fell first to his knees, then to his side, gagging and choking.

Suddenly coming to her senses, she fled into the corridor, screaming for help. Julian appeared from nowhere and gripped her arms. "It's Michael!" she gasped. "I think he's dying!"

"Are you all right?" he demanded. When she nodded numbly, he released her and ran into the room. She could not follow him. The sounds of Michael's agony could be heard in the hall, and that was bad enough. She stumbled to the head of the stairs and saw servants approaching.

Behind them came Nina, who looked up at her expressionlessly. When Abby threw her a glance of inestimable pity, the lady's face colored with anxiety. She approached the stairs and began to mount them faster and faster, her eyes never wavering from Abby's.

"Who—who drank?" she asked when she reached the top.

Abby started to answer, then could not when Nina's words took on a horrible meaning in her mind. The moment stretched ominously. Her compassion drained away to be replaced by a white-hot anger.

"Michael," she said icily. "Michael drank the wine." Even when Nina's face stretched into a mask of horror, Abby felt no pity. "Did you kill the others, too?"

Nina moved past her as if caught in a dream, then stumbled to her bedroom with Abby trailing after. Several servants had crowded into the room to assist Julian. One or two observed in mute helplessness. Seeing Nina, they moved aside, but she did not enter. A footman exited past them, evidently running for the physician.

When Abby reached the doorway, she saw Julian holding Michael and calling his name. She wanted to go to him, to comfort him, but knew he would not thank her for it, not now. When she could no longer bear to look, she turned to Nina.

"Why me?" Abby asked furiously, keeping her voice low so the servants could not hear. "Why did you want to kill me?"

Lady Michael did not answer for a long time. She watched her husband with eyes as dead as the glass eyes in a doll's face. "I'll tell you because it doesn't matter now," she whispered hoarsely. "He can't live. I put more arsenic in the bottle than I did with Carl. Three grains. I was afraid last time that I might die myself and used too little. But I've built up more tolerance now."

Abby had no idea what she was talking about. "Why did you try to poison me?" she repeated.

"Things take time," Nina murmured woodenly. "I made them look like accidents. I did it for Michael. He deserves to be the marquess; he deserves everything."

A servant ran between them carrying a basin of water and fresh towels. Swallowing her distaste for the bizarre conversation, Abby said, "I understand that the others stood in Michael's way of the title. But what threat was I?"

"You made Michael unhappy. And Julian was a thorn in his flesh. He was always afraid of Julian, even in the old days when your husband was a boy. If I hadn't made it look like Julian killed the girl and got him banished, Michael would have fallen to pieces. Everything was all right after that. But Julian came back, didn't he? Your husband came back. And Michael started slipping away from me again."

The childlike recitation chilled Abby as much as the words themselves. "I still don't understand."

"With you dead, Julian might go away. Especially if everyone thought he'd killed you. I had to make him leave. I would have killed him, but you were easier. I *thought* you were easier." Her voice grew petulant. "But you wouldn't drink!"

The noises within the room were growing quieter. Stricken into silence, Abby waited beside Nina. The monstrousness of the woman was beyond her understanding. She could not think about it now, would have to sort it out later.

A sudden cry chilled her soul.

"He's gone!" Julian called, his voice full of anguish and disbelief. "Michael's gone!"

Abby watched him pull his brother to his chest. She closed her eyes.

There was a soft stirring by her side. Abby turned and saw a flash of color disappearing around the corner. Nina was running toward the stairs. Did she mean to escape? Abby followed, fury rushing through her veins.

Seconds later, she heard a sound, an unforgettable, unmistakable sound. A sound she knew would haunt her dreams forever.

She ran to the balcony and looked down. Nina lay like a broken toy at the bottom of the stairs.

Fifteen

By midnight, the castle grew quiet. A few servants still padded through dimly lit halls tending to duties that were as necessary as they were distasteful. Behind closed doors, others were able to ease into restless slumber.

Abby had no desire for sleep or dreams. How could she, knowing two bodies lay enshrouded in the candlelit chapel below?

Hours before, she had dismissed Charlotte Ann to her attic quarters. Now, careless of wrinkling her new gown, Abby sat alone beside her bedroom fireplace, a quilt wrapped around her shoulders. Occasionally she moved to add a log to the fire, then nestled into the blanket again. There was some comfort to be derived from the heat and the mesmerizing rhythm of the flames.

Try as she might, she could not banish the horrible events of the past hours from her mind. She wanted to see Julian, longed to console him. She was haunted by the memory of his devastated face as he held Lord Michael's body.

After leaving Michael, he had only spoken with her briefly before going to sit with Lord Donberry. As far as she knew, he was with him still.

Her gaze drifted to the connecting door. Perhaps he had come back and was in his room now. No doubt he'd find sleep as impossible as she did. In that event, he might welcome conversation. But she didn't want to disturb him.

She tossed the blanket aside and walked softly to the door.

Turning the knob slowly, she pushed the door open a crack. In the firelit room beyond, shadows leapt along the walls and within the embrasures. The bedspread was pulled taut. No one sat disconsolate and alone in the dark corners.

Sighing, she began to pull the door closed. Before it shut entirely, she heard a noise in the corridor, and Julian entered. Feeling a rush of shame—was she intruding where she was not wanted?—she closed the door and leaned against it, breathing quickly. Almost immediately, he opened it again, nearly causing her to stumble into his arms.

"Come in, Abby. I'm glad you're awake."

With a fatigued smile, he motioned for her to sit on the settle beside the fireplace. After stirring the flames back to life, he sat beside her and draped an arm across her shoulders. She stared at him wordlessly for an instant, then lay her head against his chest, stealing her arms around his waist.

"I am so sorry," she said.

He pulled her closer. "I know you are, sweetheart. I'm sorry, too. Sorry for Michael and sorry for Nina and all the ones they hurt."

Abby smoothed a wrinkle from his waistcoat. "How are Carl and Sophia holding up?"

"Very well, under the circumstances. Whether it was the medicine the physician gave him or his natural resilience, Carl is recovering from the shock more quickly than I thought. It helped to know of Michael's innocence. After I told him what Nina confessed to you, he was swift to remind me that he'd always known Michael wouldn't hurt him."

"I'm glad he's well. Did the magistrate come?"

"Yes. The deaths have been ruled accidental. Carl and I hedged the truth a bit; no good can be served by bringing more scandal to the family. Nina has already given herself the ultimate punishment."

Abby moved her face against his shirt. "She was insane."

"I'm not so certain. Nina laid her plans carefully and patiently over many years. The truly mad are unable to do so.

She was shrewd enough to make use of the arsenic the steward ordered to kill the rats; Calvin told me moments ago that some of the poison was unaccounted for. Such plotting involves logical thought. I'm inclined to think she allowed her obsession for Michael's circumstance—and her own—to overshadow any sense of morality she might have had."

"I don't know, Julian. If you had seen her eyes, or listened to her reasoning. That she was willing to kill me simply to be rid of you . . ."

"She was beginning to make mistakes," he conceded, resting his cheek against Abby's hair. "I think Michael's erratic behavior pushed her to act impulsively. She'd never employed the same method twice to eliminate someone, yet she tried to poison you as she did Carl."

"I don't understand why she didn't die when she drank the wine."

"Apparently it's possible to build a tolerance for arsenic by beginning with very small doses. According to Carl's physician, such a course of action poses terrible risk, for even tiny amounts accumulate within the body and can corrode the lining of the stomach. Fortunately for Carl, whatever damage occurred inside him appears to be healing in spite of her poisoning him more than once."

Abby shuddered. Such had almost been her death.

She was comforted when Julian gently kneaded the muscles at her shoulder. Through his touch, he had felt her fear; now she was feeling his strength. And something else. Guilt? Why should he feel guilty? She questioned him with her eyes.

"I nearly lost you this evening," he explained. "I blame myself."

Indignation flushed her cheeks. "How can you say that? You have done nothing."

He loosened his hold on her and crouched before the fire, stabbing the logs with the poker. An ember landed on his sleeve and he brushed it away.

"I'm referring to this *marvelous* ability of mine." His tone

was scornful, and it hurt her to hear it. "And its total useless-
ness."

"How can you *say* that?" she cried. "Think of all the good
you can do, and have done! Not only did you save Gordie;
you rescued me from Philip's temper."

He was not to be persuaded. "But what good is it if I allow
my prejudice to stand in the way? All these years I've blamed
Michael for my banishment. One reading, Abby; one touch
might have taught me all I needed to know to save him and
prevent the danger toward you. But I did not, because I had
already confirmed his guilt in my mind. And then, in the last
moments of his life, I found out how *he* perceived *me*. And
do you know what I discovered?"

"I know he was afraid of you," she said softly. "But without
cause."

"Not only afraid, Abby. He resented me. And with good
reason."

The bitterness had faded from his voice; he sounded re-
signed. Settling on the hearth he continued to stab the logs
absently. "As I held him, I saw events common to us from his
perspective. What an obtuse, proud child I was, boasting about
my ability to find lost objects and pets and trying to control
everyone's lives. I received so much attention that he had to
exert himself constantly to win the approval he needed. He
became my father's lackey. He fawned upon people. No wonder he hated me. It was a happy day for him when he found
Christine murdered on my bed. The fears he'd expressed about
me had been confirmed at last."

He lay the poker aside and leaned his forearms on his knees.
"Until the last instant of his life, he believed I was a murderer.
He never knew what Nina had done, never knew she killed
our brothers and the maid."

Abby pulled a handkerchief from her pocket and wiped her
eyes. "Did he know she poisoned him, though unintention-
ally?"

"He was in too much agony to speculate. The emotions I

received were long-standing ones. I know he wanted Nina to help him, not me. At the very last, though, I think he recognized me as a friend and not an enemy, but I'm not certain."

She leaned toward him, wanting to give comfort but not knowing how.

His eyes were shadowed with old hurts. "Do you understand now? My ability causes only pain. I never plan to use it again. I don't want to have forebodings and dreams and images when I touch people or objects. I want to be normal."

"You don't mean that." When he looked skeptical, Abby shook her head helplessly. There was no reasoning with him tonight. She slid from the settle and sat on the carpet fronting the hearth, then leaned her head against his knees. "If I could take this sorrow from you, I would," she whispered.

He was quiet an instant, then laughed lightly and trailed his fingers down her cheek and neck, tugging her chin upward. "Never say such a thing when you're alone with a man in his bedroom."

"But you are not just any man." She willed her heart and love into her eyes. "You are my husband."

The humor slowly died from his face. "You know I can't be a real husband to you."

"Yes, I know what you *think* will happen if you are." Her eyes filled. "I need you, Julian. What kind of life will I have without you?"

A lost look came into his eyes. Slowly, as if he could not help himself, he bent forward and touched his lips to hers. He had no doubt intended it as a chaste kiss, a gesture of gratitude for her sweetness. A moment later, they were both on the floor, he with his hands beneath her head, she with her arms around his neck. He seemed unable to stop kissing her soft skin.

Abby returned his kisses with wide, toothy ones. She could not stop smiling. She saw a brief look of inattention in his eyes, as if he were listening to some inner prompting that clamored for his notice. But then he was hers again.

His touch was driving her mad with pleasure.

While she cradled his head in her hands and timidly stroked his hair, he removed the feathered bandeau from hers, then pulled at hairpins and worked his fingers under her curls until dark strands fell wildly about her shoulders. She trembled as he caressed her hair and cheeks with his fingertips.

He drew back and stared at her as if drinking in the now-solemn look of her luminous eyes, the untamed riot of hair, the generous swell of bosom straining from her dress. She was afraid now, and he saw it. But she would not shrink from him.

"My lioness," he whispered. And kissed her mouth once more, slowly and regretfully, then struggled to his feet and offered his hand.

She had seen paradise and lost it. Reluctantly she accepted his assistance, then flew into busy activity: straightening her dress, pushing her fallen hair behind her ears, running her locket back and forth on its chain; all the while keeping her gaze turned downward. But he could not miss the dampness on her cheeks.

"Abby," he groaned.

"Do you say it, Julian," she choked. "Tell me once again that I must leave you."

He touched her arm, but she pulled away impatiently. Stepping closer, he stroked her hair soothingly, then cupped her face in his hands. "No, I won't say that. Not anymore."

A look of desperate hope entered her eyes. He saw it and felt the weight of the world fall on his shoulders.

"Michael's death has given me a new appreciation for the brevity of life and the importance of love. If you leave me, you will take my heart with you."

He laughed softly when she flung her arms around him, then tugged himself free. "Before you make your decision, you must understand that we can live together only as friends." His smile faded. "God knows it will be hard, but we must."

Abby reached for her handkerchief, which had fallen to the floor. In a fit of nervous energy, she stood twisting it into knots. A sudden thought came into her mind.

"Julian, aren't there ways . . ."

She felt a blush rising. Could she possibly be here in this firelit bedroom discussing methods to prevent breeding with a man who was afraid to be her husband? Perhaps next, the stars would fall to the earth and walk. And the moon would become a giant ball which she could roll into the ocean and ride across the waves.

"Ways to prevent childbirth?" he finished for her. "None of them are totally trustworthy. No, I can't risk losing you. Whether you mean to remain with me or go away, you must base your decision on our remaining celibate."

"I will stay with you, of course," she said immediately. "But I've always wanted children."

"We can adopt."

"Yes," she said, and rose to walk to her bedroom thinking, *It's not the loss of bearing children I'll mourn so much.*

It was obvious he understood how she felt. He was undoubtedly feeling the same, for his face was solemn as he stepped beside her to the door. Before she entered her room, he bent to kiss her once more. His lips tasted of hunger and disappointment and shattered dreams, reflecting the sentiments of her heart.

Sixteen

Two mornings later, Michael and Nina were put to rest in the family cemetery a few miles behind the castle. The graves were prepared side-by-side on a little rise of ground that afforded a view for the mourners of misted fields and steamy vapors rising from the river.

The graveside service was intended as a private affair, but the prominence of the victims and the tragic aspects of their deaths drew a large crowd of neighbors and curiosity-seekers. That many of them hoped to be issued invitations to a mourning feast in the castle became obvious by their reluctance to leave the family plot, but no such invitations were forthcoming. Finally, the last of them, a tavern owner from Chelmsford and his three daughters, bid the families adieu and departed.

Lord Donberry, who had insisted on attending even though it meant being carried in a litter, accepted Julian's assistance from his chair and touched his brother's coffin a final time.

"Farewell, Michael," he said, and fumbled for his handkerchief, then blew his nose. "I shall miss you." He turned shakily, and Julian rushed to steady him, as did Lord Donberry's valet. "I'm all right, I'm all right," he declared. "Don't fuss."

Julian removed his hand but watched him from the corner of his eye. His brother had ever been a stubborn and proud man. But he was improving, beyond a doubt.

Looking away for a moment, he saw Abby walking beside Sophia toward the carriages. He was glad the two of them had become friends so quickly. Family visits could be deuced awkward when the members did not get along.

Family visits. He had never made family visits before, but all that was changing. Although he sorrowed for his lost brothers, he still had Carl and Sophia and a niece he'd not seen since she was five. And that was more than he'd known before. And of course, there was still Colleen.

Most of all, he had Abby. He continued to watch her retreating form with a painful mixture of feelings. Would the sight of her always evoke this tender yearning, or would the dry years ahead deaden their love? Time would tell, he supposed; he could not. For now, he was content merely to look at her, to speak with her, to respond to the delicious humor and innocence in her dark eyes.

She looked enchanting as she stepped carefully across the field in her new lavender gown. Yesterday Sophia offered to have one of her own black ones taken in and lengthened for her, but Abby refused, insisting on the lavender for some reason she wouldn't explain. Her vehemence was surprising; but during the service, seeing her standing like a violet among crows, he had to think she was right.

He forced his attention back to his brother. Nina's family had been clustered around her casket, and now Mr. and Mrs. Findlay and their two grown sons were approaching Carl, taking their leave. Julian joined his brother and shook hands with the ashen-faced woman and her sons and murmured half-meant condolences.

Something must be on Mr. Findlay's mind, for he lingered until the others were some distance away. Julian steeled himself for possible trouble.

But there was no hostility in Mr. Findlay's posture. He was a tall man with bristly gray hair and a beard. A strong odor of wine accompanied him, and Julian wondered if he had overindulged or if his vineyard had laced itself into his clothes. Certainly he did not appear drunk. When he bent to speak into Carl's ear, he did not lose his balance or stumble.

In order to hear him, Julian moved nearer.

"Now that my wife has stepped away, I need to know the truth," he rasped. "It weren't no accident, was it? Nina killed herself, didn't she?"

Carl blinked up at him. "We don't know, Findlay. No one was there when she went over the rail."

The man nodded. "But you think she did, I can see that. She couldn't live without Lord Michael. I never saw a girl love a man so. It was always 'Michael says this' and 'Michael does that.' Anyhow, I want to thank you for burying her in consecrated ground, my lord."

With awkwardness, Carl accepted his hand. "Would you share breakfast with us, Findlay?" he asked abruptly.

"Thank you my lord, but no, we've got to get to my other daughter's. She gave us a grandson yesterday." Mr. Findlay's eyes became damp. "Life goes on, what?"

Carl agreed that it did, then motioned for his litter to be carried to the coach. Julian accompanied him without speaking.

That evening, Abby and Julian were sitting closely together on the sofa in her bedroom when she turned to him in a sudden huff.

"And while *I'm* being celibate, what will *you* be doing? I don't suppose you've foreseen anything about—about um, ma-married love killing *you*."

"I shall be as pure as the driven snow," he pledged.

She snorted. "You would be more convincing were your eyebrows not waving like a pennant in the wind. And who could wonder, with the lovely Harriet flaunting her charms at all hours?"

"Abby, are you jealous? I've told you there has never been anything between Harry and me. Why should it be different now? Don't you trust me?"

"Trust is all very well, and I have no doubt your intentions are good. However, it seems foolish to tempt fate."

He gritted his teeth. "This is all in your mind, sweetheart. You have nothing to fear. Besides, nothing can be done. Harry earns her living in my employ. I'll not cast her and my niece to the winds."

A look of determination entered her eyes. "Well, I have been thinking about that. You could give her an allowance. How long do you imagine it would take me to learn Harriet's part in your performance?"

Before he could speak, she sprang to her feet and walked several paces away. Terror crossed her face. She brought her hands to either side of her mouth and called, "Hallooo! Is anyone at home? It is I, Hilda of Silverwaithe Farms, come to seek shelter from the storm!"

Julian buried his face in his hands.

As the days passed, the mood in the castle lightened. Old hurts were put to rest. The bond between the brothers strengthened. Lord Donberry became well enough to dine downstairs, and many evenings were spent in conversation and laughter. Julian entertained them with illusions and stories of disastrous performances. The marquess offered reminiscences of his brothers, tenuously at first, then boldly, as he saw Julian hungered to fill in the missing years.

Over dinner one evening, Julian announced he and Abby planned to return to Avilion soon. The marquess protested vehemently.

"But we can't stay forever," the magician declared. "My wife's twenty-first birthday is next week, and we'd both like to be home for it."

"Home?" the marquess cried. "What do you call this old place?"

Julian darted a look at Abby, who pulled a face. He well knew her dislike of the castle, which, despite her fondness for

Carl and Sophia, had not abated since the beginning. "Now that you are marquess, I know the castle is my home, too. But Avilion is mine, and I must return and prepare for my next tour."

"You're wrong, my boy," Lord Donberry said, pointing his fork imperially. "You don't have to earn your living anymore. I control the purse strings now, and your portion of the estate is long overdue."

"No, no. I don't want anything."

The marquess went on as if he had not spoken. "You may think because Father cut you out that you're not entitled. But he was wrong about you and a lot of things."

"It's not that precisely—"

"And now there is Michael's portion," Lord Donberry interrupted. "I don't need it."

Julian started to reply negatively, then paused. "If you want to give Michael's money to someone, give it to his daughter and Harriet."

Next to him, Abby moved excitedly. The little minx, he'd known that would thrill her. But he had a lot of work before him. Her acting was atrocious.

The marquess eyed him balefully. "That can be arranged. If what you tell me is true, it's another long-due debt we owe. But is there nothing I can do to induce you to stay?"

Julian shook his head. "We'll wear the roads thin visiting you." He forked a bite of cranberry tart. "And we expect you to visit us at Avilion at least twice yearly."

Lord Donberry drained his glass of wine, then fixed his eyes on his brother's. "Don't forget that when something happens to me, you'll be the marquess. There's a lot to be learned about handling the estate. Much you don't know."

"Nothing is going to happen to you, Carl; you're too stubborn to die. Besides, don't pretend it's you handling estate business when we all know it is Calvin O'Reilly. Now if he goes on to his reward, *then* I'll be alarmed."

Defeated, the marquess fell silent. Sophia gave him a loving

look, then turned to Abby. "Since you are set on leaving, I
want to show you the Donberry gems. There are more jewels
than I can wear in a lifetime, and I beg you to choose whatever
you wish from them. Perhaps you'll even be able to find a
wedding ring that will fit your finger." When Abby started to
protest, she said, "No, you must not refuse. After all, you're
a Donberry now and the estate's only hope for the future. It
is too late for Carl and me; we have just our daughter in school.
But you and Julian must fill the castle with strong, young
sons."

Abby's gaze dropped to her plate, then lifted to meet Julian's
sad eyes.

"There now, Sophia," Lord Donberry chided. "You've made
the girl blush. Shame."

The newlyweds departed for Avilion a few days later. During their journey home, Abby repeatedly held her garnet-and-
diamond wedding band to the window to see it sparkle.
Charlotte Ann was forced to proclaim its beauty over and
over again.

On the second day of traveling, Julian said in an exasperated
voice, "Had you told me how much you detested my ring, I
would have bought you another before now."

"I love your ring," Abby exclaimed, caressing the filigreed
gold band that once again graced his little finger. "But this
one is so delicate, and it belonged to your grandmother." In a
sensible voice, she added, "Besides, there is no danger of it
falling into my soup."

Abby's spirits grew lighter every day. She smiled often, sometimes for no apparent reason. Only the chasm between Julian
and herself prevented her complete happiness. But she would
find a way to bridge that gap. She wanted to give him strong,
young sons, and she would not let his fears prevent her.

So confident was she of their future together that when the
gates of Avilion finally came into sight, she turned to Julian

and said mischievously, "Are you certain you have no surprises awaiting me this time, my lord?"

When he looked at her with a distracted air, she fretted momentarily that she'd offended him. "No surprises," he said, a frown gathering between his brows.

He must be worried about the coming encounter with Harriet, Abby decided.

Their second reception was similar to the first. The housekeeper and butler responded almost immediately to Bugbee's horn. Harriet and Colleen took longer this time, coming from the direction of the cottage by the pond.

Harriet approached Julian with all her former confidence, but it was apparent the stiffness of his embrace startled her. When she pulled back, she looked from him to Abby and back again uncertainly.

Colleen paid them no mind; her sharp eyes had immediately detected the dazzling band on Abby's finger. "What a pretty ring!" she declared. "Where did you get it?"

"From Julian's family," Abby said, watching Harriet.

Harriet's gaze dropped to the wedding band. A red circle bloomed on each cheek, and winter came into her eyes.

Julian lightly rested his hand at the small of her back. "Come inside, Harry. I have something of interest to tell you."

There was not the slightest change in Harriet's posture. She met Julian's gaze directly, then turned to enter the house.

She knows, Abby thought. There was no taste of joy in the victory. She looked at Francis, who stood below her on the steps. The compassion in his eyes was no more than in her own.

While Julian and Harriet were closeted in the parlour, Abby was too restless to retire to her room. Since it was hours before dinner, she decided to walk awhile before changing.

Colleen expressed a desire to accompany her and led her to the informal garden behind the house. Abby was delighted to see a series of stone walkways curving around clusters of late-blooming wildflowers. The groupings looked natural, if no man had a hand in their upkeep and guided disarray, but Abby knew better. As she walked, she sniffed their faint fragrances and sighed peacefully.

"Do you like it?" Colleen asked. "I do. I like it almost as much as my own garden."

"You have a garden?"

"Yes," the girl said importantly. "Feebur helped me plant my own herbacious border. The late-lilies are blooming because we haven't had a frost yet, and I have dahlias and chrysanthemums. Do you want to see?"

Impressed, Abby said she did.

"Good! Hurry!" The child ran ahead.

Abby maintained a more leisurely pace. Everything she saw was pleasing. Beyond the tall islands of flowers, the woods loomed darkly. They were beautiful, too, but she shivered at the shadows among the trees. Julian would have to introduce her to the forest; she was not venturing there alone. Her last woodland experience had shaken her faith in her sense of direction.

While she wondered at the reason for her disquiet, a noise popped in the woods. Abby stood very still, her heart pumping wildly.

The sound came again, like a branch breaking. Footsteps began to race, faster and faster. Searching for the source of the sound, she turned her head and saw a flash of white, then brown. She opened her mouth to scream. When a pair of dark eyes stared fearfully into hers, the scream turned into laughter.

Why hadn't Julian mentioned he kept deer in his park?

To her sorrow, the trembling doe fled away.

Smiling, she turned her steps toward the pond. Colleen would be wondering where she was. When she skirted the little man-made lake, however, Abby saw the girl was not to be found behind the cottage, though the garden was certainly thriving.

Puzzled, she knocked on the back door. It was unlatched and swung inward at her touch. She crossed the threshold hesitantly and blinked in the sudden dimness of the room.

In the darkness, Colleen's blue eyes blazed above the hand that held her mouth. Abby's numbed gaze rose to the face of the disheveled man holding the child. The pistol in his other hand was pointed directly at her. She felt the room sway.

"Hello, Abigail," Philip said.

Seventeen

"So Colleen and I are wealthy?" Harriet asked, her tone disbelieving. "Michael is dead, and we are to receive his portion?"

"There is no one more deserving than the two of you," Julian said in a distracted voice. "Carl wanted you to have the funds. He said it was long past . . ."

As though he had forgotten he was speaking, Julian stepped to the window and pushed the curtains aside to look out.

"Is something wrong?"

"I don't know. Ever since we arrived, I've felt—" His eyes sharpened. "Where is Abby?"

"I'm sure I haven't the faintest idea," she said coldly.

Julian rushed from the room.

The kitchen slowly righted itself, and Abby straightened her shoulders. She scarcely recognized the man standing before her. Philip was unshaven, his hair untidy, and his clothing unspeakably dirty and worn. His skin had a yellowish cast, as if he'd been ill; his eyes looked ravaged and desperate. Were he not clutching Colleen, she almost could have felt sorry for him. Instead, she was afraid and burning with rage.

"Release the child," she demanded.

He ignored her order. "Are you surprised to see me, Abigail?"

"Yes. No." She frowned in exasperation. "What does it matter? You're here for me, I imagine. Free the child; she has nothing to do with what is between us."

Abby saw his arm relax slightly. Colleen immediately strained against his hand and kicked her feet backward. Reflexively, he jerked her closer, then cried out when she bit the fleshy base of his thumb. His face flushed with fury, and he brought the pistol near the girl's head.

"No!" Abby screamed, stepping forward, both arms held out entreatingly. "Think what you are doing! She is only a child!"

Philip's eyes met hers defiantly for an instant, then dropped, and he lowered the weapon. "Bring something to tie her," he said hoarsely.

Frantically, Abby searched the kitchen until she found several long towels. Philip instructed her to place one around Colleen's mouth. He forced the child to sit in a chair while Abby tied her arms and legs to the wood.

Colleen's eyes pleaded with Abby as she followed his directions, but there was nothing to be done, not while he could hurt the girl. When she finished, Philip seized Abby's arm and pulled her to the door. There was only time for a final, despairing glance at Colleen before Abby was drawn outside.

She looked longingly across the pond to the manor house. Julian was in there. Julian and heaven. Could he hear her thoughts? Could he hear *her?* She drew breath to cry out.

Philip's fingers dug into her arm as he pushed her toward the forest. "Don't think of screaming. If he comes, I'll shoot him. I may do so anyway, depending on how cooperative you are."

The scream died in her throat. "Have you lost your mind, Philip? What do you hope to accomplish by this? I am a married woman."

"You are not married until you are married to *me,*" he said through his teeth, his words matching the rhythm of his steps. "I have not been through three weeks of hell to be thwarted now. I've neglected everything for you. My estate. My mother

And nearly lost my life. Can you imagine, Abigail, that I spent two weeks suffering in a vermin-infested hole populated with mental deficients? And for the past five nights I've been forced to freeze under the stars because I didn't bring sufficient funds with me?"

She had a sudden urge to laugh. If he were not so livid, if his hands weren't bruising her skin, she might have.

"I know I've made you angry," she said breathlessly, trying to keep up with him so he would not tear her arm from its socket. "I'm sorry for it, Philip. But I never wanted to marry you. Don't you see that what you're doing is hopeless? Julian will come after you. I belong to him."

They were beneath the trees now, out of sight of the house and cottage, and Philip grabbed her by the shoulders and shoved her roughly against an oak. "Never say that! Don't dare say that to me!"

She paled at the violence in his eyes. The back of her head rang from striking the tree, and her knees weakened. She braced herself against the oak, the rugged bark prickling her scalp.

His expression softened, but she took no comfort in it. "I don't mean to hurt you." He started to touch her face and looked surprised to see the pistol in his hand. Pocketing the weapon, he stroked her cheek with the back of his fingers and said soothingly, "You bring it on yourself, acting so disobediently. This behavior is not like you, Abigail. It's his fault, I'm certain. I should kill him. I *will* kill him if he doesn't consent to annulling your marriage."

From the garden beyond the trees, voices could be heard calling her name. Julian was among them.

Abby smiled rebelliously, then slapped his hand away. Fury leapt into his eyes, but she continued, unheeding. "He won't consent to it. And don't talk to me of killing. Do you want to hang? You can't force everyone to bend to your will, no matter how much you would like to do so."

In a carefully controlled voice, he said, "He'll think differ-

ently after we've been together awhile. And I do mean to spend
time with you. A long, slow time; longer than you've been
with him."

Abby refused to listen to his words. Her gaze slid sideways
toward the garden. The voices were growing closer. Stalling,
she said, "It's useless. Julian and I love each other."

Instead of answering, he clutched her arm more tightly and
pushed her further into the forest.

"He'll find us," she said desperately.

"No, he won't. Do you think I mean to go back to Prosings
right away? No, we'll travel awhile. And then, when we finally
return home, he won't want you anymore. And you won't want
to leave me, either."

"You *are* mad."

In answer, he shook her angrily and moved forward until
they reached the wall. Tugging, half-dragging her along its
length for what seemed a long time, he reached the spot where
the oak swept over the side, put his hands on her waist and
prepared to lift her over. She struggled, pummeling him with
her fists and pushing against his chest.

In the midst of her terror, she couldn't help feeling surprised
at herself. Weeks ago, she would have seen no hope in her
resistance and gone docilely. But that was before Julian.

Philip seemed as surprised as she. "Go on, Abigail, or I'll
slap you senseless and throw you over!" he spat.

Neither of them heard the sound of careful footfalls, but when
Julian spoke, they both turned instantly. "No, you won't," he
said evenly. "Release my wife this instant, Demere."

Joy swept through Abby, then dread. From the corner of her
eye, she saw Philip's hand slip into his pocket. "Be careful,"
she warned. "He has a pistol."

Philip pulled out the gun and pointed it at his opponent.
"I'll shoot you where you stand if you come any closer." When
Julian hesitated and eyed the weapon, Philip smiled grimly.
"Now, turn around and walk away."

"You have missed something," the magician said.

A question came into Philip's eyes, then alarm as he sighted the pistol in Julian's hand. "Where did that come—oh, yes. The magician." His lips twisted scornfully. He jerked Abby to him and pointed the gun at her back. "It will do you no good. Throw it away."

The weapon in Julian's hand wavered. "You won't hurt her. She's the reason you've come."

Philip drew his head closer to Abby's. "Yes, but if I can't have her, neither shall you."

Julian's face moved indecisively. His weapon began to lower.

Abby felt her weight increase a hundredfold. Behind her, Philip's breathing quickened. She felt his rage as if it were her own.

"Don't!" she cried to Julian, her voice shaking. "I'm afraid he means to kill you." Angry tears began to flow. "I'd rather die than live without you!"

While Philip's fingers clawed into her side like talons, a light came into Julian's eyes, an intense, communicating light. His lips parted in a half-smile, and his eyebrows moved in exaggerated arcs.

"Very well, Philip, you are the victor." Staring fixedly at Abby, he flexed his brows again. "I'm tossing my weapon away." When a look of cautious hope entered her eyes, the magician lifted his arm in a florid gesture and threw the pistol over the wall.

While Philip watched the flight of the weapon, his grip on Abby's waist loosened, and she swung away from him. A shot rang out, and Abby's heart stopped.

For a long, dismal moment, there was silence.

Cries could be heard in the distance, coming closer. Julian's eyes squinted in pain, and Philip crumpled to the earth.

Too afraid to look, Abby blurted, "Have you killed him?"

"No, sweetheart. I aimed for his arm." Julian picked up the pistol which had slipped from his adversary's fingers and placed it in his pocket with the other one. "But I see I have shot him in the leg instead. Well, at least I hit him somewhere.

I fear Mrs. White is going to have my skin for shooting a hole through my pocket."

"You tricked me!" Philip panted from the ground. "Stupid trick!"

Abby was giddy with relief. "Never remove your eyes from a magician's hands," she could not resist saying, then added with a nervous giggle, "Or his lying eyebrows."

With his hands pressed to his thigh, Philip glared up at her. "You have changed, Abigail. You're not the girl I knew."

"Thank God," she said, and walked into Julian's embrace.

Her husband folded her within his arms. "I nearly lost you through my own stubbornness," he whispered in her ear. "I received a warning and almost ignored it. But then I remembered what you said. Perhaps it is a gift and not always a curse."

Her arms tightened around his waist. She turned her head away from Philip's disgust and agony and closed her eyes. There was no place she would rather be than in her husband's embrace.

When Francis and the servants came to carry Philip into the house, Abby suddenly remembered Colleen, and she and Julian hurried to the cottage. They paused in the kitchen doorway. Harriet had arrived before them and was loosening her daughter's bonds.

Colleen glanced up from rubbing her wrists and exclaimed, "Lady Abby wouldn't let that man shoot me, Mamma! She saved my life!"

A long look passed between the two women. Harriet's eyes burned with tears. *"Did* she now? Did she indeed?"

Eighteen

In the days that followed, Harriet no longer cast longing glances at Julian and bitter ones toward Abby. A tenuous relationship began to build between the women, and Abby was glad for it.

According to the magistrate, Philip's wound was healing nicely. The official promised to consider Lady Julian's entreaties that the attempted kidnapper be transported rather than sent to gaol.

On the evening of her twenty-first birthday, Julian hosted a small celebration after dinner. At Abby's request, only family and servants were invited.

Colleen entertained the guests by pulling baby chicks from a hat. Harriet sang several tender songs in a pure alto, and Francis proved a surprisingly good accompanist on the pianoforte. Powell amazed Abby by juggling six plates at once and breaking only two.

She received gifts from everyone, including the servants. Julian gave her a garnet pendant necklace to match her wedding ring. Since she was wearing a new gown of gold lamé that fairly cried for ornamentation, Abby insisted he fasten it around her neck immediately.

There was a straw bonnet from Harriet and Colleen. A lavender ribbon of the same material as her day dress circled its band.

Charlotte Ann gave her a pair of handkerchiefs with Abby's new initials embroidered in the corners.

Francis's eyes gleamed mischievously as she unwrapped his present. When Abby saw he had given her a traveler's guide to England, she laughed.

But it was the seamstress's gift which made her heart flutter. After cautioning Abby to "just take a peek; don't let the menfolk see," Mrs. White gave her a package containing an exquisite nightgown she had made. It was lacy, white, and designed to enhance every curve of a young bride's body.

Abby looked from it to her husband and almost wept. Mrs. White's kindly face began to crumple. Abby quickly assured her it was her love for the gown, not dislike, that brought tears to her eyes.

If only the reason for her melancholy was so simple. In truth, her longing for Julian was driving her mad. Every time his hand touched hers, every time their eyes met, she felt a heat pass through her body that could scorch the sun.

He felt the same, she knew he did. The sadness behind his eyes testified to it.

The party disbanded shortly after nine, and with the exception of Francis, the servants moved off to bed or to attend to their duties.

Harriet had just announced her intention of taking Colleen home when someone knocked at the door. Powell rushed to answer it; and, curious to find the identity of so late a visitor, Abby and Julian followed.

The door opened to reveal a well-dressed young man holding a leather folder in his hands. He introduced himself as Mr. Jacob Siddons, representative of the Lyons's family solicitors.

"I apologize for the lateness of my arrival," he said officiously. "I only received your direction from Mrs. Lyons's butler yesterday, and I've been traveling since then. My orders, Lady Julian, were to find you by your twenty-first birthday if at all possible." An extremely self-satisfied look crossed his features. "And I have done so!"

He was admitted. After they all gathered in the parlour, Mr. Siddons informed Abby that she had inherited Sharonfield.

She did not believe him at first. "How is that possible?"

Mr. Siddons was sitting on the edge of the chair, the folder carefully balanced and open on his knees. He tapped the papers before him. "Your grandfather was within his rights to will it to you since there are no male heirs."

A deep, slow rage began to burn in her chest. "Did my grandmother know of this?"

The solicitor's face betrayed no emotion. "We made efforts on several occasions to inform you of your coming inheritance, but she insisted we wait."

Abby's furious eyes met Julian's. "No wonder she became so anxious that I marry Philip. I suppose she thought I'd force her to leave when Sharonfield became mine."

"You may do so now if you wish." Mr. Siddons's words were crisp and impassive. "It's within your power."

When she hesitated, Julian asked, "Is that what you want, Abby?"

Yes. For a week or two only, so she will know how it feels to be penniless and alone. But she said, "No, of course not. She may stay for as long as she lives if she wants, but I never plan to see the place again."

The look of approval in Julian's eyes warmed her.

After Mr. Simmons refused their offers of refreshments, he guided Abby and Julian in the signing of the papers and departed.

Moments later, Harriet and Colleen retired to their cottage, and Francis went to bed. Julian and Abby ascended the stairs, then paused outside their adjoining bedrooms. A teasing light flickered in the magician's eyes.

"I never thought to have a wealthy wife," he said.

"Now you can give up being a magician if you want," she replied.

"What, and sacrifice your ambition to play Hilda? I hardly think so."

They smiled into one another's eyes, then Julian kissed her and turned away. Abby entered her bedroom, and he entered his.

When the door closed behind her, Abby began fumbling with the hooks-and-eyes at the back of her gown and wished she had not told Charlotte Ann to go to bed. Perhaps she could ask Julian for help. But such a course would lead to disaster, she supposed. In a fit of fury, she struggled out of the dress and her unmentionables, threw them aside, and, after hesitating momentarily, donned the sheer nightgown Mrs. White had given her.

As Abby combed her hair into black silk before the mirror, the nightgown mocked her with all it promised and all she could never know.

She had been sentenced to virginity forever. *Forever.*

It was impossible. The mere sight of Julian was beginning to cause her pain. She couldn't live this way.

The face in the mirror stared back at her with growing resolution. A loud hammering pounded inside her chest. Courage sparked darkly from her eyes.

She lit the lamps closest to the door to Julian's bedroom. When she was certain there was a sufficient backdrop of light, she turned the knob.

He was propped in bed reading a book. His nightshirt hung open to the waist, revealing a mat of dark hair on a strong-looking chest. At her entrance, he looked up in surprise. The book fell to his lap, then flopped unheeded to the floor. His eyes roamed swiftly over her, then glanced away and returned. His cheeks darkened.

Why, she had made him blush!

"What are you doing here, Abby?" he choked. "Where is your robe?"

"I have come to seduce my husband," she answered, her voice cracking on every word.

"Sweetheart—," he began, but before he could finish, she flew across the room on bare feet and sat on the edge of his bed. To still his protest, she placed a trembling hand over his mouth.

"Women die in childbirth every day, Julian. Every female knows that when she enters marriage. Besides, I have survived a pistol at my back and poison in my glass. Childbirth sounds easy in comparison."

She removed her hand from his lips and began smoothing the touseled hair from his forehead. He started to touch her face, then dropped his arm as if she were fire.

"I think you are wrong about your dream," she continued. "Perhaps your fears for my safety have given you nightmares. But, nightmare or prophecy, I cannot love you halfway. I don't want to grow old and sour and empty like my grandmother, always wishing for something I never had. I would rather live my life fully, no matter how long its duration."

He closed his eyes. "I shouldn't have told you," he whispered. "I know how strong you are. Why didn't I guess you would say this to me?" When she leaned forward to kiss his eyelids, he breathed deeply and turned his head aside. "There is only one hindrance to your plan, Abby. *You* may be willing to live a shorter life, but *I* am not willing to live without you."

"Take courage, Lord Merlyn," she murmured, brushing his earlobe and cheek with her lips.

"Are you trying to kill me?" he demanded.

She pulled back. "If you force me to leave, I will go. But know this. Your love has made me more than I was. You have given me hope and confidence in myself; otherwise, I would have gone over that wall with Philip. But if you reject me now, you will crush my soul. And I have always accounted my soul to be of more importance than the well-being of my body."

His blue gaze locked with hers. A wealth of tenderness and yearning could be read in his eyes. He touched the gauzy fabric at her back. She jerked slightly at the contact and felt waves of pleasure move across her body.

"Are you certain, Abby?"

"More certain than I am of anything."

After a moment, he said, "Then come here, you brazen wench."

She laughed. He laughed with her, but there was a sadness behind his eyes she could not like. She determined to kiss the sorrow away and proceeded to do so.

Julian awoke when the morning sun lit the windows. During the night, Abby had nestled against him, and he could not resist slipping his arms around her. She stirred, opened her eyes, and smiled sleepily.

"I didn't have the dream last night," Julian whispered. "I don't know what it means, but for the first time in weeks I didn't dream about you."

Her lips curled. "Coming from anyone else, that would be an insult, I think."

"Well, in the event I've hurt your feelings, allow me to make amends." He kissed her until her toes ached, then raised himself on one elbow to stare into her eyes. "Better?"

"You are a magician indeed," she said breathlessly. "More magic, please."

He threw back his head and laughed. "Do you know, Abby, I've been remembering the night we met, when I read your hand and saw marriage as the only solution to save your life. I'm beginning to think I was wrong."

"Oh?" Her voice inflected worriedly.

"Yes. There was a more obvious reason for our wedding, only I was too thick-headed to see it."

Her heartbeat steadied, then began to race again. She had never seen such a beautiful mouth in her life.

"What reason was that, Julian?"

"Why, that I was going to love you, of course."

With her lips almost touching his, she whispered, "It doesn't require a prophet's talent to see that. I have known it from the beginning." She drew back and scowled playfully. "Now, do you plan to continue pontificating, or are you going to kiss me?"

Without another word, he pulled her to him.

1826

mere followed her son to America, it has deteriorated dreadfully. I suppose we'll remain where we are. Besides, the old lady keeps threatening it will kill her if we leave."

Abby shook her head. "No worry there; she will never die."

While Harriet smiled, the marchioness turned to survey the house. Memories stirred to life; memories of countless performances when she had served as Hilda by her husband's side. But those days were long gone, buried in the greater responsibilities of raising children and fulfilling her duties.

Thank God Sophia maintained her interest in the castle. Since Carl's death the year before, the dowager marchioness had channeled her grief in constructive ways, freeing Julian to remain at Avilion for months at a time. Abby had never grown used to the castle, and it was better at Avilion for the children. Michael and Edmond had legions of friends in Coventry, and Carlotta loved the woods.

Carlotta, dear child. Abby's eyes misted at the thought of her only daughter. Julian's old dream had been fulfilled, though not in the way he thought. Their oldest babe had nearly died— in fact, they thought she *had* gone; but after a moment of not breathing, the infant filled her lungs and survived. Beautiful, beautiful Carlotta. She was growing up, and they were all spoiling her sadly. Charlotte Ann was the worst.

The curtains parted, and an expectant hush fell across the auditorium. It jolted her pleasantly to see the haunted castle set again. Julian had changed the act many times over the years, but this one had remained his—and the audience's—favorite.

The performance began.

Thunder sounded. A knocking could be heard. The door swung open, and a young, red-haired beauty entered. She was attired in a modest dress that swished the floor as she walked. It was not at all like the milkmaid's costume another Hilda had worn years ago. After all, this beauty's mother was in the audience, and Queen Victoria was on the throne.

While Colleen asked if anyone was home, Julian came to

Epilogue

The crowded theatre buzzed with excitement. It was not often a marquess was willing to entertain London society, even for charity. That Lord Donberry had once earned his living as a magician only added to the attraction.

No one guessed that the two lovely ladies sitting in the foremost box seat had at varying times served as his assistant on stage. Like the green-eyed gentleman behind them, they were too regal and elegant to have done anything frivolous in their past.

"I'm so nervous," Harriet said, fanning herself.

Francis leaned forward and placed his hand on her shoulder. "Calm yourself; you'll agitate the little one. You never used to get stagefright."

She patted her rounded stomach soothingly. "This is different."

Abby's eyes twinkled. "If you can manage my grandmother, you can manage anything."

Harriet laughed. "I'm not managing her well. She can't move from her bed yet tries to rule us all."

"But you've bought Prosings and joined the estates, haven't you? That's what she always desired."

"Yes, but it's not *hers*. She wanted the Lyons name exalted, not Francis's. We're still discussing building our own house, just as we have since we bought Sharonfield from you. Of late we've even considered moving to Prosings, but since Mrs. De-the wings and peered up at the box seats until he found Abby. When his eyes met hers, he shrugged back his cape and pulled a rose from his lapel pocket. He pressed his lips to the blossom, then lifted it toward her. His hands moved rapidly, and the rose disappeared.

A smile broke across Abby's face. Pretending not to have heard Francis's sudden movement, she lifted the rose that had fallen into her lap and kissed it.

On stage, Colleen was peering into the top hat. Julian winked, flashed his teeth, and vanished.

ZEBRA REGENCIES
ARE
THE TALK OF THE TON!

A ⬚⬚⬚⬚⬚⬚⬚⬚⬚⬚ **DATE D** ⬚⬚⬚⬚⬚⬚ ⬚⬚⬚, $3.99)
by ⬚⬚⬚⬚⬚⬚⬚⬚⬚

Af⬚⬚ governess Harri⬚ Cole helped her young charge flee to France — and the designs of a despicable suitor, more trouble soon arrived in the person of a London rake. Sir Frederick Carrington insisted on providing safe escort back to England. Harriet deemed Carrington more dangerous than any band of brigands, but secretly relished matching wits with him. But after being taken in his arms for a tender kiss, she found herself wondering — *could* a lady find love with an irresistible rogue?

A SCANDALOUS PROPOSAL (4504, $4.99)
by Teresa DesJardien

After only two weeks into the London season, Lady Pamela Premington has already received her first offer of marriage. If only it hadn't come from the *ton's* most notorious rake, Lord Marchmont. Pamela had already set her sights on the distinguished Lieutenant Penford, who had the heroism and honor that made him the ideal match. Now she had to keep from falling under the spell of the seductive Lord so she could pursue the man more worthy of her love. Or was he?

A LADY'S CHAMPION (4535, $3.99)
by Janice Bennett

Miss Daphne, art mistress of the Selwood Academy for Young Ladies, greeted the notion of ghosts haunting the academy with skepticism. However, to avoid rumors frightening off students, she found herself turning to Mr. Adrian Carstairs, sent by her uncle to be her "protector" against the "ghosts." Although, Daphne would accept no interference in her life, she *would* accept aid in exposing any spectral spirits. What she never expected was for Adrian to expose the secret wishes of her hidden heart . . .

CHARITY'S GAMBIT (4537, $3.99)
by Marcy Stewart

Charity Abercrombie reluctantly embarks on a London season in hopes of making a suitable match. However she cannot forget the mysterious Dominic Castille — and the kiss they shared — when he fell from a tree as she strolled through the woods. Charity does not know that the dark and dashing captain harbors a dangerous secret that will ensnare them both in its web — leaving Charity to risk certain ruin and losing the man she so passionately loves . . .